# PRAISE FOR PREVIOUS VOLUMES

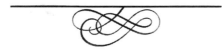

## 2 0 1 5

"...a good representation of the gay-themed creativity across genre journals and small presses right now."
**Publishers Weekly**

**Locus Recommended Reading List**

## 2 0 1 4

"There's a sort of stretching-towards-new-things, a rough but enthusiastic and charming spirit to this volume that I think we could often use more of. Year's Best anthologies sometimes tend toward the same roster over and over again—but there's something to be said for a retrospective that looks toward what's new in the field as well."
**Brit Mandelo for *Tor.com***

## 2 0 1 3

"An impressive collection brimming with originality."
**Kirkus Reviews**

# Wilde STORIES 2016

## THE YEAR'S BEST GAY SPECULATIVE FICTION
### STEVE BERMAN *ed.*

LETHE PRESS
MAPLE SHADE, NEW JERSEY

Published by Lethe Press
118 Heritage Ave, Maple Shade, NJ 08052
lethepressbooks.com

ISBN 978-1-59021-613-2 / 1-59021-613-X paperback edition

"The Astrakhan, the Homburg, and the Red Red Coal" copyright 2015 by Chaz Brenchley, first appeared in (*Queers Destroy Science Fiction*) *Lightspeed* #61 / "Camp" copyright 2015 by David Nickle, first appeared in *Aickman's Heirs* (ed. by Simon Strantzas, Undertow Publications) / "The Duchess and the Ghost" copyright 2015 by Richard Bowes, first appeared in (*Queers Destroy*) *Fantasy* #59 / "Edited" copyright 2015 by Rich Larson, first appeared in *Interzone* #259 / "Envious Moons" copyright 2015 by Richard Scott Larson, first appeared in *Joyland*, February 2, 2015 / "He Came From a Place of Openness and Truth" copyright 2015 by Bonnie Jo Stufflebeam, first appeared in *Lightspeed* #56 / "Imaginary Boys" copyright 2015 by Paul Magrs, first appeared in *Speak My Language* (ed. by Torsten Højer, Robinson) / "To the Knife Cold Stars" copyright 2015 by A. Merc Rustad, first appeared in Escape Pod 480 / "The Language of Knives" copyright 2015 by Haralambi Markov, first appeared in *Tor.com* February 4, 2015 / "Lockbox" copyright 2015 by E. Catherine Tobler, first appeared in *She Walks in Shadows* (ed. by Silvia Moreno-Garcia & Paula R. Stiles, Innsmouth Free Press) / "The Ticket Taker of Cenote Zaci" copyright 2015 by Benjamin Parzybok, first appeared in *Strange Horizons*, February 2, 2015 / "To Die Dancing" copyright 2015 by Sam J. Miller, first appeared in *Apex Magazine*, #78 / "Utrechtenaar" copyright 2015 by Paul Evanby, first appeared in *Strange Horizons*, June 1-8, 2015 / "Wallflowers" copyright 2015 by Jonathan Harper, first appeared in *Big Lucks* January 2015. / "What Lasts" copyright 2015 by Jared W. Cooper, first appeared in *Daily Science Fiction*, July 28th, 2015

Cover and Interior Design:
Inkspiral Design

Cover Art:
'Bread and Roses' by Marwane Pallas

# Introduction

STEVE BERMAN

The cardinal points of our minds are: Reality, Memory, Imagination, and Oblivion. We learn to embrace these directions as children, through play with real and imaginary friends, discovering loss and believing in impossibilities (such as my favorite, a local devil haunting the Pine Barrens of New Jersey); we discover the benefits of navigating all as adolescents through daydreaming through school, fancying boys, wet dreams, and broken hearts; as adults we become introduced to transience, which guides us towards the barren landscapes of oblivion. We make our lives have purpose by straying from such a course by choosing to invest in new memories, remaking our reality when possible, and imagine better things…or worse, depending on the emotion of the hour. Speculative fiction may seem to be the fiction of lies but, in truth, it is a genre of many truths. Whether the stories instill us with wonder or catharsis, they provide comfort in times of stress and loneliness—or offer hints of agency we wish we possessed, could possess if we just dared—just because something eerie or strange has happened does not mean we cannot return to our mental map, those four directions we found so many years ago.

So please enjoy these tales of chimerical friends and lovers, illusive paradises and purgatories of our own design. 2015 was a *very good* year for gay-themed speculative fiction; I borrow a sommelier's hackneyed phrase with justification: more and more traditional spec fic venues are featuring queer authors, queer storylines. The wealth of stories we can read and identify with the leads grows every year! While within our heads we are so often Outsiders, the physical world, in slight, but not insignificant, steps is recognizing our presence. And one day we will no longer be the boogeymen, the lisping curiosity, the anomaly—when I was a child, I could not comprehend identifying as gay. But I read a recent study that the new generation entering schools is less likely to define themselves by gender and sexual orientation. I need to dwell on that—we all should— and adjust that quadrant of our mindscape for more favorable destinations within the realm of Reality.

But now, please, step with me into Imagination…

STEVE BERMAN
*Still Devil-Haunted NJ*
*Spring 2016*

# CONTENTS

*David picked himself up and limped home. He was winded from having his balls kicked. And I—Lawrence the Novelizor—followed him home. Always a few steps behind.*

# Imaginary Boys

## PAUL MAGRS

DAVID TAYLOR WAS WALKING HOME from sixth form college, through drifts of orange leaves during the season known as autumn. He was seventeen, of medium height and build, with brown hair that needed cutting. His eyes were downcast and dark as stewed tea. He wore a blurred, vague sort of expression as if his thoughts were far away.

It was starting to get dark and David kept looking over his shoulder as he hurried back to the council estate where he lived with his female parent.

This seemed like the most stressful week of David's life. Besides everything going on at home with his mam, there was Lawrence as well. The new boy in the sixth form.

Awkward and hanging on the sidelines and always there. David had felt watched by him these past two weeks. Was he imagining it?

"Why are you walking along with me, Lawrence? I never asked you to."

David stopped walking and Lawrence almost bumped into him.

"And will you stop...narrating me?" snapped David. "It's driving me mad."

I'm sorry about that, David.

"Are you trying to wind me up?"

I can assure you I am not. It's a compliment, really.

"To have you following me around?"

Lawrence could see that David was at the end of his tether.

"Just get lost, will you? Leave me alone."

But this is where I'm meant to be.

"You what?"

I'm doing my job. And it's all to do with you, David.

"I mean it – shut up. And go away!"

There was a slight pause.

I'm sorry if I seem like a "weirdo" to you, David. That is what you think, isn't it?

"I don't think you're a weirdo."

I'm Lawrence. I'm new in town.

"I know, you're in my class. Where are you from?"

Verbatim 6.

"What?"

It's a small planet about 300 light years from here. I'm your Novelizor, David.

David looked unconvinced. "Okay." He frowned. "Bye, then!"

David turned and walked quickly away.

His mam was watching a quiz show when David came home.

"Where have you been?" she called from the front room. "Your tea's all black in the oven."

He shrugged. "I'm not really hungry."

"Here. Have one of these. I've left you all the soft centres."

He peered at the mostly empty box of chocolates. "Have you finished another box?"

"I can't help it."

"I'll get you some more when I'm in town."

"Are you all right? I usually get a lecture about how my cravings are no good for me."

"I'm fine, Mam, really."

"No one's been picking on you or anything, have they? Or giving you any trouble?"

"No, no. Nothing like that. Just some strange lad on the way home. New guy in our year…"

"Cos if those rough lads are bothering you again I'll…"

"Mam, I'm seventeen. I can look after myself."

She watched him carefully as he went to leave the room. "Where are you off to now?"

"Up to my room."

"Yeah, don't whatever you do spend any time with your poor old pregnant mother who's been sat here alone all day."

Lawrence was watching this unfold from outside. He was crouching down by the window, in some bushes. He hadn't been invited in yet. He wasn't close enough to his subject. Not as close as a Novelizor needs to be.

Through the window he could see a room with a large television screen and sliding panels of glass that opened onto a flat concrete area with green moss growing on it and plastic chairs. He saw the distended form of the female parent supine upon a settee that was decorated with a floral design. She was fabricating a tiny pair of shoes out of strings of coloured twine using two metal rods that made an insistent ticking noise. Then she left the room and walked upstairs.

She knocked on her son's bedroom door.

"Can I come in?"

"No," he said.

She opened the door.

"What are you doing?"

He was on his bed. There was a bunch of old books from the library on his duvet, as usual. "Reading poetry," he said, holding one up. "Keats. 'Ode to Autumn.' 'Season of mists and mellow fruitfulness.'"

"Oh yes?" She laughed at his put-on poetry voice.

He went on: "'Close-bosom friend of the maturing sun'…"

"Sounds a bit saucy. Bosoms in poetry."

"Mam!"

"You and your poetry," she said, rolling her eyes. She wanted to sit down with him. Ruffle his already-messy hair. "You've had to be the man of the house since your dad went. But you have to be even more so now, with the baby nearly here."

"I know that, Mam."

"It's a long time since I went through the agony of giving birth to you and it's scary just the thought of going through it again."

"I'm here, Mam."

"There's all the bringing up baby, too. I'm going to be what they call an older mother."

"We'll manage."

"I suppose you'll be swanning off to university soon and I won't see you any more…"

He burst out: "Oh, give it a rest!" Then he took a deep breath. "Sorry, Mam. I'll be home to visit."

"I was used to being a young mother. With you, I was sixteen and I got all the catty remarks. I had to fight everyone to keep you."

"I know, Mam."

"It's always been me and you, David."

"You and me against the world."

"Your Dad never really fit in, even when he was here. He was always so bound up in his bloody police work. We hardly even noticed him gone last Christmas, did we?"

"Cos we still had each other."

"Oh, come here. Give your old mam a hug…" Just then, a funny look went across her face. "Oh…!"

He sat up quickly. He was on his feet. "What is it?"

"I think…I think it's coming… The baby's coming!"

"Are you sure?"

She looked stricken. She was grabbing hold of the bedroom door. "David, call an ambulance!"

"You know what happened last time."

She was holding onto the door, shaking her head. "Ow! This is really it. Owww!"

"You're sure this isn't another of your false alarms?"

"Call it," she shouted. "Call them up, David, now!"

FOR THE THIRD NIGHT THAT month, David and his mam raced to the hospital prematurely. Another late night while the doctors looked at her and felt her all over and told her the baby wasn't ready yet, and she should get herself home. Another ride back home in a taxi.

Next day, in the sixth-form common room, David seemed to be prone to opening his mouth and making sudden, wordless noises and then looking embarrassed. This, Lawrence discovered, was "yawning."

Then David went off to somewhere called the "Boys' Bogs" and Lawrence followed him for a quiet word.

He stood outside the cubicle David was in and gave a polite knock.

David?

"What?"

It's Lawrence.

"Can't I get some peace?"

I wanted to explain something.

David flushed the toilet and came out of the little room, banging the door.

"Yeah?" he snapped. "You can explain why you're following me about for a start."

It's my job, David. This is what I'm here on Earth to do.

"Yeah, yeah…"

I've come a very long way to see you, David. To watch your early years here. It's all very interesting.

"Did anyone see you follow me in here?"

The thing is, David, I'm only in disguise as a new pupil. This isn't who I really am at all. My job is to collect stories and keep a record of interesting lives. And, well, I chose you.

There was a long pause.

Then David asked, "You chose me?" He frowned and stared at Lawrence. "What for?"

Said David, his heart rate increasing and his pulse pounding in his ears.

"And why do you keep on doing that?!"

Narrating, you mean? I have to keep an account of your actions.

"I really don't need this right now. Just stay out of my way, okay?"

He started to leave the "Boys' Bogs".

Aren't you going to wash your hands first? I believe that is the custom.

THE FOLLOWING MORNING AT BREAKFAST, David's mam was fixating on the idea that her son might put another person—an undetermined female person—in a condition she described several times as "the pudding club."

"Mam, seriously, I'm running late. Can't this wait till later?"

"All I'm saying is, you're seventeen now, and I don't want you getting caught out like I did."

"Yeah, well, I won't."

"You don't know what girls are like."

"You're right about that."

"I'm just saying. You've got to watch out. Don't chuck your life away like I did."

"Thanks!"

"You know what I mean."

"Mam, I'm going to get caught out, as you put it. When would I ever get the chance, even if I wanted to?"

"Don't get smart," she snapped.

Their late-night false alarms and ambulance trips ensured they were both over-tired and cross almost every morning.

Then the front door went.

"Who's that knocking at breakfast time?"

"I'll go," David said.

It was me! Lawrence the Novelizor from Verbatim 6. I had decided to take things to the next level in my campaign to get closer to my subject, and had learned of these things called "friends". I had decided that I would become David's, and to that end I had brought a small offering.

"Lawrence! What are you doing here?"

I want to become closer to you, David.

Mam was shouting from the kitchen. "Who is it? It's not religious, is it?"

I've brought you an offering, David.

"Oh! I don't really want…"

Here!

"What is it?"

It's a journal. You have to write in it.

"Okay…"

You've always wanted to be a writer, haven't you? These empty pages are for you to fill with all your secrets and dreams and ideas.

"Right," said David. "Thanks."

David looked—as he would put it—"freaked out" by the whole thing.

"Do I look freaked out?" he asked.

Of course. But you're getting used to me, I think. Can I walk to college with you?

"Go on then. Hang on. I'll get my bag." He yelled back at the kitchen: "I'm off now, Mam!"

She yelled back: "Aren't you going to kiss me goodbye?"

"See you tonight!"

The boys walked in silence for a while across a building site and then Lawrence said that he thought David should have introduced him to his "mam".

"I don't think so," said David.

But I need to know everything about you. She gave you life, didn't she? She was one of your progenitors.

"That's why I can't introduce you to her, Lawrence. You'll go saying something like that."

I think I'm getting the hang of life on Earth.

David pulled a face. "I wish I was."

David and Lawrence climbed through a broken fence and across damp playing fields to get to the low, blocky buildings of the school. As they joined crowds of younger human beings, Lawrence sensed David draw away from everyone else. He really seemed happiest when he was being most distant. In his classes he sat on his own. Which was good, because this made space for his Novelizor to pull up a seat alongside him. He did this in every classroom David went to and, eventually, David seemed all right with that. Do you mind if I sit here?

"Fine. As long as you don't describe everything I do."

Said David.

Sorry. Couldn't resist.


DAVID HAD ANOTHER FRIEND CALLED Robert, who was into "bands" and was very keen on football as well. At the end of that particular day at college David was walking alongside Robert, and Lawrence lagged along behind, listening in.

Robert was describing something he had seen happening during a game of football. Apparently somebody involved had "nutmegged the defender" and "planted it in the top corner".

David appeared to follow the meaning of this about as much as Lawrence did. "Wow! Great. Er, is that good?"

But then Robert had noticed who was following them down the street. "Don't look now, Davey boy, but your mate's following you again!"

"Oh," said David. "Yeah."

"Do you want me to have a word?" Robert asked him. "Or something a little harder?"

Lawrence gathered that Robert was offering to do something violent. David was alarmed. "No, it's okay. He's all right." He stopped and turned round. "Lawrence? You can walk with us if you like."

Pleased, Lawrence hurried to catch up with them.

"What are you doing?" said Robert.

"He's all right. Give him a chance."

Here we all are then! Walking home through the dark streets of the estates and the deep autumn leaves, and talking about…what are we talking about?

"Football," said a glum-looking David.

"And I was telling David he should come and watch the match down the Turbinia," said Robert.

Should he?

"I can't," said David. "I should be getting home for Mam."

Robert was keen for his friend to come to the pub and see the game.

"Come on. You should come down. We'll get leathered."

What is "leathered"?

David told Lawrence: "He means drunk."

But David is only seventeen. It would be against human law for him to consume alcoholic beverages.

Robert looked at the Novelizor incredulously. "Just…forget it."

Lawrence turned his attention to his subject. I can't help noticing that you're dawdling, David. Won't your "mam" be worrying?

Robert looked from one to the other. "What is it with you two? It's like he's got some sort of hold over you, Davey."

Lawrence nodded eagerly and happily explained how, in the old days, Novelizors used to have a literal hold over their subjects and if anyone tried to escape their brains would be burned out. Very nasty. Of course, it wasn't like that nowadays.

Robert tried to pull David aside. "What the hell's he on about?"

Embarrassed, David said: "Just some science-fiction thing. Lawrence is into sci-fi."

"Oh, he's a geek as well, is he? Fine. I'll leave you to your boyfriend."

"Shut up," David said, looking cross.

Lawrence shrugged. I am indeed a boy, and I'm his friend. What of it?

Robert was bored with the pair of them by now. There was something funny about the way they were going on and he didn't like it. "Look, I've got better stuff to do. See you tomorrow, maybe."

"Robert, wait..." David called, but it was hopeless because Robert was already running off and turning the corner at the end of the street.

David was left walking along with Lawrence, who grinned at him.

Robert seems nice. What would you like to talk about? Shall we continue that very interesting conversation from our English class? About Woolf and the Brontës and how every human relationship seems, in your opinion, to be ultimately doomed to failure?

"No," snapped David. "It's fine. I'll see you later, maybe. I ought to be getting home..."

"Hey, buggerlugs," Mam said. On the telly, someone was taking something out of an oven really carefully while a couple of other people watched on. "Come and watch the Cakey-Bakey show with me."

"No thanks."

"What's the matter with you?"

"Oh, I'm just knackered, that's all. Too much coursework and...stuff."

"Stuff?" Mam pressed the mute button on the remote. "I thought as much. Is it...a girl?"

"No!"

"Huh—I know troubles in love when I see them. Oh, come on, David, you can confide in your mam!" She reached for her box of Celebrations.

"It's nothing. It's just..."

"What?"

"Dad was...he was your first, wasn't he?"

She laughed bitterly, fishing around in the chocolates. "Yeah, first and only—and look how that went!" She stared at him. He looked so awkward standing there. "Hey, you're not worrying about ending up like him, are you? You're more like me than him. You've got my nicer nature."

"Yeah, so I've heard." He rolled his eyes. She'd been saying that stuff forever. "So... if you could go back in time, would you...would you change things?"

"Of course not! It was worth going through every moment of those eighteen years with that stupid tosser. Because out of all of that I got you, didn't I?"

David smiled. "Thanks, Mam."

"Think nothing of it. My best years were wasted, my confidence was ruined and my looks have gone to pot, but you make it all worthwhile, son." She gave him a great big smile and then she turned the sound back on, just in time for judges' comments.

It was a few days later that David next saw Lawrence at college. The Novelizor had been minding his own business, observing David's world. David found him sitting alone in the common room.

Lawrence thought he would sit here quietly, trying to blend in.

"I want to ask you something…" David said.

Have you started writing in your journal yet?

"Listen, I've got a free afternoon so I came to ask you if—you wanted to…"

It's important that you start writing quite soon. You've got a lot of work ahead of you, you know.

"I've an afternoon off. And actually, I was going to ask you…"

Yes? What were you going to ask me?

"If you wanted to come to Darlington on the bus with me. There's a place I'd like to show you."

Lawrence could hardly believe it.

I would be delighted, David.

"Really?" David grinned. "Great!"

David and Lawrence caught the 723 bus to Darlington. In the market place they visited a small shop. David led the way inside, as if it was a place of worship. There were pale wooden shelves and a long table in the middle, with paperbacks laid out in luridly colourful rows. The air was scented with exotic spices and that was apparently because these were foreign imports. These books had travelled from far afield.

David said, "I brought you here because you like sci-fi."

Do I?

"This bookshop is the best. They're all American remainder copies. And comics, too." He started poring over the stacks, and picking up particular books that caught his attention. "Have you read this? *The Grisly Space Fandango* by Penelope Faith Conquest? Or this series, *The Eternal Mayhem Chronicles* by Everard Donat." He stopped and looked at the close confines of the shop around him. "I've been coming here for years…"

Lawrence studied everything that David pointed out to him.

Some of these illustrated covers are very interesting, David. The being on this one who is strangling the Earth astronaut has a look of my fifth eldest aunt on my female parent's side.

"What?!"

That was me joking. She has far too few secondary sexual characteristics.

"Right…. Oh, look: *Entrails by Moonlight* by Marcia Sopwith."

Lawrence peered over his shoulder.

I like finding out what you like.

David was pleased to hear this. He'd never had anyone share his enthusiasm for books like this before. "Come and take a look at the Paranormal Romance section! Some of these are brilliant!"

Lawrence frowned.

What is…Paranormal Romance?

"It's where people fall in love with unsuitable beings," David explained. "Vampires, werewolves, shape-shifters and stuff. And it usually all goes wrong."

I myself am a shape-shifter. Have I told you that?

"Er…no."

I can turn into just about anything.

LATER, IN THE CAFÉ NEXT door, David and Lawrence had organic cheese scones and Lady Grey tea and David talked once more about the futility of human love.

David started quoting: "'I am the only being whose doom / No tongue would ask, no eye would mourn.'"

Lawrence stirred his tea.

Pardon? Could I have the sugar, please?

"Emily Brontë," said David.

Ah, yes. A very nice lady. I did some of my early fieldwork in nineteenth-century Yorkshire, probing into the psyches of the Brontë sisters.

"Right…" David said. He supposed he was getting used to Lawrence's strange sense of humour. "I guess she was saying that we're, like, all on our own in the end."

Novelizors can't stand being on their own. Lawrence frowned and examined his scone. We begin to lose our faculties if we have no one to observe.

"I actually think human beings are made to be on their own," said David. "We're better off being solitary. Everyone ends up falling apart otherwise. Look at Mam and Dad. And Mam and my nanna. It all goes wrong. Even Mam and me are falling out more lately."

Not good examples there, David, since the common denominator is your mam.

Might it just be that she causes rows with everyone?

"She's had a tough time!"

David was cross whenever Lawrence criticized his mother.

"I'm all she's got since Dad walked out, just after she told him about the baby. And she had me so young. I owe her so much. She was like sixteen and her own mother chucked her out and wouldn't even visit the hospital..."

Is this why you read such sad poetry all the time? Because of your guilt and attachment to your mother? Perhaps you are identifying too heavily with her view of the universe?

"I...er...don't know about that..."

I haven't been on planet Earth for very long, but I will venture an opinion. I don't think quite all human relationships are doomed.

"I feel like mine are," sighed David. "It's like I've grown up wrong, somehow."

Lawrence was surprised to hear that. He thought David was probably okay, actually.

David looked up at him, surprised to hear this. "Erm, thanks."

They stopped to look at each other over the table. Lawrence suddenly thought that David's eyes really did look like the very dark, very sweet tea he favoured.

David took a deep breath. "You know...I think I might fancy you. A bit. Is that okay?"

Lawrence wasn't sure how to react to that.

"I've never said anything like that to anyone before."

This was obviously a big moment in David's emotional development. It was most interesting.

"Right," said David briskly. "Well, let's just forget it, shall we? I never said anything."

Lawrence made a note of it.

"Just forget it!" snapped David.

THAT NIGHT, DAVID STARTED WRITING in the journal Lawrence had given him.

> I kept a page-a-day diary when I was a kid, years ago. I stopped because I thought nothing was happening in my life. It was all about what was on TV and having pizza for tea and Mam fighting with Dad and everything they said.
>
> Maybe now is when things start to happen. I feel jumpy and tingly, like my whole body knows something. Does that sound daft? Maybe I should write this in cipher. I know Mam goes through my stuff

*when she's bored. And if you're reading this, Mam, don't try to deny it…*
     *I met this boy called Lawrence. He says he comes from a world*
*called Verbatim 6. He says that he has chosen me.*

THE FOLLOWING EVENING, LAWRENCE WAS following David home as usual, looking forward to another of their chats.

"Oi!"

But then he saw David get stopped by an older boy called Simon Grainger – and his spotty mate, whose name David never knew.

They were bored and dizzy after an afternoon spent drinking a local beverage known as White Lightning.

"Hey, it's that posh git. You. Yes, you."

David tried to move past them. But they planted themselves either side of him.

"Excuse me."

"Listen to his manners. He sounds like a puff."

The spotty friend laughed at this. Lawrence stood watching from the top of the hill as Simon shoved David and he fell down in the mud.

"Whoops – look out. You've slipped on the leaves!"

David tried to tell him to leave him alone.

"Come on then, you faggot. Fight back, won't you?"

David couldn't get up.

"Where's your boyfriend today, then?"

"He's just a mate, that's all."

Lawrence realized they were talking about him.

"You ought to watch out. We don't have queers round here."

"Get off me!"

David stayed on the ground. They kicked him. And they spat on him. All the shouted words were blending into one then. Faggot. Puff. Queer.

They kept kicking him.

The bigger boy was shouting, "Come on! Get up!"

The other one noticed that kids were gathering round and taking pictures of the fight on their telephones and posting them on social networking sites and getting "likes".

The Novelizor watched all of this from the top of the hill. He was making careful mental notes. He wondered if David was getting hurt.

This had to happen. He knew that it did. It was a part of the story.

There was such a lot going on. A small crowd had gathered. Some girl was calling the police on her phone.

And then the two aggressors both turned and ran away.

Lawrence came to join his subject. His face was bleeding. I saw what happened. Are you all right?

Lawrence tried to help David up, but he was shrugged off angrily. Kids were still staring, fascinated. Then the last of them ran off.

"Why didn't you do something?"

Did they really attack you because you are a queer puff?

"It's because you hang around me, making them think you're my bloody boyfriend. It's all your fault and when I could do with some help you're not even there!"

I am a Novelizor. I can't get involved. I can only watch and narrate.

David looked at him in disbelief. "You what? Oh, just piss off, Lawrence. Leave me alone."

David picked himself up and limped home. He was winded from having his balls kicked. And I—Lawrence the Novelizor—followed him home. Always a few steps behind.

"Piss the hell off, Lawrence."

LAWRENCE WANTED TO SEE THAT David was safely home. His mam was so shocked by the state of him that she almost went into labour there and then. But she didn't. She did something even more disturbing.

She went and phoned David's dad, who David hadn't seen since he moved out the previous year.

"I know you don't want to see him—neither do I! He made both our lives a misery."

"Then why did you phone him?" He was horrified at the idea of his dad turning up.

"He's a copper. He's got power. He can get them—those animals—who did this to you."

"I'm all right. Phone him again and say we don't need him."

"You're not all right. Look at you."

"Just cuts and bruises."

"You were lucky to get away. And where was that friend of yours? That so-called best pal?"

"Lawrence?" David shrugged. "Lawrence didn't want to fight, he…"

"Some pal he turned out to be."

"It wasn't his fault."

There came an abrupt knocking at the front door.

Mam squeaked. "That'll be your dad. I've got to get changed. Answer it, will you?"

"Why are you getting changed?"

"I want to show him what he's missing."

"What?!"

She was halfway up the stairs. "Just answer the door."

David took a deep breath before opening the front door. And there was Dad. In his work suit. Looking more or less the same as ever.

"David. God, look at you. What the hell happened?"

"I've been beaten up."

His dad gave a mirthless laugh. "I can see that!" He stepped forward. "Can I come in?"

"I guess."

Dad led the way to their front room. "When your mam phoned the station she was lucky to get me. I should be in Sunderland right now."

He turned to study David's face. "That's a nasty shiner you're going to have there, son."

David looked away from him. "There's not much to make a statement about . . ."

"Young thugs can't go round attacking people like that. I understand that's what happened." He sat down heavily on the armchair and tugged his trousers neat. Then he fetched a little notebook and pen out of his jacket.

"It was unprovoked," David told him. "They got me on the way home from school."

"Did they say anything?"

"Nothing. Just laid into me."

"And do you know who they are?"

"Simon Grainger and some mate of his. They left school last year."

"I see," said Dad. "There was a lad hanging about outside the house when I pulled up."

"What?"

"Blond lad."

"Oh. That's just Lawrence. He wasn't involved."

"Okay," said Dad, as David came back from peering through the net curtains. "Now, you are going to tell me the details slowly and I'll write them down and then yourself can sign it and we'll see about getting these lads picked up tonight, all right? I'll get them. They can't do this to you. Not to my son."

"They already have."

"This wouldn't have happened if I was still here. I could..."

"It would have happened anyway."

His dad looked cross with him. "I could have taught you better how to stick up for yourself. I should have..."

Mam came breezing in, wearing a floaty aqua-print maternity dress. She looked glamorous with her hair down. She gave off a kind of carefree vibe.

"Oh!" she said, looking at them both in the middle of their interview. "There you are…"

Dad nodded at her. "Mary."

"Have you seen what those scumbags have done to your son?"

"We'll sort it out." He looked her up and down briefly. "You look nice, Mary."

Her eyebrows shot up. "Me? I'm in my rags. And I'm huge. The important thing here is David. Your son. Have you forgotten about him, eh? Look at him. You've not seen him since before Christmas. Not so much as a card!"

"Look, Mary, I've got to get this statement done and then…"

"Oh, you get on and do what you have to. I remember all your bloody 'procedures' and paperwork. Nothing ever changes with you, does it? I suppose you'll be wanting a cup of tea."

"Milky. Lots of sugar. For the shock."

Mam laughed. "He's the one who's had the shock!"

"I meant him," said Dad.

Mam waltzed off to make tea.

So David made his statement to his dad, who laboured over it, scribbling away. David was dismayed to see his words being changed, simplified, misspelled. His mam brought the tea and went on sitting there in her colourful frock the whole time, with the best china out and French Fancies on a plate. The telly sound was down and she was shooting glances at his dad.

When the statement was all taken, Dad stood up again and studied Mam. "And you, Mary. You must be…close to time now."

"Yes."

"You'll let me know, won't you? When the baby comes…"

"Will do."

"I could be there…"

"I'll let you know. If you're that interested. Look, if you've finished taking his statement, just go, would you?"

Lawrence the Novelizor had been waiting outside. He waited until the policeman left and drove off.

"Er, hullo. Is David home?"

Mam wasn't impressed by Lawrence standing there on the doorstep. "Oh, so this is your mate who didn't help you, is it?"

David let him in. "Mam, it's fine. Come on, Lawrence. We'll go to my room."

David flopped down on his single bed and let out a huge sigh. He lay on top of scribbled essay notes, paperbacks and his new journal.

"That was awful."

Lawrence had never been in David's bedroom before. It was messy and dark and musky-smelling.

"Just shut up, will you, Lawrence?"

Lawrence sat down carefully on the desk chair.

I was interested to see your male parent. Will you look like that when you are older? Balding and blotchy?

"I don't even know why I'm still talking to you."

I believe it's because you don't have many other friends in your peer group. Tell me more about your reunion with your male parent. This is a very significant moment.

"He wanted to know what names they were shouting at me. Not how I was getting on at college, or how Mam and I are doing without him. Just what words they chose to use when they beat the crap out of me. And what was I going to say? Puff? Queer?"

Did you?

"What do you think?"

Lawrence thought about this. He thought about everything that had been happening during the past few, interesting hours.

He seemed like a nice man, your father.

"No he didn't. And then he said—he said…"

What?

"He said I needed a proper man's influence in my life. That I'd been missing having him around all year and it was doing me harm."

Is that true? Do you miss him?

"I don't know. Not really. But . . . I end up actually feeling guilty. Because I haven't been in touch with him either, have I? I agreed to go out on Saturday with him. To the shops."

You are going to spend "quality" time with your male parent.

"He's offered to help me choose a suit for my university interviews."

You don't look very pleased about this.

"I just want to die."

I'll come with you, if you like.

"When I die?"

I meant in the car with your dad. To the shops. On Saturday.

"No! Absolutely no way. No!"

LAWRENCE LOOKED OUT OF THE car window at the motorway, streaking by.

I've never been in a police car before.

"It's not a police car. It's a Mondeo," said David's dad, keeping his eyes on the road. Next to him, David was being very quiet. "What do you think of this suit I'm wearing, David?"

"Very smart, yeah."

"I thought we'd get something like it for yourself."

"Great."

Lawrence had noticed that David's dad would use the word "yourself" instead of "you". It sounded strangely formal and oblique, as in: "I'm taking yourself to the biggest shopping mall in Europe!" and "Can yourself drive a car yet?"

"What's your friend saying back there?" Dad frowned.

"He often talks to himself, don't you, Lawrence?"

"I don't mind bringing him along, even though it's literally the only time we've had together in months."

"Thanks," said David.

"Do you see much of that Robert Woolf still? He was a good lad. Still into his football, is he? He had a natural talent, I always thought."

"We've kind of drifted," said David. "He hangs around with a dodgy crowd."

"That's not good."

"Yeah."

"Your mother's looking well. I hope you'll both cope. Just the two of you."

"We can manage."

Dad shot a glance at him. "Not fair on a young lad like yourself, though, is it?"

"It's okay."

"I would have stayed, you know. For the little one. And for you, as well. It's just…"

"What? It's just what, Dad?"

"It would have been worse if I'd stayed. You know that. Me and your mam, you know, it just couldn't go on like that…"

David wasn't sure what he was supposed to say to all of this. "Well, it's better now."

"That's how you feel, is it?"

"But it is, isn't it? Your life is better too. Away from Mam."

"Yes… You'll be away soon as well, won't you? Which universities are you applying to?"

"Lancaster, York, Middlesbrough…"

"You'll look the part in your new suit. I could drive you there, to the interviews and stuff."

"Yeah?"

"What are dads for?"

David bit his tongue.

AT THE SHOPPING MALL, DAD made him try suits on and David was mortified by styles, prices, by the things his dad said. By the matey way he had of going on.

"What you want is something that will last for years. Quality, not something trendy..."

"I suppose."

Dad's favourite menswear shops weren't appealing to David very much.

"You needn't spend a fortune to look stylish and smart. Are you listening, son?"

But David had seen someone.

"Oh no."

"Isn't that your mate? Robert? Go and talk to him, David. He's waving you over."

Robert Woolf was hanging around with some girls, next to a fountain.

"Davey," Robert greeted him.

"You remember my dad?"

Robert nodded. "Mr. Taylor."

"Hello there, Robert. What are you up to, then? Shouldn't you be at football practice? I remember yourself being a smashing centre-forward at one time. Do you still play?"

"A bit. When I can."

"We're getting David kitted out with some new gear."

Robert grinned. "Gear, eh? And what about his pal? Are you kitting him out as well?"

The two girls giggled, and everyone turned to look at the Novelizor.

"That's Lawrence," Dad said. "He's David's new friend."

"Yeah, I know," Robert said. There was something funny about his tone of voice. "His 'friend.'"

David was turning away. "Look, can we just go now?"

Dad chuckled. "He's just in a bad mood."

Robert called out: "You could hang out with us if you want, Davey."

Lawrence piped up.

David is going to the Terrace Café for high tea with his father and his friend, Lawrence. That's what's going to happen now.

"Uh...right," said Robert. "Go on then. Do what you want."

David, Dad and Lawrence moved away from the small party by the fountain, in the direction of the food court.

"You should be nicer to him," Dad said. "He's just a pleasant, normal lad."

David didn't look convinced.

Dad snapped, "Would you stop butting in all the time, son?"

"Leave him alone!" David said, louder than he'd meant to.

Dad was getting angry now. "I'll tell you what you've got to learn to do better, David. And that's mixing in more. There's all types of people in this world. Don't be getting ideas about yourself."

David had had enough for one day. "Can we...can we just go home now?"

So THEY DIDN'T CHOOSE A suit in the end. They went home empty-handed. All the way home Dad talked about his police work.

"When you're in a position like mine, you've got to be sure about things. I banged up a vicious cross-dresser from Ferryhill who was abusing his foster kiddies. There's no shades of grey in a case like that. It's stark black and white. He's the baddy and I'm literally the goody."

He was playing them his Simply Red CD.

Are we nearly home yet?

"I think Lawrence is feeling carsick," said David.

"We're almost back," Dad told him. He didn't really care if Lawrence felt unwell or not. "Look, did they really call yourself a puff?"

"Who?"

"Your assailants. They admitted in their own statements that they used terms of homophobic abuse and all that." There was a pause then, and David stared at the green fields sliding by, and clouds that looked to him like galleons. "Look, son. You can tell your dad anything. If yourself has anything to say..."

"I've got nothing to say."

It was like a police interrogation.

"I'm just asking."

"Well. Okay," said David.

"Cos if yourself has any worries on that score—they are wrong. Those lads. You're just sensitive and clever, like your mam used to be. That doesn't make yourself a homosexual or anything. You needn't worry. You can still be a normal lad."

"You what?"

"I don't think you've grown up wrong and perverted. I really don't."

Now they were pulling into their town. They were almost home.

"Oh. Okay. Thanks," said David. Then, a few minutes later, they were parked outside

David and his mam's house. "Bye, Dad."

"Bye then, son."

The car raced off again.

Lawrence thought he preferred David's female parent.

"You're not the only one," David told him.

That night was the night David's female parent went into the throes of the state known as labour—and this time it was real.

"What?!" David gasped.


THEY COULD HEAR MAM SCREAMING in the front room, even before David got the front door open. The pair of them went running through. She was on the settee and the cushions had been flung all over. Her knitting and all the remotes were on the floor.

"Mam! What's happening?"

"What do you bloody well think is happening?"

Lawrence the Novelizor had been quite correct in his earlier assessment of the situation.

"Lawrence, just stop! Mam?"

Mam was gasping with pain. "You've been too busy running about with that pig of a father of yours."

"Oh God," said David. He was frozen in the doorway.

"Can you…phone an…ambulance…" Mam panted. "I couldn't find the cordless—nnnnnggh—bloody thing…or my…flipping mobile…"

"Will an ambulance get here in time? Mam!"

David's mother was hauling herself onto the settee with her legs up.

Her "waters" had apparently broken and her knitting was ruined.

Mam was struggling to sit up. "Your father spoiled—nnnnnggh—both our lives. Aaagghh. I hate bloody men. Don't just stand there, David!"

For a few moments he couldn't move. He couldn't even think straight.

"David, man! It's going to happen right now. What did he say about me? Nnnnnggh. Your so-called father? Aaagghh. Slagging me off, I suppose?"

"What do I do?"

She was trying to get both her legs onto the settee, grunting and breathing hard. "Did he buy you anything? Nnnnnggh."

"Shut up about Dad. He doesn't matter."

"He's useless. AAAGGHH."

David seemed to come back to his senses. "Hot water and clean towels. That's what we need."

Lawrence wasn't sure what you did with the hot water and towels once you actually had them. Neither was David.

"Mam, can you wait until the ambulance comes?"

"AAAAGGGHHHH!"

"And shouldn't you be doing your special breathing or something?"

"NNNNGGGHH! What special bloody breathing?"

It was getting very noisy in their sitting room by now.

Mam had both hands on her huge belly. "This won't wait for the ambulance."

David was worried in case it was like the boy who cried wolf and the paramedics had stopped believing her.

"Lawrence, shut up!" David shouted at his friend. "Stop saying stupid stuff and help me! Boil the kettle and I'll phone."

Lawrence stared at him, trying to be calm.

I shouldn't interfere. I'm not supposed to.

"Just do it! You have to help! You can't just stand there!"

Lawrence just stood there, feeling unhappy and torn.

You don't understand, David!

"I do. You're scared. I'm scared. But you have to help."

But Novelizors aren't supposed to get involved! You saw me! I just stood there, didn't I? When they hit you and kicked you.

"It doesn't matter about that now," David told him.

Lawrence stared at the carpet and the sopping bundle of knitting.

I tried so hard not to get involved.

Then Mam started shrieking: "HURRY UP! NNNGGHH!"

"It's really true, isn't it?" said David, in an awe-struck tone of voice. "It's really going to happen. On our settee."

Lawrence nodded.

She is going to give birth to another person, yes. A smaller one.

David was at the sideboard, fumbling with the cordless phone.

"Maybe it'll take ages," he said. "They sometimes do, don't they? Maybe the ambulance will have time to get here…"

Mam was screaming at the top of her lungs by now.

Lawrence shuddered.

It could put you off for life, this.

Mam's screams ebbed away for a few moments and she caught her breath. Her face was bright red and wet with perspiration. "I wish I'd bothered with more of them classes now. I thought I'd remember everything from last time."

"That was seventeen years ago," David told her. "Do your breathing!"

"You popped out easy as anything," she told him.

"Mam! You have to remember! Your breathing! Do it!"

"I can't!"

"Mam—look, I don't know what to do. I..."

"Nnnggggghh! Aaaaaaaagh!"

David turned to his friend for help. "Lawrence...I...I can't...What do I do?!"

Lawrence the Novelizor from Verbatim 6 took a huge breath and made the biggest decision of his life.

Stand back, David.

"What are you doing?"

I'm taking off my school tie. And I'm rolling up the sleeves of my shirt.

"But what are you going to do?" David shouted.

I'm getting involved.

Mam yelled out croakily: "I'm going to die."

No, you're not.

She had her hair plastered all over her face and gently, Lawrence helped her brush it aside.

Can you push?

"I don't know. I'll have to take my pants off."

"Oh god," David said.

Mam screamed and David stepped backwards, watching in horrified fascination as Lawrence took over looking after his mam.

"Listen," Mam grunted. "Listen—if I die..."

You're not going to die.

"Women die in childbirth all the time," she pointed out, her voice full of panic.

Lawrence considered this.

I suppose they do in novels. In the Victorian ones that David loves so much.

"Lawrence!" David yelled, thinking his friend was getting distracted.

Mam was shrieking again. She looked wildly at David. "Who is this bloke, David?"

David swallowed. "He's—he's..."

"He's your friend, it's fine," Mam said.

More than that, really.

"Yes," David agreed. "More than that."

I'm his Novelizor.

Mam couldn't really get the gist of what they were on about since she couldn't stop howling. "What?"

"Never mind that," said David, steeling himself. "It's about time I told you, Mam..."

"AAAGGGHHHH!"

"I'm..."

Mam screamed at him: "Can we leave this till later?" Then she lapsed into a frantic burst of panting.

Lawrence stepped in, speaking as calmly as he could.

Breathe, Mrs. David's Mam!

Mam tried her best to breathe properly.

In the relatively peaceful pause, David spoke up. "I'm gay, Mam. That's what."

"What?" said Mam. And then she was wracked by another wave of pain that had her screaming, fit to burst.

Push, I think, Lawrence told her. I believe this is the time for pushing.

"Did you hear, Mam?" shouted David. "What I said? I'm gay."

Mam screamed back at him, through gritted teeth: "I already knew!"

"What?"

"Mothers always know!"

Then her screams reached a crescendo, and pretty soon after that, the ambulance arrived again at their door.

At the hospital, David and Lawrence found a coffee machine and drank soupy lattes. Then they had Twixes and Twirls—splitting them to be fair—and Lawrence decided they were the very best kind of food he had eaten since arriving on planet Earth.

"What if she's not all right, Lawrence?"

She will be. Lawrence was sure.

"What if they both die and it's all my fault?"

Lawrence was amazed how long and complicated this human childbirth could be to accomplish.

"Stop pretending that you're not human!" David was glad that the waiting room was empty apart from them.

But I'm not, David! I'm not human. I'm here with a very particular job to do, and I've already compromised that.

"Whatever."

Do you want to hear how Novelizers are born on Verbatim 6?

"Not especially."

"We begin as the merest inkling, and then someone says..."

"Listen!"

Suddenly, there was all this noise of doors opening and closing, and a baby crying. A nurse appeared before them. David and his Novelizor were gently asked to enter a room, from which the most unearthly racket could be heard…

"COME ON, DON'T BE SHY…" Mam said. "Say hello to your baby sister."

David peered close at the little bundle. "Oh. Wow." He stared at the bright pink squidgy face. It was easy to believe the baby was already having her own thoughts inside that tiny head.

Lawrence took a long, thoughtful look at the baby, too.

She has really long feet.

"She's amazing," said David.

"Thanks for your help, boys. I'm sorry it was so fraught."

David was entranced by the baby. Her black scrap of hair, her red fists, which were punching the air, like in triumph.

"I'm calling her Katherine," Mam announced. "After your nanna, even though I hate the blummin' woman."

David nodded. "Lovely."

"Pick her up. Don't be scared."

David did as he was told. He lifted the baby so carefully. "She's heavy!"

Mam laughed. "Tell me about it."

David held the baby up to Lawrence, too.

Greetings, small human. Greetings from Verbatim 6.

"Ha!" sighed Mam. "What's he like?"

"He's hilarious." David rolled his eyes. Then he said, more quietly: "I texted Dad. Just so he knows…"

"I wish you hadn't." Then she glanced at him again, curious. "Any reply yet?"

David shook his head. "Not yet, but he's probably at work. I'm sure he'll come by later."

"I'm not sure I want him to."

"But look at her," said David. "Look at Katherine. He's missing all of this."

"He walked out. We've got our own lives to get on with. And you've got yours, too. With your university stuff."

"That can wait. I'll take a gap year, or something; stay and help with the baby."

"Don't you dare!" Mam said crossly. "I might be what they call an 'older mother', but I'm not geriatric."

"We'll see."

"It's your life, David. You have to make sure you live it."

He chuckled. "Is this the gas and air talking?"

"I mean it. You do what you want to with your life. And if you do, I'll feel I've done a good job of bringing you up right. And it's true, you know."

"What is?"

Mam met his stare. "I already knew about you."

"Oh, right."

"About being a puff."

"Let's talk about it later."

"I like him. That daft lad. Your boyfriend. That's what he is, isn't he? He's a bit odd, I suppose, with the way he goes on."

Lawrence was only half-listening. He was busy trying to communicate with the newly born human.

David said awkwardly, "Well, he's not really my…my…"

"I think he is, you know," said Mam decisively. "Now go on, take him home. Get some rest."

David smiled. "Thanks, Mam."

As they left the hospital and went out into the cold to catch the early morning bus, Lawrence was dwelling on the thought that he was now far too close to his subject.

Boyfriend. It was a strange word. Wrong, somehow. But nice. Nicer than Novelizor.

A FAMILIAR FORD MONDEO PULLED up at the bus stop in front of them.

Dad called out of the window, "Hey, lads!"

"Dad, what are you doing here?"

"You yourself texted me with the news…"

"I never thought you'd come." It was freezing out on the pavement.

Dad had Simply Red playing on his car stereo again.

He said heavily, "I literally still care about you both, you know."

Lawrence beamed at him.

Thank you, Mr. David's Dad!

"Not you, daft lad."

David told his dad, "She's sleeping now. But she's got a little girl."

"Lovely."

She has extremely long feet, Lawrence pointed out.

"Still got your mate with you, I see," Dad sighed.

"He's not just a mate, Dad," said David, with sudden resolution. What did he have to lose? "He's my boyfriend."

"Oh!" said Dad, taking this in. He looked at them both and went slightly pink. "Right! I see." He nodded. "Well, I guess you'll both be wanting a lift home, yeah?"

TWENTY MINUTES LATER, DAD DROPPED them off and the boys went straight upstairs to David's room. It was early morning and everything was very quiet and still.

Lawrence watched as his friend and subject flung himself down on the bed.

"I could do with a hug," said David, softly.

Novelizors from Verbatim 6 aren't really trained to give hugs.

"Just give me a hug, will you?"

THERE WERE A FEW MOMENTS of rustling then, as Lawrence lay down awkwardly on the bed. They tried to work out who was lying on top of the duvet and who was getting under. David pulled off his jumper and shirt and, after a moment of hesitation, unzipped and shucked off his jeans. Lawrence watched all of this, wondering whether he ought to get undressed too. He wasn't sure what the protocol was. In the end, he lay down stiffly, fully dressed, on top of the duvet, quite close to David. He could smell the milky coffee on his warm breath.

You've got a little sister.

"I know. It's amazing."

Lawrence thought about that for a bit. Still, your planet is horribly over-populated. I hope your mother puts a stop to her reproductive urges now.

David shoved his shoulder. "Can't you drop the space act now?"

The what?

"The space act: saying you're from space." David looked straight into his face and Lawrence felt uncomfortable for a few seconds. "It's like a neurotic thing. A way of deflecting attention somehow, away from who you really are…"

But this is who I really am.

"Oh—if you can't be serious about anything…"

I am serious. This is as serious as it gets.

"No, it isn't." David smiled at him. Suddenly he felt daring and conscious of all the covers between them. "Come here."

They kissed.

It took several hot moments and a few delicate manoeuvres.

Oh.

"Wow," David whispered. It was like they were in a bubble of secrecy. "That was my first kiss. I've never…"

Yes. Um.

"Is that all you have to say about it?"

Um.

"You!" David laughed, but he was becoming slightly annoyed too. "You're never lost for words! You never shut up! Now look at you."

Er, yes.

"Is that it?"

Lawrence realized that they had crossed a line. This had gone too far.

"What are you on about?"

Lawrence was seized by a sudden idea. He sat up in the bed. "Come with me, David. There's something I want you to see..."

MINUTES LATER, DAVID WAS FULLY dressed again and they both had their coats and shoes on. They were out in the early morning light, hurrying together over the rubble and rough terrain of the building site.

Lawrence was leading the way to the edge of town and the wasteland.

"What are we doing out here?" David shouted at him.

Come on, and don't ask questions.

"It's the crack of dawn, Lawrence." David was stumbling over heaps of bricks and sand and scrubby plants.

Maybe it was a mistake to come out like this but the Novelizor had been seized by this sudden, mad impulse.

"When you said you had something to show me..."

Sssh. This is secret.

Eventually, they came to a halt. Lawrence waved his arms about and they stood stock still. Then Lawrence crouched down in the undergrowth and David joined him. Lawrence started pushing aside the overgrown vegetation.

"There's nothing here," said David. "What are you looking for?"

I'm going to prove to you, once and for all, who and what I am.

"You don't have to," David told him. "You're Lawrence. That's all I need to know..."

We've gone this far. I might as well show you everything.

"Lawrence. It—it..."

He could hear it before he saw it. There was a wonderful chiming noise that filled the morning air. Then there was all this multi-coloured light glittering about, and all at once, something appeared before them. Something that was as big as a council house, that hadn't been there a moment before. It was a grand and futuristic vision.

David stared at the rainbow lights at the heart of the wasteland.

"What...what is it?"

My spacecraft. It's been hiding in hyperspace. Sort of tangential to this dimension, you see. Here but not here. I thought it was time to show you. What do you think?

"I…I don't know what to say."

I used to know the future. I thought I knew how you'd react.

"It's magnificent."

They're quite common, where I come from, but this one…this one is mine.

As if on cue, as if responding to the pride in Lawrence's tone, a hatchway opened in the side of the ship and a shining ramp extended to meet them.

"It's opening," gasped David. "Does that mean…. Are you…?"

I don't know how things are going to turn out any more. For the first time ever I don't know the end of the story!

A louder bass note accompanied the chiming noise. It sounded very much as if strange and powerful engines were gearing themselves up.

Lawrence the Novelizor turned to his subject.

Will you come with me, David?

"Uh…" David was flabbergasted. "Where to?"

Into space. It's all true—everything I said. I come from your future. I fell in love with your books.

"My books?" This brought David up short. His books?

They were why I came to this place to find you. All this way. I was meant to just observe, but then I changed things and we kissed and now…will you come with me?

"I write books? What are they called?"

I can't tell you.

"But…what do I write about?"

All kinds of things. Time. Friendship. Love. How to keep people together. Learning to love them.

"And you want me to leave Earth?"

Will you?

David had to think hard about this.

"Lawrence, my family needs me. I've got a new sister. And my mam gets panic attacks when she can't get a supermarket trolley through the revolving doors. And I write books, do I? And I get…I get published?"

Fully activated, the semi-sentient ship from Verbatim 6 began to signal its readiness to depart.

I've said too much already, David. We shouldn't even really be in the same story. I used to know how it all worked out. The future was set. But I got too involved.

David took hold of him. "I do want to go with you, Lawrence. But I can't. I've got to stay here. I've got stuff to do in this world…"

But you can write in space. Just think what you might see out there!

"I have to stay. For Mam. And Katherine…. Besides, you said you loved my books. If I'm not here to write them, then you'll never read them, and you won't come back to see me, will you? We'd never have met."

Lawrence knew that he had messed things up. Now everything had changed.

David shook his head. "Do you know what? I reckon it all changed when you first gave me that journal."

The ship's noise and brightly shining lights were intensifying now, as if it was eager for the off.

Lawrence made you want to write?

"You did. Mission accomplished, I reckon."

But I was sent to observe! Not to change your life.

"But you have!" David grinned. "You've changed it forever, I think."

It's only been a couple of weeks…

"Maybe that's enough." David hugged Lawrence hard, and felt him relax into it at last. "Will you come back, then? One day?"

If I can, I will. I promise.

Then Lawrence kissed David, and stepped away.

Goodbye, David.

"Goodbye, Lawrence. I'm really going to miss you…" David had to shout to be heard over the spaceship engine noises. "And thank you!"

For what?

"You've read my books—you tell me!"

Lawrence turned and hurried away into his beloved ship. David watched as the ramp slid back and the hatchway smoothly closed. Then the ship seemed to glow in a satisfied kind of way before lifting off, gloriously, into the brightening air of the morning.

HOME AGAIN, LATER, DAVID WENT back to writing in his journal:

*When I turned seventeen I didn't really know who I was, or what I might become.*
*And then, all of a sudden, I did.*
*I knew exactly who I was.*
*And I knew who it was I was writing for. And I knew that, when he read it, he would love my story.*

*We all agreed, Jonas was the best thing to happen to us and could not remember what life was like without him. He gave us permission to talk freely, to think aloud. He gave us a sense of purpose. Even if we couldn't remember what we specifically did each afternoon, we basked in the glory of our endless laughter. While in the house we were insulated from the outside world, its cruel mechanisms, its falsehood, and the more we knew we were better off alone.*

# Wallflowers

## JONATHAN HARPER

THE HOUSE WAS A PHONY, a fraud, a fake. It was tucked away on the far side of Cavalier Park near the old abandoned post office. Why anyone would choose to build in this part of town we did not know. In comparison to our homes it was far too big and gaudy, a pretentious mix of stone and wood. The gardens were full of red plastic flowers that bobbed gently as we touched them; the front door was painted black like a gaping mouth. We had only come to see it because summer break was ending, our freedom slipping away, and it was the only place left to explore.

"A Craftsman," Margot called it. She was the new girl. Her daddy was a builder and had moved to this side of the Chesapeake Bay to bring great changes. We didn't know what that meant. To us the town of Henderson was already a sunken ship. Each year it got smaller. Not in size, but in mentality. It was falling into disrepair, its good citizens getting too fat and complacent. They liked tradition and church and most of all, the unambiguous. None of them knew where we were that afternoon. Nor did they care to know that change was coming.

Margot kept a brass key tied around her neck. She claimed she had one for every house her father built. She led us through the garage, still just a skeleton of wood beams and a plastic canopy nailed on top, and jimmied open the back door. Inside were the bare bones of an unfinished project: blank drywall, exposed pipes and wires; the kitchen cabinets were still stacked in the corner awaiting assembly. Thankfully, we discovered the toilet didn't flush before we regretted using it. As we wandered the first floor our footsteps echoed. We left hand prints on the walls, picked at the loose tiles of the fireplace, kicked open doors, searched every crevice even if we didn't know what we were looking for. What we wanted was a mystery or a haunting. But what we got was just a house, as lame as anywhere else in Henderson. We realized it must be abandoned for a reason. We had no business being there. So we left, a little disgruntled, barely giving Margot enough time to lock up behind us.

"Carpe diem," Mrs. Burkett said and wrote it on the chalkboard. "Can anyone tell me what this means?"

Our first day in Henderson High School ended in Latin class. We had no interest in dead languages. The latest trend in school electives was the cinema studies class, where students sat in a dark auditorium and pretended to watch films. Latin, with so many empty seats, was the safer choice for students like us.

"Carpe diem means 'seize the day.' It's a very common expression." Mrs. Burkett's hair was jet black with a thick gray streak. She wore dark lacy dresses and looked like an undead princess. We liked her. "Say it with me: Carpe diem!" Her face beamed with enthusiasm but again, we didn't answer. "Come on, now. There's no place for wallflowers in this class."

Funnily enough, we had never heard that word before, but instantly knew what it meant. We were wallflowers. Scarred, ugly, odd and untalented, we rarely spoke, never participated. We were all acutely aware that while the adult world mostly ignored us, the young were in the habit of attacking their weak.

"One more try, class. *Carpe diem*," she commanded.

A voice came from the back row. "Carpe scrotum!" and Benny Robertson erupted into self-congratulatory laughter. No one liked Benny, not even us. "Get it? Seize the balls!"

"That was very clever," Mrs. Burkett said and escorted him out to the hall. This was why Benny was left out of our plans. He was too loud, too vulgar, too starved for attention. Wallflowers were calm, dignified. We knew how to disappear.

We returned to the house simply because we could, but mostly because we had nowhere else to go. We were so bored, so boring, waiting for something to happen. This was the peril of our age, no more than fourteen: scornful of adulthood, offended by the mundane. We had orphan fantasies; we wanted to feel transformed. And worst of all, we were terribly self-conscious about it.

It was Margot who invented our games. She was willing to do anything to keep us from being quiet. She would start with a name, one picked at random, and we were asked to fill in the details. The goal was to cause discomfort and laughter. We described them in ugly detail, gave them dirty habits and addictions. We took turns inventing their lives, these shameful lists of mishaps and failures, always leading to their demise. The death scenes we created were far better than any horror film. Without realizing it, we had soon created an entire community of imaginary misfits, the old tenants of the house, and began writing their histories upon the walls until every bit of white space was covered.

None of us could recall how Jonas was created. Some blamed Mrs. Burkett's strange lessons. "Household deities," she said. "Di tenante." She taught as if we sat around a campfire swapping ghost stories. Lares, spirits that hovered over places, protectors of the hearth and home. This was a lesson that stuck. If we wanted a haunting, we'd have to do it ourselves.

Margot was the first to really evoke the name. "Jonas," she said and let it echo throughout the house. We uttered it like a dare, as if it tickled, as if Jonas were some ghoulish apparition who threatened to appear if we called him too many times. We wandered the house searching for him, from the concrete basement to the empty rooms on the upper floor. We began to greet him as we entered the house each afternoon. He became the center of all our games. We told him our secrets, our revenge fantasies, as if he was standing there amongst us. And when his name appeared in scrawled letters above the fireplace, we nodded to each other with approval.

In Latin class, the words "Carpe Scrotum" appeared on the chalkboard. Mrs. Burkett came waltzing in, tardy as usual, and observed the letters with cautious amusement. "All right, who wrote this?" she half-sang. Someone whispered, "Jonas," and the classroom filled with hideous laughter. We watched quietly as she escorted Benny Robertson out of the room. The entire hallway could hear him protest. This happened only once.

A MONTH PASSED AND OUR parents grew suspicious. They watched us enter well after dark, their eyes darting between us and the clock. They were curious but not concerned. Henderson was still a small town without much trouble and we were not the types to cause any. The evenings continued on as normal: in front of television sets, our families hovered over their dinner trays, always struggling for something to talk about. When they finally asked what kept us out so late, we told them we were out with Jonas and did our best not to grin.

WE ALL AGREED, JONAS WAS THE best thing to happen to us and could not remember what life was like without him. He gave us permission to talk freely, to think aloud. He gave us a sense of purpose. Even if we couldn't remember what we specifically did each afternoon, we basked in the glory of our endless laughter. While in the house we were insulated from the outside world, its cruel mechanisms, its falsehood, and the more we knew we were better off alone.

Then the "No Trespassing" sign appeared and everything shattered. We stood there, dumbstruck, looking at the heavy block letters. Perhaps we had grown too comfortable with the emptiness of the park and the boarded-up post office. It no longer occurred to us that we were trespassers. But Margot still had her key and coaxed us inside. Our graffiti was painted over, the kitchen cabinets restacked, the loose tiles of the fireplace removed. Every mark we'd left had been erased and yet, even in all that emptiness, there was a terrible sensation we were being watched.

We didn't return after that, no matter how much Margot begged. She'd flash her key in the middle of class or stalk us to our lockers. "This changes nothing," she said. To us, our time together had been fun, but now we felt depleted—as hollowed out as the empty rooms. The games were over and it was time to move on. None of us said this to Margot. She was turning possessive and hysterical. One day she gave a long rambling speech about reclaiming what was ours. She shoved us roughly, demanding not to be ignored. And when we still said nothing she slapped her fists against her bag and stomped off towards the park alone. What she did out there all by herself we could not imagine. It was the first time we wondered if there was something seriously wrong with her.

Instead we tried meeting in our own homes, a different one each afternoon. The problem was our parents. As soon as we came through the front door they openly stared, almost horrified by the size of our group. They could not comprehend where we all had come from or what we wanted. All we wanted was privacy: soundproofed walls and dimly lit spaces. We wanted to feel abandoned. While our parents barely spoke, they still hovered in the periphery. Sometimes they brought us little offerings of cookies and soda cans. Other times we caught them peering around the doorways, staring in bewilderment before they rushed away when we turned to face them.

OUTSIDE OF LATIN CLASS WE barely saw each other.

HALLOWEEN APPROACHED AND THE HIGH school exploded with paper ghosts and foam gravestones. A gallery of jack-o'-lanterns grinned in the front office. Mrs. Burkett wore a black witch's hat for a week and cast spells over the Latin texts. Benny Robertson continued to interrupt class with his embarrassing outbursts. Every time he spoke we rolled our eyes. We'd begun to accept the new routine, waiting for each day to end so we could go home and dread the next. But Margot broke her silence. She whispered that her father planned to resume construction on the house and dangled her key. Then all we could think about was our boredom and our desire for one last gathering. When you are young and neglected you don't just kill time, you slay it dead.

Halloween seemed like a night for last chances. Even the students in film class knew that. We waited for the sun to set, ate lukewarm dinners and donned our silly costumes. Across the park, we marched to the house, which had grown even more rundown in our absence. Margot unlocked the back door and we each muttered "Hello, Jonas" as we passed through. The stale air reeked with the smell of paint. In the foyer we sat cross-legged, our flashlights cutting the dark, as we struggled to remember the old games. Mostly we waited. One of us had stolen a bottle of vodka from his father's study. It circulated a second time, then a third, our lips puckering at the astringent taste. Somehow we were back at the beginning, morose and fuzzy-headed and a little relieved when Margot took a boy upstairs.

We only meant to stay an hour but we got lost in trying to prolong the moment. It was pitch black outside, far later than we'd ever stayed out before. And then we heard the siren as the windows illuminated with blue and red lights. None of this surprised us— we had been expecting it. When the front door opened the police officer peered inside, a hand on his holstered gun. He was surprised to find us lined up patiently waiting for him.

Outside we were presented to a large man with tattoo sleeves. He stood with his arms crossed, his mouth contorted into a monstrous sneer. We had never seen him before but we knew who he was. Margot stepped forward. "Hi, Daddy," she said with nothing but crude indifference. Her father didn't flinch. He grabbed her by the arm, pulled her into his car and drove off, leaving the policeman speechless.

Our parents were summoned, bringing with them that confused apathy we had grown to detest. They could not seem to grasp the situation and stared blankly as the officer said the owners would not press charges, that we were free to go with a warning. For this we were grateful. We moved towards the cars, thinking we could put this awful night behind us.

But instead, one parent asked, "Which one of you is Jonas?"

We looked at one another but said nothing.

"These are the only kids I found," the officer told them. But our parents insisted there was one more child not accounted for. "You mean the girl? Her father took her home," the officer said.

"No. There's a boy. Jonas." Our parents tried describing him, each having heard so little but confident they knew enough. Together they fumbled through a generic description, no one willing to contradict what was previously said. The night grew colder as we waited by the cars, shivering in our stupid costumes. Most of the trick-or-treaters were home, feasting on their spoils. Our mothers asked, "Where is his family? Where will he go on such a cold night?" Our fathers said, "It's not right to leave a boy all alone in an empty house." They were so upset they forgot to punish us.

WE RETURNED TO SCHOOL WITH our heads low, dwelling on the past few weeks. The previous night had left us in a dazed state. Around us, the other students congregated in their usual hierarchies. They were all preoccupied, aloof, talking amongst themselves in heavy overtones. They acted like they knew something we didn't. Gossip traveled fast in our town.

Over morning announcements, Principal Whately addressed us in her chalky smoker's voice. She explained a local boy had gone missing. Anyone with information was encouraged to come forward. Our classmates nodded to each other and continued to whisper. All day the chatter continued. No one knew the full story, but enough of the details. They knew about the house and the park. They knew that the builder's daughter was involved. In the end they seemed delighted that something had finally happened.

In Latin class, Margot's desk was empty. As we took our seats we realized how anxious we were to speak with her. Would her father change his mind and press charges? What had she told him about us, the games, about the boy we made up? She didn't return the next day or the next. Without her we lost our appetite for Latin altogether. Mrs. Burkett struggled to keep our attention and, much to her discomfort, only Benny Robertson raised his hand.

"I know this is a rough time," she finally said. "It's horrible to lose a friend under these circumstances. So, let's take this week easy and just get through the lessons." We thought she meant Margot. Apparently she did not.

Later, we learned our parents had filed a missing-person report and were assured the police would take the matter seriously. Not that they mentioned this to us. We were still young, emotionally fragile and susceptible to danger. We read about it in The Henderson Herald. They ran a cover story about the craftsman house, the developers and the break-ins. That was the first of many times we saw Jonas's name in print. The newspaper published article after article and sold a lot of ads. In church, a plump woman in a canary-yellow pantsuit stood behind the pulpit. She commanded us to pray for his safe return. Even the local tavern held a fundraiser, though no one really knew what they did with all the money.

The following week the investigator arrived like an uninvited guest. His presence unnerved us. In an assembly, he addressed us in a dull monotone voice, detailing the sad plight of teenage runaways and abducted children. He wandered the halls in his gray trench coat, his righteousness steaming off him. We averted our eyes as he passed us by. He didn't seem to notice. Instead he interviewed the upcoming valedictorian, the football quarterback, the student-body president—only the kids who would have known Jonas. He didn't ask us any questions. In fact, no one did. We had been effectively stricken from the record. After a few days we didn't see him anymore. He might have figured it all out, that there was no point searching for a person who didn't exist. Maybe the town realized it, too, because people didn't quit talking about the disappearance—they forgot about it altogether.

Until December, when somebody found the body.

It happened over the winter break, after the ice storm knocked out power for two miserably cold days. We overheard the reports as our parents sat in front of the news. Some dog walker in Cavalier Park had stumbled upon him, laid out under the frost-coated branches of a pine tree: a young man about fifteen years of age, olive complexion and dark curly hair. Hypothermia, said the newscasters. They speculated he was homeless and had died during the storm. The newspaper ran a grainy picture for its front page story but as we reached for it our parents snatched it away. "Don't worry about that," they said, patting our hands. They underestimated us. We were observers, sponges for information, and we knew how to use the internet. We knew instantly what name the reports were using: Jonas.

All of Henderson took the news like a punch in the gut. For a day or two the neighborhoods went silent through the slow thaw of the storm as people sullenly trashed their Christmas trees earlier than usual. The town hall assembly was the worst kept secret. Our parents disappeared for a few hours and returned home muttering to themselves. We were dragged by our wrists to the New Year's Eve festivities, held annually along the town square. Somehow, in the dwindling crowd, we found each other, huddled by the frozen water fountain while our parents drank mulled wine and discussed the tragedy. Children scattered about in their boisterous play, hurling ice pellets, blowing out breath clouds and playing with their sparklers. Little by little people left early, adults hunting down their young, and the town square was deserted before ten with no reason to set off the chimes at midnight.

New Year's Day, a town-wide curfew went into effect. All unaccompanied minors had to be indoors by sundown, much too hard to enforce at this stage of winter. Not that it mattered to us. There was no point in staying out. There was no place to go. We still eavesdropped on our parents. There was talk of another investigation and then a memorial service. Some morbid part of us actually wanted to see a funeral, to see Jonas's name carved in stone. We imagined Mrs. Burkett standing over an empty casket, mournfully reading a Greek poem.

At school we were greeted by Principal Whately's omnipresent voice from over the loudspeaker. "Be home by dark," she commanded. We wondered when the school would realize there had never been a Jonas registered.

We could barely hear her over the chorus of chatter. Everyone was talking about the dead boy as if it were the only thing that had ever happened. They discussed him with the enthusiasm of a delightful mystery. They talked about the house on the edge of Cavalier Park, a place no one had ever thought to go. When they mentioned the unnamed group of teenagers who met there, their voices filled with envy. We exchanged dark glances and smirks, but did not say anything.

We saw Amanda Sharpe, a horrid pretty girl, stomping down the halls with her entourage. In between sobs, she told her friends she had dated Jonas the previous summer and could not bear the idea of his loss. Together we swallowed the urge to laugh. In the locker room we overheard Craig Morey mention he and Jonas had been best friends when they were little and later on Peter Coleman angrily claimed Jonas still owed him twenty dollars. Then Benny Robertson, picking off the dead flakes of skin from his lips, said it was all a mistake—that Jonas was alive and well and he had seen him just the other day. That was until Leisha Malone publically reprimanded him for having no respect for the dead. That, and Leisha knew Jonas was a fallen Catholic and we should all be concerned for his soul.

The stories grew. Soon the entire freshman class could recount where they were the moment Jonas had died, the various circumstances in which they had known him, loved him, remembered him. There were candlelit vigils, midnight excursions to the park, all sorts of events we were excluded from. Our teachers were obviously unnerved by the stories. They forgot their lesson plans and fell into stunned silence. In response, the school brought in a team of grief counselors who annexed part of the gymnasium, setting up makeshift cubicles, and encouraged all students to make an appointment. Hannah Burns was there every afternoon, wailing loud enough to ensure we could all hear her over the bell.

If the rest of the high school was caught up in the fever of Jonas, then our beloved Mrs. Burkett was miraculously immune. She seemed unaware of the growing hysteria outside her classroom door. Every day, she greeted us with near manic delight. Her movements were still ethereal, her black dresses swaying as she pranced around our classroom. Only Benny Robertson brought up the subject. He told her he couldn't understand how she could be so cheerful when a student was rotting in the morgue. Of course Mrs. Burkett had a way of brushing such things aside. She gave a haughty laugh and said, "My lovelies, there are five acknowledged stages of grief: denial, anger, bargaining, depression and finally acceptance. It appears your fellow students have invented a sixth. Self indulgence." And then she picked back up where she'd left off.

OF COURSE THE TOWN GREW impatient with the high school's grieving process. Urban legends about dead boys were bad publicity for developers. As far as the city council was concerned, the children were no longer in danger. They said we were now the problem. Overnight the grief counselors were banished and the gymnasium returned to its usual sadistic mechanisms. Teachers were ordered to continue with the curriculum. An ordinance was put in place: they weren't even allowed to mention his name.

Without us noticing, construction on the Jonas house resumed. Demolition teams tore down the old post office, sectioned it off with a chain-link fence. Even the vacant lots around Cavalier Park were bulldozed for more Craftsman houses. We heard rumors of the break-ins and the vandalism.

The *Herald* ran a story about a group of teens caught inside, holding a séance. The "No Trespassing" sign disappeared and was replaced every other day. Our group rushed after school through the park, hoping to leave enough time before curfew. Spray painted along the side of the house were the words: "Jonas was here. And we will not be silenced."

We thought Jonas would be a shortlived phenomenon. Our peers were simple minded with short attention spans. But the stories kept growing and the high school was drunk on them. It was no longer enough for Jonas to be a simple runaway who died during the ice storm. With each retelling his death became more grandiose. They said he was impaled by a fallen icicle, bitten by a rabid dog, hit by a car and left for dead. Mike Daniels claimed it was a drug overdose and Clara Halberson said she had heard that he was on the run from the law. Murder became a favorite theme. His head was smashed in by a lead pipe. He was strangled by his abusive father. Shot twice in the head. They continued to speculate in the most grotesque ways, as if wishing him alive and well so they could kill him all over again.

The school brought in hall monitors, old ladies dressed in polka-dot muumuus. Their task was to suppress the chatter. They lurked in pairs and eavesdropped. They stood sentinel by our lockers, waded in between cafeteria tables, armed with rulers to slap at those who mentioned the name. As soon as they passed, some brave troublemaker would hiss the word "Jonas" and the old crones spun around, flailing their arms, searching for the culprit.

Someone created a website detailing the many theories about the dead boy. They called it a conspiracy. We found Reggie Guntherson distributing tradable "Who Killed Jonas" cards that he had made on his computer. They were crudely printed with bad art and listed the suspects, locations and manners of his death. It didn't take the hall monitors long. All the cards were confiscated within a day. Then Reggie died a few weeks later over Spring Break. It was a car accident, one of those brutal wrecks that smashes a body beyond recognition. And that wasn't enough for a single lit candle.

Jonas became a ghost story used to frighten our young and gullible. How many times had we told the tale? Don't walk through Cavalier Park at night or else he will come for you. Entire sleepovers were dedicated to summoning him through Ouija boards, all the players insisting they hadn't moved the pointer. Some claimed you could raise his ghost in the mirror by saying his name three times: Jonas, Jonas, Jonas. Our younger siblings went through a phase when they couldn't use the bathroom with the door closed. We'd walk by and see them squatting on the toilet, refusing to look towards the vanity. Disgusted, we'd slam the door shut and hold it tight while they screamed in terror, pulling against the knob, leaving soft trails of shit behind them.

Towards the end of freshman year, as the Memorial Day parade approached, the theater club announced the theme of their float: the Life and Death of Jonas. They did so early to prevent competition from the jazz ensemble, the student socialist party and the horticulturist club. But the city council put an end to that. They said they'd sure enough cancel the whole damn thing before they would let us go on promoting dead runaways. We didn't know what that meant or what was at stake. Many of us said we would boycott the parade altogether and yet, like every year, we all showed up along the main drag, stuck to our parents' sides.

We watched the long processional flow down Main Street: decorated cars and crappy floats, local business owners handing out coupons. The mayor and his wife rode in the back of a pickup truck, waving like royalty. As the high school band approached the center of town, we thought this was it: the grand finale and the end to another ridiculous parade. But suddenly the band stopped, halted in place, and left a startling quiet over the crowd. Our parents looked unnerved. Then one lone trumpet player started up with the military taps and from the crowds marched a group of black-garbed teens carrying a long black coffin. They were led by Mrs. Burkett herself, dressed up as a grieving mother. And from the stands and street corners came the council members and their crony police officers, ready to break up the trouble. The teenagers were prepared, calmly placed their fake coffin down, and braced themselves for combat. When the riot broke out, the police twirled old-fashioned batons and the marching band fought them off with clarinets and drumsticks. Even Mrs. Burkett was seen tackling Principal Whately as the crowds rallied and smashed windows and set the city hall on fire. And amidst the chaos the coffin's lid popped open and out jumped Benny Robertson, who ran screaming down the street.

OR MAYBE I DREAMED UP that last part and the parade finished without interruption. Maybe that's how I wanted it all to end. Maybe I had overheard several kids at school talking about such a stunt but knew none of them had the guts. Maybe these were the same kids who whispered insults as I passed them by. Maybe some of them used to be my friends. Maybe we were once called wallflowers by our eccentric Latin teacher and for a while that meant we were connected. Maybe we never really liked each other. Or maybe we did until we became just as shortsighted as everyone else.

Here is what I know: Jonas made a good distraction, but he couldn't last forever. I don't know what happened with the police investigation or the memorial service, but apparently both things did occur before being erased from public knowledge. Eventually, Henderson simmered down to its usual tepid pace. The adults maintained their authority and teenagers stayed self-absorbed, only now there was an increased sense of distrust between them. The real tragedy, at least from my perspective, was after we were expelled from the house and the rumors began, my group never met up again. We created Jonas and in the end he was our destroyer. One by one my friends were absorbed into the Amanda Sharpes and Craig Moreys and Peter Colemans until they were all indistinguishable from them. They kept adding to the myths, adding so many lies that they probably couldn't remember the humble truths. It was enough to purge us of each other until suddenly I found myself standing alone, quietly judging as they pretended I wasn't even there.

In those last few weeks of freshman year, when students were burning out and cutting school, I maintained the same indifference I always had. I kept my head low, studied hard and when the bell rang I rushed straight home without a word to anyone. Except one afternoon, I lingered too long after Latin class and found myself alone with Mrs. Burkett. It was my first private conversation with this strange woman, who wore costume jewelry and loved dead languages. She lavished her affections on me, insisting I take her intermediate course next year. She said I was her favorite student. I thought, Why? She didn't know a thing about me. Like the fact that I loved astronomy and slasher flicks, that I suffered night terrors and still wet the bed, that when I got too big and my uncle quit our secret wrestling matches, I actually missed them. I don't know why any of this was important, but I wanted her to know something.

"There was never any Jonas," I said. "I should know. I was actually there. We made him up."

She didn't even flinch. "Of course he's real. He's real because people wanted to believe in him." I called her nuts, but still agreed to take her class next year and left the room feeling oddly at peace.

In the hall I stumbled upon the impervious Benny Robertson. He stood alone, leaning against his locker with his head bowed, as if he was patiently waiting for someone to come collect him. For the first time, I felt nothing but empathy for him and, against all rational thought, decided to make him my friend. As we walked home through uncertain territory, other students coldly remarked that of course the two of us had ended up together. And yet, when we reached my door, Benny was still beside me, smiling. We spent our weekends avoiding our families, watching anime films, crafting plotlines for comic books we would never draw. We confessed every embarrassing thought in our heads. Together we quit the confirmation classes at church and, much to our parents' chagrin, announced that we were atheists. We found others like us, experimented with Dungeons and Dragons and circle jerks. Eventually Benny became my first lover. It was a doomed relationship from the start, but one that I would return to at various stages of my life. Even as grown men we joked that we were the perfect mates as long as we never saw each other.

I never told Benny or our new friends about my role in Jonas's creation. That was one secret, unlike all the rest, I actually kept. I wasn't ashamed; I had more fun playing along. Whenever that old topic surfaced, which it did, we would lay out the theories like a deck of cards. Jonas was killed with a pickaxe, Benny said. I heard they buried him alive, I'd whisper back. Gutted with a hunting knife. Throat slashed with barbed wire. Murdered by Mayor Thompson. By his evil twin. He still haunts Cavalier Park. Jonas lives, we'd both say and burst out laughing. And then I'd think, if you find Jonas, you should kill him. That way he'll live forever.

*They both had a vague idea of what cormorants looked like. There had been a colony of the birds in the city, on some parkland near the lake. The birds were ugly up close, and they ate too much fish, and their shit killed trees, and there'd been a hand-wringing debate about whether to kill them off to save the waterfront and a long segment on the CBC with some breathtaking pictures. But what did James and Paul know about cormorants, really?*

# Camp

## DAVID NICKLE

BEFORE EVERYTHING, THEY HAD TO get married.

That had happened just two days prior, at a little woodland bed and breakfast outside South River. There was some family, but it was mostly friends—in from Ottawa and Toronto, and Chicago where James had grown up. They laughed and drank and danced among the black flies and pine trees, the vivid afternoon light that laid the land in such sharp relief. When finally the friends and family went home they swapped out wedding luggage for camping gear from James' sister Evelyn's van, strapped their sea kayaks to the roof of the Honda... and James and Paul Berringer headed alone into the northern Ontario high summer.

The truck passed them the first time on a straight-away outside New Liskeard. It was a big silver GM pickup that rode high and was designed for sport more than work. James, driving, gave a polite wave, and Paul had thought he'd been waving at some road-weary toddler. Not so, as it turned out. *Some old bat*, James'd said. More than that it was hard to say, because the truck rode a good two feet higher than the Honda. To show what he meant, James gunned the motor the next straight-away and sailed past the truck. Paul waved out the window as they passed. He bent to look in the side-view mirror, saw a hand emerge, salute off the top of the cab like it was a captain's hat.

The truck made its next pass on a curve, as the highway cut down close to a lake of tufted islands and wind-warped conifers. Two hands emerged from the passenger window that time, bestowing garlands of air kisses down onto the Honda. Paul tried to return the salute by jutting out his passenger window, propping ass on car door and waving over the top of the roof. But he remembered that the kayaks were there, about the same time as James shouted at him to quit fooling around and put his goddamn seatbelt on.

They laughed and drove, and turned up the music, and turned it down again when they wanted to talk and back up when they'd made their points, as the highway cut through blasted-out shield rock and trees that seemed to hang just over their heads. The truck showed up in the rear-view from time to time but it was gone as often as it was there. After awhile, they stopped checking for it. They were two guys on their honeymoon. They had other things on their mind. Christ.

They stopped, finally, in the late afternoon—at a place called Curt. The town wasn't much more than a co-op grocery store, a liquor store and a filling station, all along the highway. They slowed down and pulled into the grocery store's parking lot. It was late in the afternoon, and things didn't stay open that long up here. And the truck appeared again, pulling into the spot right beside them.

"You two are beautiful," said the man behind the wheel of the truck. "Don't know if you knew that. But you're goddamn beautiful. You're glowing."

Paul leaned out the passenger window and smiled wide and toothy.

"Just married," he said. Beside him, in the driver's seat, James grinned and waved and Paul wondered if that might just be that. The man was about seventy—with close-cropped hair and a deep tan over a heavily lined face. His beard was longer, and it was winter-white. Sharp blue eyes twinkled in deep-set lines. His own wife rode shotgun. She was plumper, and more tanned, with reddish hair pulled in a ponytail that reached out the back of her sun visor. *How do a couple like them deal with a couple like us?* Paul wondered.

But when she said, "Honeymooners?" both Paul and James nodded and grinned.

"Honeymooners," he said, and James said again: "Just married."

The old man opened the door and stepped gingerly out of the cab. He was wearing a pair of walking shorts, and his legs were thin as sticks. Sandaled feet crunched on the gravel.

"It's not hard to tell," he said, and grinned. "Did your wedding go well? I don't even have to ask that, do I?"

"Now you're off on an adventure." His wife came out from around the back of the truck. She had a canvas bag that looked like it was stuffed with other canvas bags. "Those are beautiful boats you have on your roof." She and her husband made a show of admiring them.

"They're our wedding gift to each other," said James, and explained that they were just the right size for hauling the two of them and a full camp kit, and how they hoped their camping trip wouldn't be too much of an adventure. Paul started introductions, and it developed that they were talking to Stanley Green and his wife Nancy. Stanley once worked in natural resources. Nancy used to be a compositor for a newspaper. They had been married for forty-three years. The last ten, they'd lived up here.

"We bought an old YMCA camp on Scout Lake," said Stanley, and Nancy said, "It was his idea," and Paul said, "Oh, it was like that, was it?" and everybody laughed.

Paul leaned on the hood of the Honda, and James easily wended under his arm. It was getting cooler here than they were used to, although the late afternoon sun made the town look lovelier, warmer. Nancy brought out a silver steel thermos and four plastic travel mugs. IF YOU DON'T STAND BEHIND OUR TROOPS, WE CAN ARRANGE FOR YOU TO STAND IN FRONT OF THEM, was written on the side of Paul's.

She set them on the wheel well of the truck, and poured. Paul sipped his. It was Irish coffee, with an emphasis on the Irish. He grinned like a baby. James wasn't as pleased – he had to drive, after all, and they weren't planning on stopping. But like Paul, he liked the Greens. They'd seen a "glow" about them. Where was the harm, really, in a bit more glow from Nancy Green's thermos?

They finished their coffee, gave the mugs back and made it into the store just fifteen minutes before it closed and checked out with a box of supplies five minutes after it closed. Paul looked around for the truck – but it was long gone.

"That's too bad," said James when Paul pointed that out. "They were nice folks. Would have been good to say a proper goodbye." Then he craned his neck, looking at their car, and said, "What the fuck?"

Paul set his box of groceries down in the gravel and pulled the folded sheet of paper from underneath their windshield wiper. He unfolded it.

"It's a map," he said, and held it up. "Scout Tourist Region." James checked it out. The lake was a maze of inlets and islands. It suggested the shape of a horse with a rider. Kind of like an old time scout, Paul thought. There was a big X on one of the islands, toward the western end. The highway was at the east. There was a note in a spot of clear water, written using the same thick pencil as the X.

GREAT MEETING YOU 2! WHY DON'T YOU JOIN US AT THE Y? BRING A BEDROLL & THOSE PRETTY KAYAKS—JUST SHOW UP & WE TAKE CARE OF THE REST! XOX YR HWY 11 FRIENDS STAN & NANC

THE WHISKEY IN THE COFFEE made James too sleepy to drive and Paul couldn't say he was in any better shape, so they found a little roadside motel twenty odd kilometers on, and sacked out for the night.

When they settled in, Paul opened up the map on the pine-covered breakfast table and did finger measurements. "Shit," he said. "That's about twelve kilometers in."

"Give or take a thumb," said James. "You're not seriously thinking about this?"

"Scout Lake's a lot closer than Quebec. Just another hour up the highway, the way you drive."

That drew a playful slap, and James bent over the map, made Paul show him what the route would be. He commented that it looked like a pretty run, but he counted more than twelve kilometers.

"But that's not here nor there," said James. "Fact is, that's a long way in. And we don't know these people."

"Sure we do. Stanley worked in natural resources. Nancy…worked in newspapers or something. They carry open liquor in the cab of their truck."

"They pick up glowing men on the highway."

"I'd pick up glowing men on the highway. So would you."

"That's why we're together."

They laughed, but James wondered about that: whether they might just be old-school swingers with a dose of bi-curiosity. "I don't want to go there just to find we have to sponge bath old Stan while Nancy watches on the webcam," he said. Paul thought about that, and agreed: *Yeah, it's possible.* But he didn't take that impression from those two, and cornered on the subject, James admitted that he didn't either. They both took another look at the map.

Depending on the wind, they agreed that, twelve kilometers or fourteen, they could probably make the run in under four hours. Just to be on the safe side, they'd pack some food and a tent—the camp stove—the first aid kit—and the rifle. They could camp out on an island, if it turned out they had to.

THE MAP SHOWED THE MARINA as being right on the highway's edge, but that wasn't how it played out. There was a little sign on the side of the road with an arrow pointing to a long dirt road, that first wound through bush, then dropped on a steep slope between high rounded rocks. Here and there, the dirt road passed a driveway that climbed those hills—and sometimes, Paul could peer up and see parts of houses poking out of the trees overhead. Twice, they had to deal with oncoming traffic: pickup trucks that appeared in front of them with terrifying suddenness and speed.

But they made it. The rocks and trees finally spread, and the marina appeared, in a little natural harbour rimmed with low cliffs and right across from a pair of knuckly little islands. There was a place to park, and a boat launch, and a couple of long docks with outboard motor boats tied up. There was even a little general store that sold wine by the box.

It wasn't an hour before they were in the lake and paddling over still waters, to the sweet space between those first two islands.

AFTER TWO HOURS ON THE lake, they stopped on a little island that seemed to have been furnished for the purpose – with a firepit and a weathered wooden bench for fish cleaning—a box with a toilet seat on it that was not, as it developed, a proper chemical toilet.

The wind was picking up, and they were paddling into it. As they chewed on cold cuts and breakfast bars, James and Paul looked at their maps, and revised their estimated arrival time. Paul wished they could call ahead to say they were coming later—but as James reminded him, Stan and Nancy left no phone number on the map. Just the pencilled-in X.

After lunch, they crossed from the horse's tail to the wide expanse of Scout Lake's belly. Here, the winds were fierce. They moved along the shore, taking shelter in tiny inlets where water lilies grew.

A front blew in from the east and rain came and went, as they crossed the horse's hind legs. This time, they didn't take shelter, and the rain soaked them. The sun came out, and the wind died back, and they poached in their wet clothes as they pushed along low rock faces and cliffs.

"Not far now!" shouted James, and Paul laughed, and James said, "Wow."

"What?" Paul shouted. They were maybe forty feet apart, drifting a moment in the stilled water.

James pointed with his paddle, ahead of them. They were coming up to a promontory—a long tongue of rock and dirt, where a patch of tall, brambled branches— you wouldn't call them trees—clustered. Although it was the height of the summer, their twisted limbs had no leaves. At every crook in the branches, they could see a black speck.

The two kayaks drifted nearer one another as they watched. "Birds," Paul opined, and James added that there were "a fuck of a lot of birds." They dipped paddles and pushed nearer, and although they were as quiet as kayakers could be, before long it was clear they'd set off some sort of alarm. Black wings cut across the water and long sine waves of black-bodied birds emerged from the water. One snaked directly over James' boat, and Paul looked closer and said: "Cormorants!"

They both had a vague idea of what cormorants looked like. There had been a colony of the birds in the city, on some parkland near the lake. The birds were ugly up close, and they ate too much fish, and their shit killed trees, and there'd been a hand-wringing debate about whether to kill them off to save the waterfront and a long segment on the CBC with some breathtaking pictures.

But what did James and Paul know about cormorants, really?

They lifted their paddles from the water and sat still, watching as more of the birds took flight, spun off in lines around them—circling, as if the birds were watching them, making sure they didn't tarry too close. Protecting their nests... their families.

Paul wondered about adopting.

"Where did that come from?" asked James—they hadn't talked about having kids, not really—and Paul shrugged.

"It's the future," he said. "It'd be nice, having a son. In the future."

A cloud thinned, and the sun came pale and yellow through it.

"A son?"

"Or a daughter. But if we get to pick—"

"—a son." James considered. "We'd need a bigger place," he said.

Paul thought their place was fine for raising a boy. There were three bedrooms and there could be one for the two of them, another one for the office, and a third for the boy. The place was small and there wasn't much of a yard—but it wasn't much of a hardship, surely it couldn't be much of a hardship.

Paul didn't say any of that, though. He looked back at the shore, watched as the birds returned to their perches—to the bare soil and rock there. They had shapes like vases, standing upright.

James dipped a paddle into the water and started to turn his kayak about. "We should keep moving," he said, and Paul agreed. They both turned the boats away from the colony, and continued further along the shore of the lake.

It was only when they were far away from the birds and their squawks and their black, jagged-looking wingspans, that it occurred to either of them: what a stench the colony carried. It was the foulest thing either of them had ever smelled.

Although neither remarked on it, both of them thought it stank of death.

THE SUN CAME OUT PAST the noon hour, and all the clouds vanished, and the lake grew quite warm indeed. James stripped off his fleece, and lashed it to the front of the kayak. Paul kept his on just a little longer, and pulled off his and his shirt too, and strapped his lifejacket back on over bare skin.

"Okay," said Paul, "you win. No boy right now."

"I didn't say we shouldn't."

"You didn't need to."

They laughed, and Paul asked: "Where are we on the map?"

James fumbled for the paper.

He'd stuffed it in his fleece jacket's pocket, which was lashed to the front of the boat. He raised up, and leaned forward—and took hold of the cloth. The kayak seemed to wriggle as he did so.

Paul thought: *Oh shit*, just as James thought the same. And all at once, the kayak tilted.

James threw himself back, slapped at the water with the flat of his paddle, and tried to twist his shoulders away from the tilt, reclaim his centre of gravity. It was no good. He started to pinwheel the oar, as though he thought he might paddle through air the same as water.

The kayak pitched over. James shouted, maybe screamed, and splashed into the water as the kayak pitched the rest of the way.

IT WAS VERY STILL, AND hot. The two dry bags that were lashed to the kayak came loose, and bobbed up, one at a time, alongside the kayak's sky-blue hull. James' fleece spread just beneath the water, like a torso-shaped oil slick.

Paul called out James' name: first in the quit-fucking-around tone that James had used the day before, on the highway, when Paul was trying to prop his ass on the edge of the chute

Except for the ripples radiating out from the dry bags, the kayak, the water was a looking glass.

"James!"

Paul shattered that glass with his paddle and drew himself closer to James' still kayak. There had been no struggling, no bubbles, still, as there would have been, if James had pulled himself free of the cockpit, or even if he were trying.

When Paul got close enough, he slid the paddle underneath the hull, where James would be. He might be able to catch hold of it—use it as leverage to pull himself up again, pull himself out. To safety.

Paul didn't let himself consider certain matters: there was no sign of his husband underneath the boat. Even if he were sitting as still as he could, inverted in the kayak, there would have to be some sign of it on the surface: some small stream of bubbles. But how could he be sitting still, under the lake in an inverted kayak? Why would he be sitting still, fully conscious, aware of the fact that he only had so much air, and not struggle to right the kayak – to get out and save himself, before his air ran out and he drowned?

The paddle cut through empty water, and clunked against the plastic gunwales of the little boat, rocking it easily in the water, and this forced Paul to consider: nothing was underneath the boat.

James was not under the boat. He was not, in fact, anywhere.

A DOZEN CORMORANTS FLEW so low their feet trailed in the water. They came close to Paul—so close he might have caught one with the blade of his paddle. But he kept still, watched them until they passed, then returned to the water, which he regarded with empty fascination. The air grew cool as the sun fell beneath the line of trees. Insects buzzed in his ear as James' kayak drifted off, the dry bags scattering in their own directions.

As the first star emerged—probably not a star at all, but a planet, maybe Jupiter—in a deepened sky—Paul drew a breath.

He thought it might have been his first.

HE DIPPED HIS PADDLE INTO the water, and drew it to the kayak's bow, and slid backward through the dark water. There was no moon. There were stars, scattering thick across the middle of the sky, but they weren't enough. They left the world black.

He paddled backward twice more, and turned himself in another direction—by how much, he couldn't tell—and proceeded. James was gone. The dry bags, the kayak—he left them all.

The night air was cool and numbing, and he warmed himself with exertion – paddling harder and driving the kayak faster across the lake. The water was still as it had been in the afternoon, and the stars reflected in it, dully, stretching infinity below him.

And Paul shut his eyes against even the pale light of the twinning stars, and thought: *It's just me now.*

DID HE SLEEP?

He must have, for when he opened his eyes, it was to a bloody red dawn. The air was hot, and mist rose off the water and swirled about him. He was near a shore, but not one he recognized—this was high, round rock, topped with trees that looked to have been denuded by fire. Nearer the waterline, sharp stumps and rocks like broken teeth rose out of the mist. In their midst…a dock lolled, like a grey and splintered tongue, from the base of the rock.

He guided the kayak through the rock and wood, until its tip touched the wood. A moment later, he was stretched on the dock, pulling the kinks from his legs.

He lay back, and looked up the rockface. It was a strange place to put a dock, for there was no easy way to get up the rockface; it was nearly sheer here, and a good twenty feet up to the remainder of the woods, branches peeking over the lip of the cliff like an untrimmed brow. He felt a smile grow on his face.

And he thought again: *I am alone.*

His smile wavered. He sat up. Looked out through the mist. Its slow swirl fascinated him, and he cocked his head to watch it turn and bend, and as he watched, his smile vanished, as thoughts of speeding down a highway – hanging out the car window, feeling the wind…laughing, with him…

He bent his head away from the lake, and shut his eyes, and tensed, as a part of him fought…fought to return, to remember. He was having a difficult time remembering, anything really.

He gripped his own thighs, and rocked, and his lips struggled with the word, with the name of what he'd lost…

…of what he'd come for…

He opened his eyes, and stood on the dock. The kayak, he saw, was starting to drift off—so he bent over, and reached with his foot. He dragged it back, and took a breath, and put it together, and said it aloud:

"James."

He was losing himself. There had been a second kayak, just like this one—the day before, the time before. As this kayak bumped back against the dock, he considered that moment—James, his husband. And the still water, beneath which he'd vanished.

He tried to hold that in his mind. James. The second kayak. Their wedding.

The long paddle through the night, across the lake of stars…

With an effort, he hefted an end of the kayak onto the dock, and hauled it the rest of the way along, until the length of the boat was safe on the dock.

Then, he turned his attention to the rock face.

It was smooth; there didn't seem to be a way to climb it without gear. But it didn't make sense that anyone would put a dock here, if there weren't some way up. Most likely, this was set up to be a portage.

There had to be a reason for the dock. It had to lead to somewhere.

He ran his hands along the stone, and peered into the thinning mist at the base. There was no way up immediately, but there was a slick ledge, at nearly the water's edge, that fell off into the water. Tentatively, he put a toe on it. Maybe there was some stairs, some kind of a ladder, further along. Tentatively he put a foot on it. He slid into the water, ankle-deep, then came up against a cleft that seemed as though he could balance on.

He put his weight on that foot, and drew the other into the water. It was icy cold, but he endured.

He made his way along the rock face in this way.

And as he proceeded, memory started to become clearer, and his situation clarified – and he thought about James, and the overturned kayak... and how he froze, and sat there in his kayak, as his new husband vanished. Why had he not jumped in? Finished the search? Why had he left... so easily?

He made it a dozen feet along, so disquieted by these new thoughts that he only heard the outboard motor when it stopped.

"Well hello!"

Stanley Green waved from the back of the aluminum boat, as his wife Nancy sat at the bow, binoculars fixed on him. They were wearing colored windbreakers—Stanley's blue, Nancy's a brilliant yellow. A fishing rod hung over the side of the boat, lure glinting in the mist.

He didn't wave.

"Where's your friend?" said Stanley Green, and Nancy clarified: "Your husband?"

He turned in the water so he faced them, leaning against the rock face. The boat was maybe three dozen yards off, and they had to shout to be heard.

He shouted an answer.

"Oh my!" Nancy said, and Stanley shouted: "Where? Where'd it happen?"

For that, he had no answer. He'd crossed the lake at night, paddled through the stars. It was the other side of *that*.

Stanley and Nancy conferred, and Stanley turned back to him, and shouted that he'd bring the boat in, and get him, and they could go look for his friend together.

He trembled, and slid, and he steadied himself in the water, as Stanley bent over the outboard. What was Stanley doing there, this quiet morning, tugging at a rope on the top of the thing?

There was a terrible coughing sound, and a roar—and it sent his heart pounding... and he spun about in the water, and felt it sheathe off his feet, his long and slender legs—

He rested a moment, on top of the rocks, the scoured forest at his back. The view of the lake was more commanding from here; the height made him feel better... safer.

The two in the boat were talking to each other. He couldn't understand what they said. But they were pointing at the dock as they spoke. They were confused, and frightened. The boat made close to the dock, and they both climbed out. He craned his neck over the edge of the rock, peered down curiously at them. She looked up, and pointed, and her husband looked at him too.

Their eyes were wide, and wet, and afraid, and above all—
guilty.

And he had enough of it. So he spread his arms wide, and pushed down on the
heavy morning air, and left them there on the dock.

PAUL FINALLY FOUND JAMES THAT afternoon, in the cleft between a small rocky island
and the shore. It wasn't difficult – he had eyes for this kind of thing, and Paul would
recognize James anywhere. He circled twice just to be sure, then narrowed his wings
just so, and let the earth pull him down. James flashed silver, as though signalling him,
making a perfect target... and when the surface of the water broke, Paul took James
around the middle, and his gills twitched in recognition, as Paul broke the surface again,
and took back to flight.

The two didn't speak after that. There were no words necessary.

They flew in silence, close to the water this time, as Paul guided them both, by
prehistoric instinct, to the camp—the place where they were both expected, where
hungry mouths waited.

*Later at night, he sat in bed and stared up at the ceiling and felt lonely and horny. He imagined Ronaldo's kiss on his lips and chest. He couldn't sleep so he opened a beer and read a literary magazine for an hour, carefully avoiding the stack of poems he'd come here to complete. One of the magazine pages had a caricature of the President of Mexico and he drew a Mariachi mustache on him in pencil and then cut it out of the magazine.*

# The Ticket Taker of Cenote Zaci

## BENJAMIN PARZYBOK

As Eduardo sold the tickets, he liked to imagine the duendes' approval, the ones Angelita had told him about in a hushed voice. He had laughed and hurt her feelings. Now he imagined their little goblin faces nodding thoughtfully in praise of his work ethic. *The cenote's gatekeeper*, they would say in their cricket voices, *the ticket taker. He pleases us with his diligence.*

The cenote, a perfect circular pool, lay inside a cave. The water was so blue and clear that you could see deep into it, its rocky sides like a tunnel, as if a great worm had long ago dug to the center of the Earth. To stand at the edge of the cenote gave one vertigo. Acrophobes gripped the cave's walls, their lunch in their throats. A slim spear of sunlight from an opening in the cave's roof stabbed into the center, making the pool glow.

In this town he'd adopted he was to finally live up to his promise. His small self-exile, a hermitage, to finish his book. Except after work he succumbed to trivial pleasures. There were the peanut dulces Doña Merced sold at the market. Or how with every traffic light in Valledolid lined up just so, he passed through town as if on the back of a great wild hare instead of his old motorbike. That was pleasure. *Ding.* Or like when— but sure, this dinged everyone, did it not?—a pretty boy let his eyes linger for an extra instant, locked with his, as if they were sockets to plug into, *oh.*

But there was a thing about the tickets.

He had a good memory for faces, and a good mind for numbers, Eduardo did. He lined up the torn stubs from the day's sales. When a tourist exited he threw the stub away. Inside he had carefully placed six torn ticket stubs against the back edge of the desk. These tourists had not returned.

The first time a stub remained, he'd hollered into the cenote to make sure no one lingered. He brushed it off as a counter's error. Perhaps a quick-footed tourist snuck by without his noticing. On a whim he pushed that first extra ticket to the back edge of the desk. Three days later, there was another counter's error, and this stub he set next to the first. But in the night he woke in his bed and stared toward the dark ceiling and had an uneasiness that sat in his lungs like a cockroach had taken up residence there.

After that he annotated the torn stubs with a code so that he could remember to whom they belonged. The blond Canadian with the pink backpack whose voice sounded of helium. The round Mexican from Guadalajara with a smile like a slice of grapefruit. The towering, stooped German who had plugged into his eyes. They did not speak each other's language but they spoke each other's language, too. The viejo with dentures from town who brought his lunch with him, hobbling slowly down the stairs, asking if he'd seen any duendes, wink wink.

No, he had not seen any. He did not believe in them. He hazarded a glance toward Angelita's ice cream cart. And you? Have you seen the duendes? He asked the viejo.

Yes, the viejo said, his eyes glimmered with mischief and cataracts, the pupil of one milky blue like the cenote itself. Yea big, he gestured, the distance between his hands indicating the size of a two year old. Skinny things, with great beards, and for hair? Green moss and twigs. Teeth like broken sea shells.

Eduardo leaned forward into the ticket window, suddenly enraged. I mean really.

Joven, I can barely see as it is. If they wanted you to see them, you would see them.

Angelita operated the helados cart that roved the park, sometimes parking next to Eduardo's ticket taker booth. He felt like they, the two park workers, were like husband and wife, siloed each in their little houses, one peddling sweet ice, the other sweet hereafter, or the portal to it, at least.

The tall German? Eduardo said. The one who bought the lemon cone? With the blond hair.

You like him?

No, I just—have you seen him exit?

Ooh. Going to ask him on a date? There was a playful hostility to her speech whenever they spoke of boys.

Angelita. I mean did he come out yet?

Why should I keep track? You keep track of your own boyfriends.

Two days later Eduardo showed Angelita his collection of ticket stubs. She entered his booth and they stood close together. In her hair he could smell sugar and cream mingled with sweat. The stubs were lined up like little tombstones on his desk.

So?

None of these tourists have come back.

What do you mean?

I mean, they went down to the cenote, and they never came back up.

She eyed him for a long moment. No, she said, you weren't paying attention. You're too busy selling tickets.

Angelita.

She turned and frowned, and he could see that she considered him for a moment. OK, she said. So maybe they're still down there. Did you go and check?

Of course I did! Eduardo felt the hair raise on the back of his neck. This one—he held up a stub—went down eleven days ago.

She shrugged. Mexican or foreigner?

Foreigner.

What do I know about foreigners? Are they all foreigners?

No! See? Young, old— he separated the tombstones into the two groups. Extranjero, Mexicano, he reshuffled them again. Men, women.

If someone was missing we'd hear it. The police would get called. People don't go poof.

Poof, Eduardo said. She was right. A small stack of leftover ticket stubs did not make a mystery. He gathered up his ticket stub graveyard and made a short stack of them at the corner of his desk. He'd been careless, he was loathe to admit. He'd miscounted. He'd start fresh tomorrow.

They are long gone, Angelita said. They've traveled far from here already. Don't worry about them.

LATER AT NIGHT, HE SAT in bed and stared up at the ceiling and felt lonely and horny. He imagined Ronaldo's kiss on his lips and chest. He couldn't sleep so he opened a beer and read a literary magazine for an hour, carefully avoiding the stack of poems he'd come here to complete. One of the magazine pages had a caricature of the President of Mexico and he drew a Mariachi mustache on him in pencil and then cut it out of the magazine.

Deep in the night he dreamed the cenote hung above him, pooling there darkly in the ceiling, pulling him in like a black hole. He clutched the edges of his bed and held on. In his dream, he remembered feeling sure that some day he would be sucked in. The whole town too, and then all of Mexico.

SATURDAYS WERE BUSY. HE SOLD ticket after ticket all morning. The sounds of swimming echoed up the stairs and through the gate. The torn and coded ticket stubs he set aside on his desk like sheep in a field. He watched Angelita sell ice cream, her face shiny with sweat as she dug in the buckets. When she left for the bathroom, he jogged to her cart, opened the heavy lid and took a finger-full of limón for himself, then unfolded the mustached caricature of Presidente Enrique Peña Nieto over the top of the vanilla.

Back at the booth he looked over his tickets, organizing them in his mind by the various subgroups. With sudden horror he realized children under six got in free. They had no tickets. They were uncountable.

Just then a scream issued from across the park and he jerked his head up, seeing only an approaching horde of schoolchildren. But beyond, Angelita held up the president's head, dripping with vanilla. She shook her fist at him. He giggled; she was an easy scare.

At the end of the day two stubs remained. There had never been more than one. As the sunset dimmed he hovered anxiously, hoping they would show.

Come down with me, he asked Angelita as she served her last cone.

It's too dark.

We'll still be able to see if we hurry.

I don't want to, Eduardo.

You're scared. It's just a dumb little tourist site. A silly little underground pool.

The Mayans sacrificed people in it.

No, you're just saying that. You're trying to spook me.

She shrugged. Anyway, I'm not going.

Eduardo sighed. Wait for me.

She looped her arm through the cenote's gate. Hurry, she said.

His footsteps rang out as he reached the stone path in the dim light. The stubs had belonged to a couple, Americans or perhaps Canadians, a man and woman near his age.

As the cenote yawned blackly into view the echoes diminished.

Hello? he called in English. Closing time!

For a moment he struggled with an urge to turn back. If only Ronaldo could see what strange place he'd sent himself. He'd fashioned the perfect exile. And now he was trapped within its concerns, as far away from his work as he could possibly imagine. He walked carefully around the pool. A drip sounded and then it went eerily quiet.

Angelita? he called back up the path, but there was no answer.

Where the path turned toward the stone swimming platform, his shins bumped into flesh and he strangled a scream. It was too dark to see what was at his feet, and for a moment he breathed hard and did nothing.

He reached his hand out slowly and found a face in the dark. It was warm and alive and he said, hello? He moved to the shoulder and shook hard. Hello?

Oh, it said, a woman's voice in English.

Closing time.

Brad, she said. Wake up.

You are two? Eduardo said. In the dim light he watched her silhouette rise from the ground.

Come on Brad. She was shaking the other. He won't wake up, she said.

How? he said. How did you fall asleep! We have to hurry. Here, I will help you pull him up. Are you *borracho*? Drunk?

Here is his arm.

Eduardo got hold and began to pull. Fuck, he said in English, working against the muscular weight of the Canadian. We can't be down here right now.

When Brad woke they hurried along the path. Then they were at the gate with Angelita. Eduardo put his hands on his knees and breathed. The park was completely dark.

Goblins? The Canadian girl said, did you say something about goblins?

What? No. If I did I was joking, Eduardo said.

Brad chuckled and put his arm around his girlfriend and said: That was spooky, and weird. We must be tired, eh cookie?

EDUARDO HELPED ANGELITA CLOSE DOWN her cart and then he looped arms with her and steered her toward his motorcycle.

Please, he said, let me buy you dinner. I can't go home yet.

Ooh la la, she said.

Wherever you want. I am haunted by sleeping Canadians.

And afterwards, dancing?

Maybe.

And then after that?

After that I will give you a ride to your house.

Good choice, my bed is softer.

They talked about everything but the cenote and the duendes. He didn't want to think about them. He wanted the idea of them alone in his mind. See, she said—two missing ticket stubs, two sleeping tourists. There's nothing to worry about.

Nothing to worry about, he repeated.

Right, she said.

You believe that?

Yes, she said.

No you don't, I can see you don't believe that.

She shrugged and held her tequila. Cheers.

LATER AT HOME HE SAT at his table and for the first time in a long time he tried to compose. Just like that three poems materialized, one after the other, in a sweaty fever of productivity. He laid them across the table and studied each one with exuberant surprise, feeling enormously pleased with himself. He wondered where they had come from, all of a sudden, after so many weeks of stalling. This, *this* was what he had come for!

He regarded his day with superstition then. Something had led to this, an atmosphere in his mind ripe for output. The dinner with Angelita? The sleeping Canadians? What sequence of events had made it happen? What secret, coded recipe of the day could he re-enact for the same outcome?

But the next day was a rout. He sold tickets and counted stubs. No one went missing and for that he felt relieved. Angelita already had dinner plans with a real suitor. At home, he dispiritedly ate undercooked black beans from the pot and drank a six-pack of Tecate. The blank sheet of white paper he'd carefully laid out for himself on the table garnered nothing but drink rings and pornographic doodles.

In the morning he felt awful. He had slept in his clothes and his mouth tasted of rot.

At work he had trouble keeping up with the ticket stubs, remembering who was who. Angelita felt sorry for him and gave him a free lime ice cream. In a moment of distraction he tilted the cone so that the scoop landed plumply on his desk like a dollop of green shit and he had to close his eyes to keep a tantrum at bay. The ticket booth felt like a hot closet and he wondered why he did this to himself, when he could be back in Mexico City sitting in a cafe and pretending to work on his oeuvre like all his other comrades.

At the end of the day, one stub was left. When he read his code he remembered this one clearly, a vieja, a bent old woman. She had come alone.

He eyed the gate and wondered if she were down there still, asleep on the stone path.

No, he decided. He'd simply not noticed her. He'd been distracted. He locked the gate and drove fast for home, giving Angelita a defeated wave.

In bed he stared at the ceiling and thought guiltily of the vieja and it made him angry. Why did she go alone?

He fetched a piece of paper to write a letter and instead another poem effortlessly filled up the page. But the poem's existence only made him more upset and he crumpled it and threw it at the trash.

A few minutes later he went looking for it and carefully smoothed it on the table. It was good, he admitted, startlingly good.

HE NEEDED A VACATION, HE decided. He proposed to Angelita that she take him around the area on his motorbike and show him the sites. *He* could be a tourist for once. He hid his collection of tombstone stubs and prepared the booth for the high school student who occasionally filled in. At home, his four completed poems shone in his mind like pearls, a secret wealth that gave him comfort. But instead of a thing he looked forward to fashioning more of, they felt like a pile of ill-gotten cash, which he hoarded with greed.

THEY DROVE NORTH, ANGELITA ON the back of his motorcycle. In a couple of hours they were staring into the Gulf of Mexico off a wooden pier. *Querido Ronaldo: I have gone on vacation with a girl.* They sat and dangled their legs in the water and talked about boys and smiled and lay back on the pier and stared at the sky. Great pelicans flew by overhead, fish in their beaks.

When they arrived back at the park the substitute ticket taker was closing up the booth.

I'm just waiting for my parents, the kid said.

He was fifteen or sixteen, Eduardo thought, and cute as a stuffed bear, so cute that Eduardo lost track of what he said. I'm sorry?

The kid gestured toward the cenote. Just waiting for my parents.

Eduardo stared toward the entrance and tasted vomit suddenly at the back of his throat. The sun was going down. Give me the flashlight, he said.

Don't go, Angelita said.

What's happening? the kid said.

Eduardo staggered and nearly fell on the way to the stairs, overcome with nausea. He spit out the sour taste and then went into the cave opening.

In the dim light he saw the deeper black of the round cenote. The amorphous walls of the cave. With the flashlight on it was spookier: he could see only what was directly before him then, obscuring everything else. He called out but there was no response, only the *plink, plink, plink* of a drip. As he came to the swimmer's platform where he'd found the Canadian couple, he paused and called out and his voice echoed against stone.

God damn you, he yelled at the cenote. He leaned to look in, shining the beam deep into its throat, and then lost his grip on the flashlight. With terror, he watched it sink. The firefly glow receded deeper and deeper, continuing to diminish past all reasonable expectations of time, eerily illuminating a streak of blue in the water, until it was only a pin-prick of light and then gone altogether. Eduardo backed slowly away from the cenote, gripping the wall and held still. He heard rustling in the undergrowth that lined the inside of the tall cave, but when he turned his attention to each sound it went quiet.

Walking along the path his foot kicked an object that skittered on the stone. He went to his knees and felt along the ground in the dark and found a bowl filled with some hard organic matter, seeds or wood chips. He gathered up what he could of the spilled substance and carried the bowl back to the entrance.

Angelita talked to the substitute ticket taker gaily about his school. He shook hands with her and handed Eduardo the keys and then said he was off.

What about your parents? Eduardo said.

Yeah, the kid rolled his eyes. I know.

Eduardo watched him go, gripping the bowl he'd found.

But his parents? Eduardo asked Angelita.

What about them, Angelita said.

He was waiting for them!

Angelita put her hands up, a sarcastic ward against his angry exasperation. Eduardo stumbled into the ticket taker's booth and turned on the overhead light. The bowl was rough-cut stone. He puzzled over its contents, which appeared to be desiccated white corn or broken seashells. He didn't want Angelita to see.

Hey amor, lock the gate for me? he said and handed out the keys.

He sifted through the pieces and then he knew what they were—whole, human fingernails. They had lost their translucence. Some were chipped and broken, others perfect and complete. There were hundreds. He was overcome with dizziness. He lurched from the booth and threw up in the bushes.

OK, he said, hunched over. He wiped his mouth.

Are you all right? Angelita called.

Too much sun I think, I'm fine. No, ugh— he leaned in and threw up again. OK. Let's get out of here.

At home he sat and drank a beer and felt numb.

He picked up his phone and pondered calling Ronaldo but wasn't sure what to say. Come get me? Take me home? I'm scared shitless?

There was a white sheet of paper laid out for him and ready and he could feel the itching of a poem there in him somewhere. It repelled and horrified him that he could even think about work.

On the third beer he gave in and composed two poems without ceasing and didn't bother to re-read them afterwards. He stood at the refrigerator and ate bites off a block of cotija cheese, then brushed his teeth and went to bed.

But in the morning he loved them. He held one in each hand and stared at them. Stacked up with the others the pile was short but hearty, poems that could form the core of a book. With them outstretched like wings, he leapt about his small room, unable to tamp down the loft they gave him.

THE FOLLOWING NIGHT HE DREAMED. He walked around the cenote along the path, and it was crowded with people who did not speak or move. They did not look at him as he passed. They stood facing the cenote, their eyes transfixed on its center, the tips of their fingers soft and pulpy.

BEFORE WORK HE DROVE TO the police station and browsed through the missing persons files. There were many, dozens of them, but not a single one that he recognized. Each had hints of a terrible story, with the official record of their life reduced to startlingly few details. Age, height, weight, moment last seen; the similarities to his ticket stub records were unsettling. The photos seemed dug up from some family album, in each the subject smiling, with no precognition of what would befall them.

You find somebody, or lose somebody? A policeman asked him.

Eduardo wasn't sure what to answer and he felt a moment of panic rise into his throat. No, just having a look.

The policeman was, Eduardo thought, the spitting image of a small town Mexican policeman, as if he'd set out to fill his own stereotype. A giant mustache, a large belly, police cap slightly askew. He leaned on the night stick holstered at his belt.

Look all you want, hijo.

A question for you sir, the cenote?

Cenote Zací?

Any crimes ever happen there?

The town's treasure, the policeman said. El tesoro del pueblo. Doorway to the underworld, the Mayans thought. *Xibalba*. Oh sure, there've been crimes. He sat down on a chair across from Eduardo as if about to tell a long story, but instead said: Hot out, right? and wiped his forehead.

Any recently?

The policeman worked at his loaded front shirt pocket until a chili-lime lollipop manifested from it.

Eduardo accepted the sucker and the policeman produced another for himself.

Let's see, he spoke around his lollipop. Last year about this time a girl went missing. We had ten, maybe twelve policeman looking for her. She never turned up. Even sent divers down to the bottom. Later her brother confessed to pushing her in. Little bastard.

But the divers…?

Oh, the bottom is far down and not exactly straightforward, so I'm told. Never been in myself. The policeman chuckled suddenly and then began to cough and Eduardo wondered if the proper thing to do was to clap him on the back.

Funny thing with those divers, he said, one of them found a human skull. It'd gone greenish brown with I-don't-know, algae. Not the girl, obviously. Guy who found it pretty well propelled out of the water. Wouldn't go back in.

A policewoman paused next to them with arms the circumference of drainpipe and impatiently motioned for a lollipop to be provided.

No diver's been in since, the policewoman said. Extranjeros keep asking the city to do an archaeological survey but it's never gone through. Why do you get the ones with chili, Carlos? They're disgusting.

Beggars choosers.

You've been there? the policewoman said.

I'm the ticket taker, Eduardo said.

There was a pause which later Eduardo couldn't figure out if it had only been in his mind, his own heart slowing in expectation of their reaction, stilling time, so that they both seemed to stare at him with a vacant sort of alarm, for a moment which seemed to have no end. Then their faces softened thoughtfully around their lollipops.

And you're not from here? Carlos said.

No sir.

Well that's nice, the policewoman said. El tesoro del pueblo. Get to meet a lot of people, I expect.

He didn't go back to work. He rode the streets, circling closer to Cenote Zací, and then at each approach chose another detour for himself, circling away again, until he found himself home.

In the mailbox was a letter from Ronaldo.

Querido Eduardo:

I hope you will not be too disgusted with me. The piece you sent was *oh-my-god* lovely, it still makes my hair stand on end. I know we're here for each other, et cetera, as in love as in artistry. We're each other's life support, and so of course you're not going to believe *my* praise.

But…: After reading it, and before my jaw had adequately recovered itself from the floor, I impulsively re-posted it to *La Revista Nacional*. Three days later I received the enclosed check and one of the most insanely over-the-top letters of praise I've ever seen an editor write, you bastard *bastard* bastard.

I didn't think editors even *knew* how to use such words! I'm overflowing with envy and, of course, such pride. Your piece, *Blue*, will appear in the review this month (. . . do you suppose they pushed someone out to fit you in on such short notice?)

When can I come visit? Don't give me that nonsense about exile and the work and such. I want to see you and this pond! I'll behave myself.

Amor,

Ronaldo


Eduardo read the editor's letter and wept. After, he pulled a beer from the fridge and sat with a pen and paper to compose a letter to Ronaldo. He had another beer and sent the editor of *La Revista Nacional* three more poems, which she'd requested and for which she'd promised a sum of money he felt entirely in awe of.

Then he pulled out his bottle of tequila from above the stove. He thought: Only I remember, and that can be fixed. He thought: I am celebrating! but there was no celebration in it.

Sometime in the night he woke up on the floor, his clothes soaked through with sweat. He was still drunk and had had another dream he couldn't quite put his finger on. He wished more than anything that Ronaldo were there and thought about rewriting his return letter. *Please come*, he would say. *I miss you more than life.* But he did not. Instead he showered and changed clothes and drove to the cenote, where a few angry notes were taped to the booth about the unexpected closure, some in mangled Spanish.

I saved your lives, shitheads, he said in English and tore the notes down.

He unlocked the gate and walked down the stone path to the cenote. As the sun rose it sent a sparkling ray into the center of the blue pool. He leaned against the cavern's wall and watched and waited. It was breathtakingly beautiful, and for a moment he saw it as he'd once seen it, when he'd first arrived, and was filled with awe.

As it neared 9am he laid out his own notebook next to the window and wrote LIBRO DE VISITAS / GUEST BOOK across the top of it, with columns for NAME/NOMBRE and HOTEL.

He obsessively catalogued them. Fat ones, thin ones, tall ones, short ones. Brown and pink. Angelita came and stood by the booth and seeing his mood left quietly.

As the day came toward a close he looked at his stack of torn ticket stubs with dread. It seemed far too large for the hour.

¡*La Revista Nacional!* he thought.

As a group left with one member short he lurched from his booth and made up some pretense for speaking to them.

The fourth gentleman who came with you? He's where? I have a special deal on tickets to Chichen Itza I can provide you, but only if there are four, Eduardo said breathlessly.

I don't think we're interested sir, thank you.

OK no problem—the fourth gentleman, he's right behind you?

Yes, he's taking one more photo. Is it a problem?

Eduardo waited at the gate and then the man exited, his camera strapped to his wrist, his expression vague and uncertain.

At the end of the day a single stub remained. He stabbed his pencil down next to the man's name. Francisco Velasquez, Hotel San Clemente. In a group of three, Eduardo recalled. Mother, father and daughter.

He raced his motorcycle to the hotel and asked for the room of Velasquez's.

A young woman in her late teens answered the door.

Is your father, Francisco, here? Eduardo said, not realizing until he spoke that he was out of breath. He leaned over to ease the pressure of his side ache.

No, the girl said.

Please, he stuck his foot in the door.

The older woman appeared behind the girl.

I'm looking for Francisco, he said.

The mother frowned. There are no Franciscos here.

OK, Eduardo said, then where is he?

No I mean to say there are no Franciscos staying here, with us.

Where is your father then? he asked the girl.

The girl turned and looked back at her mother.

Her father is no longer with us, the mother said. Who are you? What do you want?

Jesus Christ, Eduardo said. What happened?

Nothing happened, the daughter said. He had a heart attack eleven years ago.

Eduardo sunk to the ground. He felt suddenly as if he were having a heart attack himself. And today? he said, his breathing more difficult. At the cenote? Did you not come with someone?

Young man are you alright? the mother asked. Help me pull him in.

Mother!

He needs help, Rosa! Put him on the bed. Go get the clerk, hurry!

Please, Eduardo said, I'm fine. Just a moment. He rolled off the bed and found himself on the floor, and then came to his knees. Just answer please! He stared at the rug. His head seemed packed full of gunshot or sea pebbles or fingernails.

AT HOME HE PUT HIS remaining supply of blank paper in the sink and ran water over it until it became a pulpy mass. Then he unwrapped a new bottle of tequila and lay on the bed. After a while he realized that every thought was organizing itself into verse. The leaden chaos of his mind kept crystalizing out lines. Shut up! he yelled. The verse came about the girl's father, who had lived these last eleven years for Eduardo only, it seemed. Shut up! Shut up! He took a deep pull of tequila and stared at the ceiling. The poem hung in his mind as if on fire, written in the air. He let himself tinker with it, change lines about, edit and hone. And then he gave in. For lack of paper, he sat on the edge of the bed and removed his pants and wrote out the poem in ballpoint pen along his leg. When he was finished he took another long pull of tequila and admired it. It sprawled in blue from his knee to the top of his thigh.

There was a knock at the door and then Ronaldo's face appeared from behind it. Oh, love, Ronaldo said.

How? Eduardo said, but he could hear the words slur on his tongue and felt embarrassed and stopped speaking. He watched Ronaldo pick his way across the room, over strewn clothes intermingled with beer cans and thrown manuscript papers. In the sink, a pulpy mass like some deep sea creature.

I hope it wasn't written on? Ronaldo pointed. He smiled down at him sitting on the bed with his pants down and his hands wrapped around a bottle of tequila and said: Looks like I'm just in time. Then he took a draught from the bottle and leaned in and kissed Eduardo. What's this? He went to his knees and read the poem upside down, his hands gripping the outside of Eduardo's thighs. Wow, amor.

Ronaldo pulled his laptop from his shoulder bag and set it next to Eduardo. Don't move, he said. We will soon smear it, you and I, so I better do this now. You know paper doesn't have to be washed, right, caballero? He typed in the poem. Poor love, out here on the frontier alone, making do and going native. When he was finished, he kissed his way up the other thigh. Eduardo allowed himself to fall backwards onto the bed.

RONALDO SAT ON A STOOL in the doorway of the ticket taker's booth and chatted while Eduardo tore the stubs and recorded the visitors. He was having a hard time following what Ronaldo was saying amid the anxious rush of traffic and his gatekeeper's obligations. He committed each face to memory. Ronaldo was giving an account of their friends: José had gotten a teaching job for way too little pay. Magrite was shooting up her inheritance. Mincho said he was working on a novel and no one ever saw him. Fé had married rich. To Eduardo the names all sounded insubstantial, like people he'd only known in a dream.

Tell me why again I can't go down there, amor? Ronaldo said. I don't see why all these tourists get to go and not me.

Eduardo could not bring himself to tell him. He had taped Francisco's torn stub along with every detail he could remember to the back of the desk where he could see and remember it. He had not, he told himself, simply made up the man.

At least let me see what you're so frantically doing there. Ronaldo leaned in and watched Eduardo annotate four torn ticket stubs. You're describing them? This trip has been hard on you.

Angelita dropped by and ate an ice cream cone with Ronaldo. How come he's so serious now? Ronaldo said.

I'm not, Eduardo said, but his voice didn't modulate well.

Angelita shrugged and smiled at Ronaldo again. I've heard so much about you.

What? He talks about me? I've got to hear this.

But Angelita got embarrassed and turned pink and licked her strawberry ice cream.

OK, then just tell me about the cenote, Ronaldo said. Why won't he let me go down there?

Angelita glanced at Eduardo and then looked away. He said you can do an amazing trick with your tongue...

Oh, he did, did he.

She blushed bright. And that you're very romantic.

Mmmm.

And that you snore.

I do not! Ronaldo reached over and punched Eduardo in the arm and Eduardo laughed and then felt sick.

Watch the booth for me, would you both? he said. Don't sell any tickets. Tell them it's full, whatever.

He walked to the park's bathroom, locked himself in a stall and stood swaying above the toilet. He was hungover and nauseous and his stomach would not settle. He put his finger into his throat to make himself throw up and when that was done he leaned his forehead against the concrete wall and breathed until he could settle his mind.

When he returned to the booth there was a line to serve. The last ticket he'd written was positioned in the middle of the desk, isolated from the others. He'd noted: A handsome Mexican man in his late twenties, with wavy dark hair, and green eyes. *Ronaldo Charmed.* What kind of a last name is that? he thought. The hotel location, he read with horror, was his own address. He could not remember writing it.

But a moment later: *Ronaldo.* He felt startled by his momentary loss of memory, as if it'd been snatched from him, like a pelican plucks a fish from the water. Ronaldo had descended into the cenote! He slammed his fist into the desktop, the ticket stubs jumped. But what right did he have to forbid him? Everyone who came to the city visited. He underlined *Ronaldo* on the stub and put it with the others.

As the day wore on, he found himself in a better rhythm. He set the torn tickets to the side organized chronologically. He looked up and waved at Angelita across the park and she waved back and smiled, each too busy now to talk to the other.

When the sunlight streamed golden through the trees and began to dim on the edge of the sky he sorted through his remaining stubs. There were ten of them. The last few visitors were exiting quickly now, making the pile diminish rapidly. It would be a no-tickets-left day, he could feel it, and for this he was relieved.

But there was one ticket left when the park closed. He reread the code and did not remember the face it belonged to.

It was a cruel prank played by Angelita, he thought, or someone who had written the street number wrong; *his own*. He looked for her across the park but could not see her. He swore and walked to the gate of the cenote with his new flashlight. A vein in his throat pulsed with heartbeat. Hello? he called into it. In the cave's entrance before the path he thought about how much he abhorred the job. But he was fashioning *his* ticket out: *La Revista Nacional*! Just the thought of the journal caused an upwelling within him, memory and thought roiling beneath the surface of his mind's lake. There would be work tonight!

Come on! he yelled from the top of the path. The cenote shimmered darkly, the turquoise pool dimming to black. He pulled the torn stub from his pocket and inspected it with his flashlight.

It was a name he liked, Ronaldo was. He proceeded slowly down the path, turning the flashlight on for short intervals, and then turning it off so his eyes could adjust to the whole cavern. Had the Mayans sacrificed here to pay tribute? Or because they were afraid of it? Señor! he called. Ronaldo!

Near the lower part of the path next to the platform he whispered the name into the dark. It didn't sound right. It was a made up name. In his head he began composing a letter but he couldn't think to whom. *Querido*.

Ronaldo! he yelled. With the water softly lapping at the edge, inches from his shoes, he scanned the pool with his flashlight. What had made the water move?

Deep in its depths he saw something. It was a body, highlighted fluorescent blue by the light, in the heart of the pool. Its arms stretched wide, suspended. He knew this body.

Eduardo dove in, swimming hard with one hand, the other clasping the flashlight as its sword beam cut through the water, making the body glow. He swam deeper and deeper but the body stayed out of reach, so far and deep and dreamlike at the bottom.

His lungs ached and he realized he would not reach him.

He let his air go and turned to resurface but every direction was the same. *Querido Ronaldo: I have followed you in.* His lungs seared, as if coal burned in them. He swam hard for the top but the body was there, too, still far away. Waving now, perhaps, or only swaying dully back and forth by his thrashing. He gulped in water, wishing to yell out in anger, to give one last *fuck you* to the cenote before it silenced him. And then his lungs could hold no longer and he dropped the flashlight and let the water in.

When, querido, the sickening panic subsides into a pleasant, deathly drowsiness, I will float down to you, and we will embrace at the bottom. He drifted this way, unsure which direction the pool pulled him.

Around him he felt the water churn, claws or strong fingers gripped the back of his shirt. They clenched his hair, the sharp nails bit into his ankles and wrists. Pinchers at his stomach and back. He was being pulled down to the strange twisted bottom. To float amongst the skulls, ancient and new. *Deep and not exactly straightforward.*

The claws struggled with him and he felt tired and closed his eyes and slept and when he woke he was on the platform. The cavern was lit by moon glow, beaming down on him through the hole at the top. He felt arms around him.

"Ronaldo?" he said, and the cavern obediently repeated the word with sharp reverberations, until the sound became meaningless. The arms tightened in empathetic response. Kiss me, he thought. But as he turned the arms pulled back into the darkness, unseen, outside of the moon's spotlight. The cenote quieted, the moon moved on, and within him rose a sense of loss so strong it felt audible. The beating of his heart like a hammer on tin, in an enormous room.

*When I met the Duchess I still gave my age as eighteen and only a few had begun to doubt it. Maybe I was a careless and lazy boy but I was not entirely a stupid one.*

# The Duchess and the Ghost

RICHARD BOWES

1.

WHEN I REMEMBER THE DUCHESS it's in vignettes, snapshots. Even when she lived that's how I saw her. Now I hope that it's how some people will remember me.

"My family lost everything in the Revolution," she sighed the first time we met. The accent was unplaceable. "The houses in Paris and Rome, the estate in Maryland, all gone." Her hands fluttered away to illustrate this. Her eyes seemed to focus on another world.

"What revolution was that?" I asked. I mean she was old but not "Tale of Two Cities," or Lenin and Stalin old.

"The Sexual Revolution," she said and appeared astounded that I wouldn't know this. In fact I had heard a little about her family disowning her. I had no doubt mine was really unhappy with me too. Though by then my only contact with them was in my nightmares.

I had turned eighteen near the tail end of 1961, about two and a half years before encountering the Duchess. A few weeks after that birthday, coming home from college on my freshman year Christmas Break, I abandoned the train in the old, original Penn Station. My one glance back had showed me a face staring with shock and horror from a train window. That face seemed like what my ghost's would look like and I lost myself fast in the noise and confusion of pre-Christmas New York City.

When I met the Duchess I still gave my age as eighteen and only a few had begun to doubt it. Maybe I was a careless and lazy boy but I was not entirely a stupid one.

On our first meeting I'd guessed that the Duchess'ss past was as twisted and hidden as a path through a dark forest. It was how I had come to see mine.

She was all about contradictions. The cheekbones were elegance itself. The voice was throaty, a loud whisper if there is such a thing. But the hands were larger than might be expected of a lady of breeding. She got away with an array of giveaways like that because this was 1964 and a significant part of the population was still blind enough to believe that Liberace was straight.

She had lived much of her life in the world I'd found in New York and read my reaction right off my face. "Silly girl, if they can recognize what I am or what you're up to, it means they're as deeply perverted as either of us. And those can be the most dangerous ones. The rest are like sleeping cattle."

She wore a maroon Borsalino hat and what I later learned to recognize as a knock-off of a Schiaparelli tennis outfit. This was daring because of the way it exposed somewhat muscular legs. And also because Greenwich Village was far from being as free and open sexually as was advertised.

The mafia ruled and the street style was macho. Women did not wear shorts unless they had tough boyfriends. Men got busted for going in drag. Shorts for males were legal but unwise. Wearing them in this city if you were above the age of maybe eight meant you were gay and for sale.

I'd found that out early in my life in the neighborhood when both my pairs of long pants were at the laundry and the Italian kids on the corner called me faggot for showing my knees. Boys I knew got the shit beaten out of them by street gangs for "walking funny."

The Duchess was brave. When I told her that she said, "Darling, bravery is a euphemism for stupidity."

2.

SHE AND I STOOD IN a small room with a view of the back garden of an Italian restaurant. The Duchess had a five-room apartment on the gentle curve of Commerce Street in the Village. It was rent controlled which meant she paid very little for it.

There was a big enough bed, a table with a lamp, a chair and an armoire. The walls were a blue that I've never been able to match anywhere.

On the table was a silver framed photo of a European guy with a dueling scar and what I saw as a sappy smile.

She said, "For those few years on the Adriatic, the Margrave and I were of the same sex, which was convenient. Then he died which was convenient in its own way." I was going to ask which sex they'd shared.

But I thought better of it because this was going to be my room for thirty dollars a month. My sugar daddy had just good-by to me. And a boy who finds himself in that situation has to take hints and detect undercurrents.

I'd studied it carefully from all angles and been shocked by how narrow the choices were for a rent boy who would not be a boy for much longer.

3.

ROGER TIPPET, THE DESIGNER, HAD turned out to be my final daddy. My occasional crying out in my sleep did me in. As he slid me out of his life (a dancer at the New York City Ballet School was waiting in the wings), he said it was time I met the Duchess.

"I knew her when she *ruled* this city. Since then she's run through her trust fund but you can learn a lot about attitude from the Duchess."

Then he added. "Never let it be said I don't take care of my old tricks." He smiled the way he did when a private thought pleased him and said, "That's how I always want to be remembered."

I paid my first month's rent and moved in. After I'd gotten to know the Duchess to the extent one could do that, I told her about how Tippet wanted to be remembered.

"When they begin to write their own epitaphs it means they want us to attribute human motives to them," she said. "People like that have an innate ability to rise above everybody else's problems."

Beyond doubt Tippet was the biggest asshole but he wasn't the worst daddy by any means. That would be Augustus who made me dress in a blue blazer and tan chinos like a private schoolboy, insisted I call him 'Uncle Augie' in public and dispensed corporal punishment when stoned.

But the one that I missed then, and that I still miss over half a century later is Garcia, my first daddy. He was tending bar at the Cedar Tavern on Eighth Street on a quiet December Sunday night when a scared, drunken kid staggered in the door carrying a suitcase. It was my first night in a city where the drinking age was eighteen.

All I knew immediately was that Garcia was as old as my father—almost fifty. He looked and sounded tough. But even as a traumatized kid, I recognized real gentleness and charm. He brought me home; had me sleep on his couch until I trusted him enough to let him take me to bed. It felt good just being near him.

He listened to my tales of untimely erections that led to my getting jumped in school showers and stomach punched in hallways, of my parents giving me hard slaps and crew cuts if I wasn't butch enough and my college freshman roommate lodging a complaint about being placed with a fag. A report about this had been sent to my father and was awaiting my arrival home the night I ran away.

Garcia introduced me to the Folk and Jazz obsessed Village, taught me the ins and outs of the neighborhood. When he was certain I didn't want to go back to my family and was afraid of getting drafted into the army, he brought me to a scary guy called the Doorman in a cellar in an alley far east on Bleecker Street.

Garcia had said he wanted me to get used to this place. He bought me counterfeit I.D. and draft cards—supposedly the best in the city. On these I was Anthony Willis, a name I had to memorize. From then on my name was Tony.

After he made them, the Doorman, big and bald, sat behind the desk where he did his forgery. At his back was a door opening onto a pitch-black room. He looked at me with these dead eyes and told Garcia, "Your boyfriend needs more than an alias. He's got ghosts."

In the dark behind him, I saw a face staring with horror from a window as a train rolled out of Penn Station. It was the face I saw when I looked back that first night in the city. The one that made me cry out in my sleep.

Garcia saw my fear, put his arms around my shoulders and blocked my line of sight to the black room. "You prick," he told the Doorman. "You didn't have to show him that! He's just a kid and when he's ready he'll make up his own mind about what to do with his ghosts. You won't cheat him out of half his life like you did me."

The Doorman told him never to come back. But I noticed he didn't tell me.

4.

LIFE WITH THE DUCHESS a couple of years later was much different from Garcia. I remember standing naked in her living room much to her amusement and that of the Countess, her transvestite disciple.

I'd paid the first month's rent but the Duchess wondered how I'd pay the next. I had savings but knew how fast they could evaporate. I had few skills beyond being a boy.

The Countess was short, dark haired and unmistakably out of Brooklyn. She ran a string of male prostitutes. "Girls that strip down and turn out to be guys are what's big right now," she said. "Not sure that's right for you."

They were trying to get me into drag, but the high heels were deadly and I hated the painful business of hiding my junk.

The Countess was vexed as I stumbled out of the shoes and the penis-gaffe dropped on the floor. "What possible use is he?" she asked. "He makes you feel pity. Not a big market anywhere."

"He isn't a stupid boy," said the Duchess, trying to put the best light on the situation.

The Countess noticed a single white hair on the back of my head, took the mirror and showed it to me.

"Eventually, I'll be distinguished looking," I suggested.

"You'll be foolish looking," said the Countess, clipping it off savagely.

"Worse than foolish, middle aged," the Duchess said and we all shuddered.

She was reading the *Village Voice*. "There's a boutique called, 'Hope is a Thing With Leathers', (Emily Dickinson, I cry for you) over on East Ninth Street. There's a string of boutiques over there. Straight ladies are getting divorced. With the alimony they hire a smart fag and open these very twee shops. Dear God, one is called, 'Hippopotami Have Feelings Too', for larger women, no doubt."

She looked at me. "I know who to talk to. Get dressed. You'll be the smart fag," she said and so it was. The Duchess was a semi-legend in the world of boutique fashion. I found out I liked selling and being the gay boy in a shop full of women.

5.

AFTER LANDING THE BOUTIQUE JOB, I began spending little time in the Duchess'ss place. I'd met Frankie who played piano around the Village when he could, the first boyfriend my age, the first sex partner who made less money than I did.

"How silly of you! Men are always disgusting but sometimes they're rich," the Duchess said when I informed her. I was caught between a new feeling of freedom and the old recurring dreams in which I was scared, alone and locked in an attic in my family's house.

That summer there was a funeral on my day off from work. An old friend of the Duchess and Countess was being seen off at St Luke in the Fields Church on Christopher Street. I was introduced to the other mourners as, 'The son of an old family retainer' and the campiness of this made me smile.

It was a beautiful day. In the church gardens were butterflies, including a large red and black one. The Duchess said, "In ancient Greece, a butterfly was thought to be the spirit of the departed."

The apartment had lots of closets and storage spaces and she was going through them. I knew from the Countess that the Duchess had cancer and knew she would never tell me directly. Cancer was a secret thing back then. You told no one and hoped it would go away was how it worked.

The Duchess, though, did say things like, "The problem with living in the moment is the crowds living in that moment with you."

I tried to be around and help her when I could. She never tried to make me feel guilty.

The funeral had made me remember Garcia. And because I thought about it a lot and she did know stuff, I told the Duchess about the strange thing that had happened when Garcia took me to get forged papers.

The Duchess's face was a mask as she listened to my tale of the Doorman and the ghost. When I said I still dreamed about the face in the train window and mentioned other bad stuff in my dreams, she changed the subject, asked me to help her go through the hall closet.

I repeatedly went up a ladder and took down boxes from Paris shops, a small safe, a hussar uniform, family records and a midget bridal gown. Occasionally, the Duchess exclaimed about something. "Dear mama's beagle whip!" or "Keys to Uncle Fargo's pleasure room."

I understood or hoped that she was making all this up. But I was self centered enough to be disappointed that she paid so little attention to something that pained and scared me.

The next morning I woke up and found on my table a Xerox copy of a *New York Herald Tribune* page from 1923. This hadn't been there when I fell asleep. It was photos and commentary about the Knickerbocker Cotillion, a very elite dancing school with young people in evening clothes. One shot was of a guy maybe twenty, "Jason Arkwright," he was called. The Countess had told me Arkwright was the Duchess's family name and that I was never to mention it.

But the guy's remote gaze and cheekbones revealed the family resemblance. He was gorgeous but somehow looked hurt like my ghost in my dreams did. I knew this wasn't a brother. It was the Duchess in an unhappy manifestation.

She wasn't home, but on her kitchen table was another copy of a newspaper page. This was 1932, The Daughters of Gotham Charity Ball. It featured guys in tuxedos and a line-up of women in evening gowns and hair made to do things hair was never meant to do, looking right out of Hollywood.

And there was Jason Arkwright in drag: those distant eyes, those bones, but with every bit of the Duchess'ss assurance. The bevy's names were under the photo. There was a Rockefeller and a Whitney. The Duchess, AKA Jason Arkwright, was identified as Bo-Bo Signee. It was obviously the same person as the one in the earlier photo. How had she managed to get away with this transparent alias? Did no one in New York society catch on?

I was intensely curious but knew better than to ask her directly about this. When I came home that night, she began talking about her disease but very indirectly.

"It's all the creams that kept my skin smooth, all the makeup and hormone injections. Write on my tombstone, 'She died for beauty.' It's so stupid."

"I don't think that's what causes..." I trailed off. I'd tried to learn something about leukemia but I'd had little experience with disease and dying. AIDS/HIV was a decade and a half and more in the future.

"It was the beauty treatments," she snarled. "I will have it no other way. Straight people die of mundane diseases. I will die of hormones and makeup or it's not worth dying at all!"

She insisted we look in the hall closet again. It was mostly empty. But I found a metal bit like a horse's with leather straps and buckles attached and handed it down to her.

"Grandmother's funeral muzzle," she said. "Prevents ones who wake up in a coffin from disrupting the ceremony by yelling that they're still alive! Make sure I'm wearing it when I go."

I was still young enough to be able to surprise myself. Standing on the ladder I started to cry.

She was very angry. "You don't know me well enough to be grief-stricken at my being gone. In any case, it's none of your business."

So I sobbed, "I'm just afraid of losing a place to live."

This was acceptably distant, as I'd hoped it would be.

"My dear," she said, "I've entangled this place in so many legalities it will take them years to get rid of you. I'll write you in as a bastard child." And so she did.

I started to climb down and saw her shake her head at my stupidity. I turned back and noticed papers on the shelf.

The Duchess had disappeared into her bedroom when I descended. Sorting through the pages, I found news and photos of Jason Arkwright's death when his car collided with a tree in 1924. There was also a gossip column from 1935, which hinted at "an unsubstantiated rumor" that "Secret Men-Women" had recently infiltrated a certain New York charity event.

By the time of that charity event, Jason Arkwright was officially dead and probably half forgotten. And back then it was inconceivable to most people that as lovely a woman as Bo-Bo could be a man. As I suddenly saw it, the Duchess had somehow managed to erase her ghost and had then given a "fuck you" to an elite that would have spurned her had they known.

7.

That night I dreamed for what seemed like the thousandth time that I was locked in the cellar of my parents' house. The ghost me in my dreams reminded me of Jason, half-formed, vulnerable. Waking in my bedroom, I couldn't go back to sleep and couldn't stop thinking of Garcia in his last days.

We'd been together for six months and more when he started to be distant and withdrawn and kept calling in sick for work. One night he had me back sleeping on the living room couch and I was afraid he was tired of me.

Next morning he sent me out on a long list of errands, something he'd never done before. When I got back that afternoon, an ambulance and a cop car were outside the building. I ran up the stairs and the apartment door was open. A cop and the nosey lady from down the hall were in there. My suitcase was by the door, completely packed and with my phony name on a tag.

"There's Tony, the young man I told you about," said the lady.

The cop's disdain was automatic. Without my asking, he looked in his notebook and said, "Your friend had a heart attack as far as they know." He saw my shocked expression and asked a few more questions about Garcia and me.

At that moment, Garcia's sister and brother-in-law, people that he'd never talked about, showed up and made it clear they found me disgusting and wanted me gone. I was reminded of home.

I carted my suitcase for the first time since the night Garcia found me. Stunned and still dry eyed I sat near the fountain in Washington Square. That's when I opened the suitcase and found five hundred dollars in bills, a big deal in 1962. That money helped me step out of some bad situations over the next couple of years.

There was also a photo of Garcia and me at the Night Owl Café that I still have. On postcards he had written, "Put the dough in the bank. Kid, I thought I could take away your pain by loving you. But my time is all used up and I don't want you to have to see me die. It twisted my heart to hear you cry last night and to know I wouldn't see you any more.

"That ghost you dream about is you hating yourself. I was dumb and waited too long to cure myself and got cheated out of a chunk of my life.

"I should have been more careful taking you to the Doorman. The place is like hell but they can get rid of ghosts. They take some of your life as payment so they can live forever. But you got plenty of life left. Demand to see the Boss and maybe the Boss's Boss if you need to. Don't settle for less than fifty years and maybe a little extra."

8.

THE MEMORY OF MY FACE in a thousand nightmares had kept me away from the Doorman. The Duchess, though, knocked me out of my Psychotic Sleeping Beauty trance.

Her last weeks were spent in St. Vincent's Hospital in the Village. Mostly she was in a morphine doze. But once, when I was alone with her she opened her eyes, looked into mine and said, "I bribed the Powers with a couple of decades of my life and they killed the cowardly boy I had once been. Do the same or spend the rest of your life crying in your sleep. An irritating habit by the way!"

The hospital johnnie only partly covered her. Arranging the sheets, I saw on her hip what looked like a tattoo. I'd seen one like it on Garcia's hip. He never let me read his. Hers had a date three days away.

Her last words, on that last day to a roomful of friends were, "Dropping dead is like getting to snub everyone you ever knew."

Most of the wake and funeral attendees reminded me of the Wax Museum in Sunset Boulevard. An elderly lawyer, present to safeguard family interests, was the only representative of the Arkwrights.

The burial was at a famous old cemetery in Brooklyn where the family owned a big plot. The Countess saved us from too much sadness by throwing herself into the grave crying out, "Bo-Bo, I followed you into Diors found in flea markets and lesbian cabaret stylings and I will follow you now." She broke her ankle and an ambulance had to come to the graveside to haul her away. I believe the Duchess would have approved.

Butterflies filled the air.

9.

NOT LONG AFTER THAT I went down the alley far to the east on Bleecker and knocked on the cellar door. I wished Garcia was with me. By then, I had spoken to a few others who had done business with the Powers. Some thought The Doorman and company worked for God, some bet on Satan. But none had ever heard of the Powers breaking their word.

The Doorman said to come in and it felt like he expected me. I'd rehearsed my lines and told him, "I'll keep fifty years of my life and a bit more. The rest is yours if you get rid of the ghost."

He answered, "Thirty years more is what you get. The rest is ours."

But I'd learned a bit about bargaining in the boutiques and said, "I want to talk to your Boss." He kept the sneer but I could tell this made him almost as scared as I was. I had to strip and kneel down inside the black room that lay behind the little office. The air seemed to be rising out of a cold cave.

Two things were visible in the dark. The first was a huge face, pale as the moon and with dark staring eyes. The second was me – or that version of me I'd left at the old Penn Station. He/I was walking at dawn along the street my family maybe still lived on. His eyes were cast down and he had a rope under his arm. I remembered bits of this dream from the last few years and knew what was going to happen and that I needed to be strong.

The cold, my nakedness, the unfolding horror as my ghost reached a park and found the right tree, was meant to intimidate. I was afraid but thought of the Duchess'ss bravery and Garcia's love.

"We will end this one who lives inside you," said a distant voice as my ghost tied the rope around a branch. "We will allow you forty more years of life and the rest of your years we will keep for ourselves so we can continue our work."

"Sixty or I walk," I said and kept my eyes on the kid who was part of me, putting the noose around his neck, standing on a branch and getting ready to jump.

The Boss's pale face before me blinked and I thought I detected fear. Then another voice even more distant—The Boss's Boss—said, "Fifty years."

I watched as the kid who was me jumped off the branch. "And a year and a day," I said not knowing where that came from. Then my nerve broke. I looked away before my ghost's neck snapped.

"Done," said the most distant voice. "Amusing," it added and I glimpsed my ghost's darkening face and bulging eyes, the hands and legs flapping.

The Doorman came in looking pale, pulled me to my feet and struck my hip. My tattoo grew there. I looked back after I got dressed. The faces of my ghosts and the Bosses had all disappeared.

## 10.

THE ALLEY IS GONE NOW along with the building that housed The Doorman's office and the dark room. A boutique tourist hotel sits on the spot. An irony is that ten years ago, my partner Luis and I did the lobby decoration. I can only imagine what the Duchess would say. I think of her and Garcia, always.

My ghost never appeared again and it's been a long time since I heard anything about the Doorman or the Bosses. Maybe they acquired enough years from those like me to live forever. But I hope it's because the supply of refugees who need to flee their own self-hatred has dried up.

Fifty years and a year and a day seems such a long time when one is only twenty. My life has had its tragedies and joys. But today is my seventy-first year plus one day.

And on a chilly November, a butterfly

flutters past

my window

*No matter how close I was, Edgar drew me closer, long fingers guiding mine over the lines that marked the pages. These were original maps, bound into a book for what had been deemed "safer keeping," and I could feel the difference between smooth ink and rough paper. Coupled with the heat of Edgar's hand atop mine, I thought the maps would smudge beneath our fingers, lost to anyone who came after. When Edgar leaned in to kiss me, I felt the line of the River Tyne on the page beneath my middle finger and drew back from both boy and map.*

# *Lockbox*

## E · CATHERINE TOBLER

If nothing else, remember this: Edgar always knew.[1]

He found the ruin by mistake, a wrong turn down a street that fizzled out and turned into a rutted dead end choked with undergrowth. Housewarming, helping friends move, whatever the event[2] would have become over the course of a sloppy October night, there was no house Edgar could actually see, until—he said with a dramatic pause—the ground crumbled under his feet and he found himself standing within the shattered remains of what he first called a cathedral. It was, he said, as if an entire abbey had been sunk[3] into the ground and buried over for a hundred thousand years.

Everyone gave him shit—said he was taking our course on Gothic literature a little too literally. *Had he seen any old gentlemen with forty-yard beards?* Thomas wanted to know. Were there women weeping upon the moors—*No moors, you imbecile, and not a single solitary soul, nor any of the others who had been invited,* Edgar said and then his eyes fell to me. The way his mouth slanted up, I knew what he was thinking, that we would go and have each other within that desolate ruin, out where there should have been a house, but there was only a buried ruin that no one could even name.

---

1   We may debate exactly *when* Edgar knew at length, but I am not convinced there was ever a single, discernable point one can reference; as the notions herein are circular,[20] I feel so, too, was Edgar's knowledge.

2   I have often been asked if there was an event at all; I cannot prove the existence of "the event," only that Edgar did leave, around 6pm on a Friday evening, and did not return until 2pm the following Sunday. He told me friends he'd had longer than he'd had me were moving and needed his help, but Edgar's hands never betrayed a lick of work.

3   *Had been sunk,* he phrased it so, as if some hand had pulled the abbey down with great intention.

But I was less careless than he and wanted to know more about this nameless, sunken place before we made to go. I had known Edgar for three years—it was our last year at University, the last year before we were to part ways, unless I followed him to London and I hated London[4] with all my heart, no matter how much I loved Edgar. He was decisive where I was not, disruptive—the kind to run shrieking through a church service, daring those amassed to consider matters outside their quiet circles of contemplation.[5]

*Surely*, I said to him as he watched me with the infinite patience of a man in love,[6] *the ruin possessed a name.* Everything in the world was named, controlled, precisely defined. We spent afternoons in the library poring over every ancient tome we could lay our hands on, asking the librarians if they had ever heard of such a place and they said no—but I saw it in their eyes. I *heard* the unspoken words clawing at the corners of their closed mouths. I didn't ask more of them, fearing they *could not* say. Edgar and I propped ourselves against the hard walnut shelves in a tangle with books of old, large maps spread across his loose-thighed lap.

No matter how close I was, Edgar drew me closer, long fingers guiding mine over the lines that marked the pages. These were original maps, bound into a book for what had been deemed "safer keeping," and I could feel the difference between smooth ink and rough paper. Coupled with the heat of Edgar's hand atop mine, I thought the maps would smudge beneath our fingers, lost to anyone who came after. When Edgar leaned in to kiss me, I felt the line of the River Tyne on the page beneath my middle finger and drew back from both boy and map.

"Exham,[7]" I breathed.

"Possible," Edgar said and I couldn't tell if his expression of annoyance was over the broken kiss or the accuracy of my guess.

As stories went, Exham Priory had housed the worst of the worst; the most depraved creatures had called those halls home and surely, it could not be that which Edgar had found in the ground. It could *not*—and if it was? Oh, I could not deny the way my heart

---

4   If one cares to look, the reasoning for this can be found in my chapbook, *Terrible London*, Meridian (2012). Everything but the food, dear reader; I found great comfort in warm beer and dry potatoes — No.

5   Edgar did not possess any religious leanings, which made his discovery of the abbey all the more curious. It wasn't something he would have made up, even to gain favor with me—and being that he already possessed much more than my favor, this only lent credence to the story he told me. It is a terrible thing, to understand the limits of storytelling and be drawn in even so.

6   Was he? Or was this merely part of the story he was telling?

7   In my coursework, I had studied the rumors of Exham Priory at length and they were simply not to be believed. There were terrible things in this world, to be certain, but I refused to believe in the numerous atrocities that were said to have taken place at Exham Priory. Inbreeding, people confined within cages, one body sewn to another to create a third thing entirely. Elephantine forms, long in places and bloated in others. Myths and legends, happenings that existed only within the fragments of ballads, ghost stories. Imagination has a way of shaping all things, including culture and politics. Perhaps especially these.

quickened at the mere idea. If I—If *we* were to discover the ruins of Exham Priory and prove every single thing about the place true—It couldn't be possible and yet, I wanted it very much to be.

"Was it an aunt you had in that region?"

His question to me required no actual answer. Edgar tangled his hand into my necktie and pulled me closer, to forestall all dialogue but that between lip and tongue. The ruin didn't exactly matter then—it *was* an aunt I had near Exham, widowed and alone for more years than anyone wanted to count—and Edgar seemed to put the place out of his mind, until the end of the week when he looked at me over a stack of fresh books we had been perusing and asked if I wanted to go. *Its name didn't matter*, he insisted, but he wanted to show me the ruin; he wanted me to see the way the setting sunlight would fill the depression the ruin made in the ground, a pool of gold draining away as the evening descended. We could also call upon my aunt, if I wished, but thoughts of her made me more uneasy. How *that* was possible, given our potential destination, baffled me. Something about women wandering alone, unseen.

He bade me pack my camera and we drove south, until Edinburgh was far behind.[8] Here, the land was untamed, streets turning to dirt before they fizzled out altogether. The idea that a wrong turn had brought him here in the first place seemed unlikely; it had perplexed me, his disappearance over the weekend, the claim of seeing friends into a new house, but when Edgar parked the car and took my hand to draw me out, I said nothing, captivated by what spread before us. It was as he said, like nothing you might imagine when a person explained it. It seemed a whole city submerged, drawn into the guts of the world where it held the last moments of sunlight from the rest of the land.

Within the dry and crumbling earth, walls made themselves known as dwindling sunlight caressed them. I picked out windows and doorways, even the remains of a sloping roof. Edgar grasped my hand and pulled me down a set of crumbling stone steps, into the building itself, and from there watched me as I wandered. The great hall rose around us to frame the twilight sky. I saw each piece of the wreck in turn, through the camera lens as the light faded and faded. Then it was Edgar's mouth lighting up the ruin, against my cheek, my ear, as he held me from behind, buckled my knees, and pressed me into the dirt. Here, the earth smelled like eternity. I watched in some measure of amusement as Edgar caught my camera as it tumbled from my hand. He set it carefully aside, showing less care with my jacket, my trousers. He was insatiable, the ground strangely warm beneath my splayed hands, as if with spilled blood, though it crumbled dry between my fingers when hands turned to fists. When we walked up that

---

8  We drove approximately two hours south, though I would be hard-pressed to pinpoint our location beyond this. Indeed, the River Tyne was nearby and we passed through a wood that was surely the Whitelee Moor National Nature Reserve, but I can recollect nothing more specific.

long staircase later, as if we were drunk on the world and each other,[9] the moonlight glossing the stone made each step seem whole once more. Each was solid beneath my feet in a way they had not been upon our descent, no crumbling debris but only smooth and worn from centuries of feet moving across them.

I could not put the ruin from my head and wanted to return. Even in sleep, which we took in a small B&B in town proper,[10] the sunken building invited me to wander its halls. I returned to that crumbling staircase and found, not Edgar there but a woman, draped in what seemed shadows, but under my fingers was vintage silk. *Under my fingers*—she stood that close, looking down at me as if she had seen me once upon a time, but now needed a nudge to remember. She did not seem quite real and I presumed her to be my aunt with her silver hair until her lips parted, until she took a breath and drew the world into her lungs.

*This*, she said in a voice that was not my aunt's, *is not right.*

Her mouth did not move, but I heard the words even so. I could not tell dream from reality, then. I meant to ask her which it was, but it seemed ridiculous as she moved past me, down the stairs—

*The night stairs*, she said as she passed, the silk of her gown evacuating my grasp as though it were running away. It flowed behind her as a black river down every stone step. I turned to follow, unable to do anything else. My feet would not carry me up and out of the ruin, so down it was.[11]

A sickly yellow-green glow illuminated the underground passages we traversed, as if glowworms congregated somewhere above our heads. No bit of light touched the lady. She seemed cut from the world, only a paper silhouette cameo in front of me, the absence of all things. But the longer I looked at her, I began to see shapes within even the shadow of her. The air seemed made of great, dark whorls, as if many-limbed creatures moved *inside* her. No matter how impossible this also was, I went with it. I followed the passage of one such creature down her spine and into what should have been the cradle of her hips. There it curled, as if making a nest, and bared its fangs at me, fangs that gleamed like anthracite. Black on black and blacker still.[12]

*Come, now. Women are not made of such things.*

---

9    Reader, forgive my indulgence. I would banish this cliché, were it not true. In trying to keep to the facts at hand, I must include my infatuation for Edgar.

10    I cannot recollect the name of the town or the B&B, but my memory of each is otherwise intact: small, historical, charming. The woman who claimed ownership of the B&B is one Mrs. Baird, but without a location to search, I have been unable to find her. Baird is often as common a name as Smith.

11    Given the nature of dreams, perhaps this account should not be present, but to eliminate it also eliminates a truth I feel to this day. I have been unable to forget the feel of that silk between my fingers or that sickly yellow light.

12    If need be, I would compare what I saw to something pilots experience: sensory illusions when your eyes grow tired of an unchanging, blank landscape. It was not that I believed myself to be flying, but seeing these spirals made me waver and stumble as if drunk. We had not, however, been drinking.

She turned down a corridor and vanished from my sight. I gasped at the loss of her—the sensation was terrible, as if I had ceased to breathe, the whole of the world crumbling atop me—I increased my stride, but around the corner, she was still gone. Screams rose in the near distance.

*Margaret!*[13] I wanted to cry, but the name lodged in my throat.

She was as the ballad said:

> Here roams the lady daemon, between childer bound and freeman.
> Hair of silver, eye of gilt; soft of foot, through blood she spilt.
> — The Lady Daemon (1512)[14]

At the corridor's end stood a door, a sliver of that sickly light visible beneath it. This light shone so clearly upon my shoes that I could see where I had scuffed them the first day I'd met Edgar—I had kicked a stone unknowingly into his path, putting a similar scar on his own shoe. I pressed my hands to the door and it was like touching ice and fire both. From beyond the door, screams like you would find in your worst nightmares—as if people were being disassembled while they yet lived. There were letters carved into the door, worn by so much time they were mostly illegible.[15] I imagined a knife held in an unsteady hand, each cut into the wood drawing forth a fresh scream from the room beyond. The latch was cold beneath my hands, but would not be freed, no matter how I tried. It was likewise steady beneath the thump of my shoulder, refusing to give.

My fall from the bed woke me, shoulder thumping against floor and not door. I had no good idea where I was until Edgar reached down, fingers stroking my bare shoulder. I cringed at his touch, retreating into the tangle of blankets. My shoulder ached. When I looked, it showed a bruise, which of course could not be. Even Edgar's face betrayed surprise at this and I felt the emotion genuine—there were things he knew and could not yet tell me, but this mark upon my skin surprised him as much as it did me. He touched me again, the bruise warmer than the rest of the arm, angry with blood and injury.[16]

---

13  Lady Margaret Trevor of Cornwall. She married the second son of the fifth Baron Exham. Fourteenth-fifteenth century, though I, like so many before, have been unable to establish any firmer dates for her. She refuses to be pinned to any single point, looping through the histories of as many as eleven distinct cultures, but none so firmly held as those along the Welsh border. Children still fear she will take them from their beds, into the priory's cellars where she will bend them, cut them apart, breed them.

14  Fragment of "The Lady Daemon," a ballad, collected within E. Drake's *Ballads of the Welsh Border* (1650)

15  Druidic and Roman origins, but nothing so dramatic or simple as HELP or GO BACK carved within the wood. Trying to draw them the following morning led to the strange sensation of having written these words before. Magna Mater — oh, Great Mother.

16  To this day, the shoulder aches. I have been subject to all manner of medical examinations, each of which shows no injury. Edgar mentioned Frodo Baggins and the ache of the wound sustained on Weathertop. I could not laugh, for yes, it has become that, an injury that draws me into the memory of an occurrence I will (...)

The ruin was different in daylight, less hostile but no more welcoming. I expected to see footprints upon the steps, but while there was evidence of my tussle with Edgar, there was no sign that anyone else had been in the ruin.[17] I pulled Edgar down the hallways I had dreamed and we found the door, the terrible door, and Edgar—

Edgar's hands closed over my own, forcing me to hold the doorknob. It burned like ice and fire, as it had in my dream, but opened easily enough under our combined strength. I gasped as the foul stench of the room rolled out to greet us. I could not withdraw, for Edgar nudged me in.[18]

The crypt was vast, vaults lining the walls, rats skittering across the floor. Some were inscribed with names, but most were not. Each was locked tight, flowers turning to dust on the ground before three of the vaults. Edgar left my side to trace the few names he found, as if he would recognize some of the dead.[19]

The floor vibrated with anguish. It was as strong as anything I had ever felt, pulling me across the floor and down another set of stone steps. Into the heart of the priory, the lowest cellars where the worst things lingered. I did not question then what I saw, took it only for what it was, endless torment that Margaret Trevor had a hand in both then and now. How could it be that such things continued long past their points of origin? Or was it that everything was a circle,[20] moving outward before curling under and down to return through the middle and move back out? There was no end to anything begun here.

The worst thing was, despite the horrors around her, Margaret Trevor was something to be worshipped, a glory even in the blood and ruin that streaked her. The stories said that she loved the old cults well, but had taken a passive role beside her husband. But here, in the horrible cellar with its collapsing girders, she was a gold-and-silver goddess while her husband cowered. He held his hands before his face, as if he could not bear a magnificence such as she, while she opened the bodies[21] laid on an altar

---

(...) not fully explain.

17   How easily my mind explained *this*, for Margaret's dress had been long and surely, it swept all evidence of her steps away. Childer bound and…freeman, the ballad goes. Alone among the horrors, only I walked free. Only I.

18   We tell ourselves that nothing awful happens in the light of day, true terrors reserved for night and night alone, but daylight hides nothing. People still vanish under the light of a noon sun. Daylight strips the comfort of blackness away and we were not dreaming when we saw what we saw.

19   When I later asked, Edgar could remember no names. I asked if any of them were De la Poers or Shrews-fields, but he did not know and the more I asked, the more it drove him mad. He had always known and then did not.

20   Eternal return/recurrence, with its roots in Egypt and India both, further deconstructed by Blanqui (1871), Eddington (1927), Black Elk (1961), Hawking (2010), and certainly, yes, Pizzolatto (2013). Had we been here before? We had, but tell me not.

21   Bodies. Those they had fashioned in their breeding experiments, made to summon the utterly divine. I—Cannot. Not even here.

before her to welcome the oldest things anyone in the world might ever know.

What emerged beneath the guidance of her hands was something my memory has forced into a locked box. When I think on it, the world shutters to black and it feels as though iced water runs through my veins.[22] My blood does not exactly stop, nor does my heart cease, but I do not think overlong on the things we saw. I cannot, because the box is locked.

When we emerged, the clouds had broken and thin sunlight dribbled onto our faces. A backward glance[23] showed us nothing whatsoever amiss. Edgar laughed and wrapped an arm around my aching shoulder as we walked back to the car.

"I would have sworn...." He trailed off, as if unsure what led us here.

And I frowned, because I almost couldn't remember, either, but then it was night and we slept, and—Only dreamed.

Lady Margaret whispers from Edgar's mouth and I know the heat of the ancient sands parting, as if I, as if *we*, are stretched upon that altar in offering. She laughs and when I wake, I cannot wholly remember because I have placed that in the box, too.

When Edgar tells me he has to help friends move, I think little of it. He remains friends with people he knew before we even met and some do not know he has a lover. I nod, because I have my studies and there is always a paper in need of writing, so it will be good to have the nights. I think on the week that was and cannot fully place everything we have done, until Edgar returns, pressing a kiss against the corner of my mouth—

(the gleam of fangs

and he's coiled in the cradle of her hips,

waiting to be born,

waiting to be loosed—

unspoken words in the corner of his mouth, his maw.)

He got foolishly lost, he laughs, and there was no house, but there was still a place I

---

22  Would that it were so easy; a *locked* box and ice water—dramatic, Harry — but of course, I hold the key to this box. Margaret placed it within my skin so I can always find this place, where she calls the deepest horrors of the universe into our very own world. She opened the body as if parting sand, and I felt the warmth of an Egyptian desert. The scarabs whispered as they flowed up Lady Margaret's arms, into her very skin. She turned blue — the way Egyptians had painted the ceilings of their tombs or the Greeks their roofs, bright as the twilight sky. Each and every scarab became a star upon her. She glowed like the heavens and from her body, and the dead before her, vomited new, strange life. Forms I had never seen entered this world, on eight legs and more, and made everyone bow, everyone but Margaret. These strange creatures bowed to *her*. When Edgar did not bow in worship, they seized him, in hands horrible and deformed. I thought they would press him to his knees in the bloody dirt, and perhaps they meant to, but he resisted. His eyes met mine and he knew, he *knew*, and was taken into that hideous maw, consumed whole. Margaret stood as round as Cybele, swollen with the life to come. Edgar, *my* Edgar. When he was spat back out, it was from Margaret's distended mouth, and he was made different, made *knowing* of things others cannot, yet.

23  Always a mistake, reader. We did not turn to salt and yet, we turned.

needed to see. A place he wanted to take me.
    Edgar always knew. And I —
    Not yet.[24]


    THERE ONCE WAS A HO liked to murder
    Adept with both knife & stray girder
    She hiked up her skirt
    Put the men in the dirt
    And nobody talked shit about her.
    — The Lady Daemon (1992)[25]

---

24  Not yet
25  Posted by user "daemon-marg" on the Her Story BBS, uk.history.myths.legends.wales (11/1/92)

*With no schematic, put him back*
*together. Shape his face with molds and*
*iron casings, give him eyes of copper bulbs.*
*Make his muscles of kinetic wire, to make*
*him strong like Kennan wasn't. Try to*
*forget Kennan. Fail. Give the bot a body*
*it—he can use.*

# What Lasts

JARED W. COOPER

STEP 1:

Dig for parts in the Gearwoman's scrapyard, through dead frames and the rotted pages of old schematics. Find one of her bots, with thin limbs not yet rusted, intact and broken like yourself. Collect, and run away.

STEP 2:

With no schematic, put him back together. Shape his face with molds and iron casings, give him eyes of copper bulbs. Make his muscles of kinetic wire, to make him strong like Kennan wasn't. Try to forget Kennan. Fail. Give the bot a body it—*he* can use. Make his legs good for running, just in case.

Make his heart. Do not skip this step. Make the core with logic mods, with those chips that simulate emotion, but fill the space with pieces of yourself. Give to him your dreams and fears, those parts of you that always hurt. Put your heart inside of his, so when it sputters and flickers and comes to life, you recognize that beat, that heat that used to shine inside you.

STEP 3:

Sit on your porch when the Gearwoman comes. Let the bot sit by you, neither of you hiding. Let her see what you made from what she threw away. Listen as she yells at you, tells you what becomes of boys who take her bots. As she barks, lean back on your hands and feel the heat of the bronze-blue sun. Let her anger build as she threatens you with death, and worse.

Let her promise. Do not skip this step. Let her point and tell you what she'll do to you, how when she's done you'll be just another body in her scrapyard, and wait. Watch as your bot rises, hearing the promise of violence in her tone.

Watch him leap at her, strong and fast and moving to the beat of your own heart. Watch him soundless and perfect as he shoves her, sending her sprawling down your grey grass yard, a tumble of leather skirts and oil-stained skin. Watch and admire him, protective, proud and powerful.

When the Gearwoman rises, notice how hollow her new threats, how laced with fear her voice. But listen, because she tells you how you might as well be one of them. She knows a bot when she sees one. Take in this idea—that you could be just like him—and thank her.

Step 4:

Build a body for yourself, one that matches his. Find the casings that will be your limbs, casts that will replace the flesh and bone. Let him help you, because he's more open, now. He remembers the still and silent pain of the Gearwoman's yard as well as he remembers the strongest types of metal. He shows you what's best, not the ones that shine but the ones that last.

Listen to the creak in his voice, and when he asks, follow him. Go to that scrapyard where you found him—take minor visceral joy in the Gearwoman's absence—and walk among the leavings of her work. All bots, all boys, limbs and chassis and heaps that don't have faces. Too far gone to be awakened, he says, even by your heart.

Say nothing as he kneels among the husks of a thousand broken souls, as he remembers how deep his pain can go.

Step 5:

Fall in love. Do not skip this step.

Step 6:

Take the best of his fallen brothers, to make yourself anew. Make your mind of stronger things so you can feel what he does. Sell your house, your clothes, all the human things you'll never need, and pay another Gearsmith to make the change.

Let him hold your hand when they rip your brain and move it, strip your nerves and hollow out your veins. Believe him when he tells you you're not dying, as if he knows.

Ask him if he ever felt like this, and listen when he says yes. When he says that's why the Gearwoman burns the pages of her schematics. Why she's so good at what she does, why her boy-bots feel so real—because they were. Because they, like you, only need to give up pieces of their heart.

Be hateful when he tells you this, and make that hate a lasting thing. Keep it with you in your new body, so when you wake with copper eyes and hollow limbs, when your heart beats like his does, remind him what that fury feels like.

STEP 7:

Love him hard and often, like you never could with Kennan. Let him give you what he never shared when he was a person, that life cut short when the Gearwoman found him.

And after, when he finds you, making that creak that sounds like crying, let him come to you. Feel his pain through the parts you share, and feel him let it go. Let him show you how to do the same—for Kennan, for your hate, for the pain once thought too deep to heal.

Make a promise, that he won't feel that pain again. As when you built his body, as when he helped you remake yours, take the best of what you find. Not what hurts, but what lasts. Do not skip this step.

*Turns out that aliens are pretty damn good at road trips. They have the stamina, yeah, to go across country like they were driving down the street for bread. They have the money, too, what with all the cash their people gave them, compensating for every possible emergency that might arise when they sent them down here.*

# He Came From a Place of Openness and Truth

## BONNIE JO STUFFLEBEAM

MICKEY AND I WORKED TOGETHER at Hillman's Horror House, and maybe the thrill of scaring people was what made me notice him. I'd never thought about another guy that way before, and so when I first got that electric jolt as his hand brushed mine in the changing room, I felt like I might puke. I went to the bathroom, where instead of throwing up I jacked off into the toilet.

Mickey was a weird one, sure as hell. He had this damn goofy laugh like he was hacking up a hairball and these glasses so thick you could probably use the lenses as hockey pucks. He never talked to anyone at school except this one kid named Allen who was really into these books with half-naked women holding ray guns on the covers. Guys liked to chat the kid up so they could get a better look at his books during class when they weren't allowed to pull their phones out. Like they couldn't go a second without looking at that shit. I never saw anything all that good about Allen's books. They were cartoon women, after all, and no way a real woman would ever look that way, where they stood with their legs spread like they were just waiting for some high school loser to come and peer up there. But how would I know? I didn't have much experience with girls. They were kinda alien to me. Mickey liked the kid for his company, or so it seemed; he hung around him even when he didn't have a book. And the way Mickey looked at me, I knew he didn't care about those covers.

At the haunted house, Mickey was a trailer, which meant that he stood at the entrance in a cheap alien mask and made people think he was a statue until he started following back behind them. I was a slider, so I slid out in front of people, crossing their paths in a shriek of black and sweat. I liked making people scream. At first, I tried not to talk to Mickey, but it was hard, him being the only other high school boy working there. Eventually he caught up to me after my shift and asked if I wanted to go out for waffles, his treat. I was hungry, and he seemed okay despite the grabby hands, so I went, though I told him straight up I would buy my own waffles. He seemed cool with this, and we talked a lot about all kinds of interesting stuff. He complimented my sliding, which made me feel good, and we laughed about all the dumb teachers at school, and it turned out that he even liked hockey as much as me. I invited him to come play with us in the parking lot one day. Next hockey game he showed up smiling but didn't play, just stood off to the side, grinning. I liked being watched like that. I fantasized about it for the next two weeks, but in my fantasies it wasn't just hockey. He watched me eat my morning bagel. He watched me read before bed at night. He watched me wash my hair during my locker room shower.

It wasn't two weeks from that day that I grabbed him by the collar after work and asked him did he want to come out back. Earlier that day I'd seen Mickey talking to some tall, skinny college guy, and it made me want Mickey's lips on my body all of a sudden.

That started a routine: every day outside of Hillman's, and then it was in my bedroom while my mom was asleep, and then it was in the bathroom at the waffle place. I started referring to Mickey as my boyfriend, in my head at least, and I even let him kiss me on the mouth after he was done.

"But I'm not gay," I told him, I said to the mirror, to the friends who teased me about how much time I spent with Mickey. "I don't ever do anything back."

"Whatever, man," my friends said. "It's okay. Be gay. Go out and get yourself a thong and some fucking glitter and a rainbow flag or whatever, just don't expect us to start watching musicals with you."

"I don't like musicals," I said. "I fucking hate glitter."

I didn't want to be gay. I just wanted to keep letting Mickey suck me off for as long as I liked it.

But I didn't get tired of Mickey. Halloween came and went, and Hillman's closed for the season so that we were both out of work and with a whole lot of free time on our hands all of a sudden, and it got to where Mickey and I were hanging out every weekend, eating lunch together with all our friends at one table, even Allen, who got weirder and wouldn't ever look me in the eye. I didn't want anything to change, so when Mickey told me that he loved me, I didn't know what to do. I didn't say anything back.

We lay in my bed, naked and warm under the covers, and I liked the tickle of his leg hairs on mine but I pushed him away anyway.

"What did you go and say that for?" I said.

"I do. I love you, Ben. I thought you would return the sentiment. I was told it was good to say this."

"Jesus, Mickey, told by who? Who are you talking about us with?"

"It is true. I love you."

"Shit, maybe it's true and maybe it isn't. But you shouldn't have gone and said it. Don't you like things like they are?"

"I like things. I like you. I like your semen."

"Holy hell, man, why do you have to talk like that?" I lurched up from bed and started rooting around the floor for my clothes, which we'd thrown all over the place as we came in. My mom never checked on us up here, and it was probably this reason that we always went to my house and not Mickey's, though I'd never really asked about his parents, or his house. I flipped the light on. Mickey squinted at me. He was thin and cute, damn it, and I felt like a prize asshole for knowing so little about him.

"What's your last name, Mickey?" I asked. I hadn't even looked him up on Facebook. "Where do you live? Why don't we ever go to your place? Is it your parents? Do they know about me?"

Mickey shrugged but said nothing, just stared up at me with these round, hopeless eyes. I wondered, did he know what I was about to say, what I was about to do? Did he even realize that it wasn't fair of me to keep him like this when I couldn't say I love you and I couldn't even tell him his own damn last name?

"I think you should get out of here. I don't think we should see each other anymore."

I thought he would argue, beg, give me something to work with, but all he did was crawl out of bed, slip on his clothes, and go without a word. At school for the next few months he shielded his eyes every time he saw me in the hallway. Every now and then he'd utter a hello as he passed. I didn't say it back.

THOSE DAYS WITHOUT MICKEY I played a lot of hockey. And jacked it. And while I could get started with porn, the girls and boys in those videos weren't enough. I had to think of Mickey to finish. My friends asked why he didn't sit with us anymore. I tried to learn more about my friends until I was certain I knew every question that might be asked about them ever. I already knew their last names, sure, but I made it a point to also know their favorite food, color, band, movie, and what they wanted to do when they grew up.

BEFORE I KNEW IT, HALLOWEEN was here again and I was sliding at Hillman's. Mickey was there, too, and on break I never saw him with another guy, and I hadn't stopped thinking about him while jacking it, so I figured maybe it was time to give him another try, but this time the right way, with dates and shit. I asked him to go out with me after work. We went to a twenty-four-hour shithole diner down the street from Hillman's and we munched burgers and I asked him all kinds of questions, which he didn't answer. He always turned the conversation right back to me. Finally I figured I knew what he wanted before he would open up so I gave it to him.

"I was wrong before, okay?" I whispered across the table. "I can tell you right now I fucking love you, Mickey, so if you would please just open up and give me something to go off here, I'd really appreciate a little slack."

He grabbed my hand across the table. I felt like everyone in the diner turned their heads to stare, but no one was looking, really. "I come from a place you know nothing about. I come from a place of openness and truth. The place I come from, we do not have to hide who we are." He never did any facial expressions when he talked, just the same gaze behind those glasses. I think that's one of the things I like about him; his no-frills way of saying things, of acting.

"Damn it." I pulled my hand away. "Is that what you want? Listen, Mick, my parents will kill me if I come out."

"I want you to be with me," he said. "I want your semen. I want you to stay with me so I can have your juices always any time."

He wanted us to live together? The prospect didn't seem half bad. Sex any time I wanted it? A warm body to hold and be held by in the night? I imagined he intended for us to get a place together; we were seventeen, almost old enough to buy cigarettes and spray paint. But as I thought about it, I realized I didn't for sure know Mickey's age.

"Are you seventeen?" I asked.

"No," he said.

"Are you eighteen?" I asked.

"No," he said.

I got queasy cause if he wasn't seventeen and he wasn't eighteen that would make him older or younger, and either he was moved up some grades and I was in some deep shit, or he stayed back, and I wasn't sure I liked that option either, since it meant that he might not have a lot going on in that head, and I always thought he was a smart dude. Given the choice, I would've chosen older, but I didn't like being wrong regardless, so I asked him even though I wasn't sure I wanted to know: "How old are you?"

"I am eighty-five of your Earth years," he said.

I laughed uneasily. "Yeah, sure, but I'm being serious. You can't be much younger or older than me, right? Are you younger than me?"

"No," he said.

"Well, thank goodness." I pumped my fists in the air, more relieved than I thought I'd be. I'd just have to take it, I figured, as he was probably ashamed of being held back and all. When I really thought about it, I realized that it might be better that way, if we were living together; he could buy cigarettes already, and maybe, just maybe, he was close to old enough to buy beer.

"Let me think on it," I said, and then we were okay again, like it had never even been brought up. That night I walked him home for the first time and expected that he would let me into his house to meet his mother and all, but he didn't, and I was nervous, so I didn't pry. I did wonder, though, if she knew about me, if she knew about me and her son, if she knew that he was planning on moving out with me and living a big gay life. I told myself I owed it to Mickey to at least break it to my mom, even if I didn't decide to go on with his plan to live together after all. But I couldn't tell her. Instead I kept on with Mickey, and it was better this time. We even did more than just blowjobs.

About two weeks later, though, my mom brought it on herself. First she asked me, straight up, why I never hung out with girls, and so I thought, well here's as good a chance as ever, and so I told her, "I hang out with Mickey."

"Well, yeah," she said. "But why don't you two ever have any girls over? You can bring girls over, you know, so long as you let me know beforehand and you're *careful* and *safe* if something like that does happen, which I know is a high possibility, but which I feel I should advise you, as your *mother*, isn't the smartest thing in the world."

"That's cool," I said. "Can Mickey come over?"

She rolled her eyes but told me that yes, of course he could come over, he could always come over so long as I kept getting all my schoolwork done. "I love Mickey," she said. "He's a smart boy. He's a much better influence than your other friends."

That's what she said, no shit, and so when, about two hours later, she walked in on us in the middle of things, as it were, she was partly mad and partly just confused.

"What are you two doing?" she screamed, picking up the closest thing to her and throwing it so hard it nearly knocked us both over. I hurried to grab up the blankets and pull them over me so she wouldn't see the hard-on shrinking between my legs, but Mickey stayed poised with his ass in the air until she yelled at him to get the hell out, and he did pretty fast for someone who never showed the least signs of sportiness.

"We're not going to tell your father," was the first thing she said to me as she sat on the edge of my bed. "Don't you dare tell him."

If there ever was a chance, it was then, so I flat out told her no, I was tired of secrets and that I loved Mickey and it was their problem, not mine. I grabbed up my clothes, slipped them on, and left the room. My mom wrung her hands, begging me to please not do what I was about to do, but I wanted Mickey to stay with me, and he'd said himself that in his house they were open, and it sounded like a good way to be.

I found my dad watching football in the living room, but really he wasn't watching. He was cracking pecans and pretending like one was the excuse to do the other, but Dad never really did like football all that much. He admitted once to me, though, that he loved cracking nuts. I laughed a lot when he said that, but later I thought it was kind of sad that he felt like he had to cover up his real love with something he thought every man should like. Huh. That's actually not a bad point, now that I think about it, and maybe deep down watching him watch football even though he didn't really love it egged me on even more at that moment, and so when I said to him, "Dad, I'm in love with Mickey," maybe I believed that because of this football-nuts thing he might take the news in stride.

He didn't. There were a whole lot of mean words, and I'll admit that I cried a little, and he teared up, even, and my mom definitely cried, and when he told me to leave the house, I was more than ready to.

There was only one place I wanted to go.

Mickey didn't answer when I rang the doorbell, and neither did his parents, but when I tried the door it was unlocked so I went on inside. The house didn't smell lived in, which I thought was weird. It smelled like a hospital, like a really sterile place, and I thought to myself that yeah, Mickey always did seem real clean, too clean maybe, for a high school boy. The house was dark, so I fumbled along the wall for a light switch, and when I found one, I flipped it.

I couldn't breathe after what I saw.

The whole of the living room to my left and the whole of the dining room to my right was filled with what looked like naked sculptures of me, only they seemed real, like wax. They stood in rows with closed eyes and were connected to these silver stands that strapped their feet in place. They were totally still except that their chests moved in sleep breaths, and I wondered what sort of bizarre motor must have been in place, cause I'd never seen breathing sculptures before. At first I was scared to touch them — it's weird seeing yourself from the outside, and that was what freaked me out right away. Then the reality hit and I remembered where I was and that was what freaked me out, but rather than get the hell out of there like a sane person, I went up to one and touched its cheek. It felt like it was real skin, but it didn't move or anything. Whatever the material, it was damn good, and it looked very much like me, maybe a little different in the nose, but otherwise it could have been my twin. I took a step and my foot squished some sort of thin rubber tube on the ground, the same color as the carpet. I looked down and saw that it was connected to the twin me at the spine. They were all attached to these tubes, which led up some stairs. I started to follow when I heard Mickey's voice behind me, saying my name.

"Stay away from me," I said as I turned, holding my fingers up like a cross, for some weird reason. My heart was beating really fast, faster even than it had that first time outside Hillman's. He stood in the door to the living room, blocking my way out, with a bag in his hands.

"Just let me leave, please, please," I said.

"I'm glad you found this. This is what I came here to do," he said. "They asked me to come do this for them. It is necessary to the continuance of our people. See, I carry your seed in my hyoglossal pouch." He opened his mouth. Something wasn't right about his tongue, and I had to look away or I'd start to freak myself out remembering how good his mouth felt when he went down on me. "And when I return home it is warm and safe. I combine it with our own special chromosomal mixture and I make these clones of you." He seemed proud of it.

"Clones?" I recalled his alien mask, the way he spoke of the place he came from. I remembered those dumb paperbacks with the blue-skinned beasts in the background.

"This is all you wanted from me? This is all I'm good for?" I said, looking around at the so many faces, like a hundred mirrors, but none of them looked as sad as I felt.

"No, no," he said. "You do not understand. I chose you. My species realized that past methods of collection were inefficient. We once collected from one specimen then moved on. We revised our plan for Earth. We would collect from one specimen multiple times. I chose you. Of all the boys, I chose you, because you are kind and you are smart and you are beautiful." Mickey stepped closer, and I realized too late that I should have backed away; that's what you do when you're scared of someone, when you're mad at someone, and damn it if I wasn't both at him at the same time. But then he got so close I could smell him, all weird and musty like he was, and he hugged me, and I couldn't stay mad. It was even kind of cool, that he was from another planet and shit.

"What's in the bag?" I asked right in his ear.

"Let me show you!" And we broke apart and he pulled all kinds of awesome shit he'd bought for me from the bag at his feet: potato chips, grab bags of candy, bananas, orange juice, chocolate chip cookies. Damn, I thought, I'm going to like living with you. He didn't ask me why I was there, even, and that night, in a bedroom where about twelve replicas of myself surrounded us, he didn't ask why I was sniffling beside him, not saying anything. Damn, I thought, I really do love the bastard.

THE FIRST FEW MONTHS WITH Mickey were pretty awesome. We ate what we wanted, though Mickey often grumbled about healthy food and how we had to keep our bodies clean and in shape and all this other alien shit I ignored on account of he was from another planet and knew jack shit about what was good for a teenage boy. We stayed out late with friends even on school nights, though we never invited them over on account of the weird replicas. They were okay not visiting our house. I think it might have made them uncomfortable, despite how cool they were about the gay thing. We convinced some homeless dude with an ID outside the liquor store to buy us booze in exchange for money; Mickey had a lot of money, sent from his parents or guardians or whatever on whatever spaceship he'd come down on. I didn't understand much about how he got here, though he explained it to me. Honestly, looking up at the sky always made me feel all weak-kneed and scared, like the whole concept of something out there I could never see meant it was all monsters and things I didn't and wouldn't ever understand, so I didn't try too hard to get it. I did ask him once how long he'd be staying. "As long as I need to," he said, and this was a comfort, and I didn't feel I needed to ask any more questions, really.

He never wanted to talk about his home, anyhow. I never talked about my parents either. I know some therapists might say how we were repressing our bad memories, but I'd say that yeah, of course we were, on account of we had way too much partying to do and not near enough time to do it, what with school and sex and all to take up our time.

Yeah, life was pretty good for Mickey and me, for a while. Until three things happened all at once.

First I found a replica in Mickey's closet, which he'd been hiding from me, on purpose, though he says he just put him in there cause he didn't fit with the me replicas. We were playing hide-and-seek like children. Mickey said he'd never played it as a kid; they didn't have it where he was from or something, and so we were playing when I hid in the closet. I thought the replica beside me was another me, of course; they were everywhere, so I jokingly slid my hand between its legs to feel what I felt like down there from outside my body and it felt pretty good, actually, until Mickey flung open the door and the light revealed me to be groping Allen.

"What the fuck?" I screamed as I jumped out of the closet. When I saw it was just a replica, I breathed a sigh of relief until I realized what that meant; he'd sucked off Allen just the same as he did me.

"What is wrong?"

"What the fuck is this?" I said, sitting on the edge of the bed, my head fuzzy.

"You are upset?"

"Of course I'm upset. When did this happen?"

"I thought Allen was to be my source," Mickey said, standing in front of me. "I did not know yet that you existed. It takes time to find the one perfect for replicating. Allen was good, but not as good as you."

"Shit, did you use a condom at least? Who knows what that kid sticks his dick in."

"Condoms defeat the purpose of our mission," said Mickey. "If asked, we are instructed to move on to the next specimen."

"Good God," I said. "You haven't done this with a bunch of dudes, have you?" The thought of all those hands all over my boyfriend made my stomach churn. I both wanted and didn't want to know any more. Openness and truth? Bullshit. What does an alien know about honesty?

"You are my third specimen. The first did not take. His emissions were not potent enough for the replication process."

"Well, I've only done things with you," I said.

"My planet needs your people there, or else we are at risk of dying."

I made the mistake then of asking one of the questions I'd told myself I wouldn't ask. And this was the second thing that ruined our happiness in that house.

"What does that even mean? Why do you need so many replicas? What's with all these clones?" I looked around at them, and they seemed creepy all of a sudden, like a sinister thing I'd been ignoring.

Mickey stood with his arms straight at his sides, as he often did, and I realized just how strange his posture was. How had I never suspected before he told me? "Our landscape is harsh," he said. "We require vast technologically advanced structures to survive and live good lives. But we have other work to do. We are too busy to build. It makes our hands rough, and we have other tasks that are more important to the survival of not only our people but people on other planets as well. Our people do not love the life of physical labor. Your people are better for this. Your brains are structured more for this than for the intellectual work that is our specialty. So we came to the conclusion that it would be best to come here and, rather than take your people off your planet, for you would likely be unwilling to go, we have replicated you so that we can take a crew of you back with us." He placed his hand on one of the clones, right on his shoulder, like he was an old friend. "When we wake your clones, we will load them into our ships. On our planet, you will build our structures for us, and then you will help us maintain them. It would be a hard, boring life for our people, but yours will feel right at home.

"Wait a fucking second," I said. "You didn't tell me that's what these clones were for! I don't want to go work myself to death on your sorry-ass planet."

Mickey shook his head, smiling. "No, no," he said. "You won't be going. It is just these replicas that will go. Don't worry. You and I will be together here, until I am asked to return to my planet."

When he said that, my mind went all fuzzy and blank, like I didn't even know how to respond. I tried to come up with something, anything, to say to him, but everything just seemed pointless, and the idea of the Allen clone and Mickey leaving and the me clones gave me this pressure in the chest that I couldn't shake. I couldn't go home, that was for damn sure, and I couldn't try to explain why I was upset, cause holy hell, Mickey and I were from different worlds, and there wasn't ever going to be anything I could do about that.

I locked myself in our room with the music turned way, way up. I stared at the replicas, and looking at them made me so mad I wanted to pummel them to pieces like those body builder punching bags shaped like men. I couldn't touch them, though. I couldn't hurt myself. I crawled under the bed where it was dark and closed my eyes and thought about what it all meant, this alien shit. Was I meant to do something here, something big, like in the movies? I could destroy all the clones. Would Mickey have to leave if I did that?

What must have been a couple of hours later, I heard this crazy echoing sound coming from downstairs and suddenly I wasn't worried about higher purposes, I just wanted to know what the damn noise was and make sure Mickey was safe out there.

I crept through the house, my heart pounding, until I found Mickey in the kitchen in the dark with some device clutched to his ear. He was making this wracking belly sound like his body was gurgling, and when I flipped on the light he didn't look at me, just kept on making those noises.

"What the fuck was that noise?" I asked, but he still didn't say anything until the gurgling stopped and he dropped the little metal device and curled into himself on the floor there. "What's wrong, Mickey?"

"I understand why you are upset," he said, not looking up at me. "Your replicas will be used by my kind and not given a choice. I did not realize that choice is important to your people. It is important to ours, too."

"What does that mean, though? Can we stop it?"

"It is stopped already. The replicas are no good. My people have asked me just now, over the communicator, to destroy the replicas. We have made a mistake once more. It is not good to have so many of one replica. That way spreads blight. They say that the blight is making your people perish in alarming numbers. My people say more diversity is needed, so that the blight does not take so many. They want one of you, and one of you only. The rest they say to unplug and let rot in here. They have ordered me home."

For once in our whole time together I thought I saw something human in his face rather than the plaster gaze he usually gave.

"But you said just a minute ago…I mean, you seemed like you wanted to go home, eventually. And I'm not so sure I'm against destroying all these clones, Mickey. To be honest, I don't know if I like the idea of so many of me existing all in the same place. This should be good news, right? After all, what, you didn't think we would stay together, and I sure never thought that."

"Stop," he said. "You lie when you say that. And as for the other part, I will quote your people when I say that you don't know what you have until it is gone. I didn't know what I wanted until just now. Ben, I chose you. I chose. And I do not want to go back. I do not ever want to go back."

Aw, hell, I thought, and I rushed across the room and wrapped my arms so tight around him I thought I might break him if he weren't so tough, built of whatever alien skin he had in him or on him, I'd never asked much about if he looked like this all the time or just here on Earth, but I figured he had to be different somehow in his chemical makeup. And so what did I do right there, to comfort him? I kissed him. I unzipped his pants and reached my hands into his boxers and then we made love, that's right, love, on the kitchen floor, and when it was over, this third of our problems, we figured out just what we were going to do next.

TURNS OUT THAT ALIENS ARE pretty damn good at road trips. They have the stamina, yeah, to go across country like they were driving down the street for bread. They have the money, too, what with all the cash their people gave them, compensating for every possible emergency that might arise when they sent them down here. As for keeping ourselves under the radar, making sure my parents didn't come looking for us, though we might, we agreed, go looking for them again someday to make our amends, we sent one of my replicas in my place. When we turned him on, he smiled at me, but he didn't even look at Mickey, really. It was weird but kind of cool to see him walking around. He already had my memories and everything, so it was easy to drop him off in my parents' driveway. I'm sure Mom and Dad loved that I came to my senses and no longer had Mickey around or even spoke of him anymore. As for the gay stuff, I don't know if that's the way the replica swung or even if I could say I swing that way or if Mickey's replicas even have ways to swing or if people do. Maybe there's just a lot of love and when it finds you, you do what you can with it.

The rest of the replicas we unplugged and drove, truckload by truckload, out to surrounding cities. This will create some confusion one of these days, to be certain, but it seemed like the best option, and besides I thought it was one damn funny practical joke. We gave Allen his replica, to do with what he wished, and he was sure psyched about that, though not so happy that we were leaving him. We told him that we'd be back one day and gave him the keys to our house, for him to do what he wanted in there. Maybe he'll do great things with it. Maybe when Mickey's people come looking, they'll find Allen and take him up there with them and he'll get some of what he's always wanted.

I try not to think too hard about what's going to happen or what did happen, just the good parts, like Mickey's hand in mine, or the open windows in the car we bought, or the look of mountains, true-to-life mountains, and the way I feel when we drive toward them. And the look of the alien mask he snuck along, which he sometimes wears when he blows me, and how it's never like you think it'll be, this life stuff, which is something new I'm learning all the time.

*Your husband floats to the top of the thick translucent waters, peaceful and tender. You hold your breath, aching to lean over and kiss him one more time—but that is forbidden. His body is now sacred, and you are not. You've seen him sleep, his powerful chest rising and falling, his breath a harbinger of summer storms. The purification bath makes it easy to pull him up and slide him onto the table, where the budding dawn seeping from the skylight above illuminates his transmogrification, his ascent. His skin has taken a rich pomegranate hue. His hair is a stark mountaintop white.*

# HARALAMBI MARKOV

A LONG, SILENT DAY AWAITS you and your daughter as you prepare to cut your husband's body. You remove organs from flesh, flesh from bones, bones from tendons—all ingredients for the cake you're making, the heavy price of admission for an afterlife you pay your gods; a proper send-off for the greatest of all warriors to walk the lands.

The Baking Chamber feels small with two people inside, even though you've spent a month with your daughter as part of her apprenticeship. You feel irritated at having to share this moment, but this is a big day for your daughter. You steal a glance at her. See how imposing she looks in her ramie garments the color of a blood moon, how well the leather apron made from changeling hide sits on her.

You work in silence, as the ritual demands, and your breath hisses as you both twist off the aquamarine top of the purification vat. Your husband floats to the top of the thick translucent waters, peaceful and tender. You hold your breath, aching to lean over and kiss him one more time—but that is forbidden. His body is now sacred, and you are not. You've seen him sleep, his powerful chest rising and falling, his breath a harbinger of summer storms. The purification bath makes it easy to pull him up and slide him onto the table, where the budding dawn seeping from the skylight above illuminates his transmogrification, his ascent. His skin has taken a rich pomegranate hue. His hair is a stark mountaintop white.

You raise your head to study your daughter's reaction at seeing her father since his wake. You study her face, suspicious of any muscle that might twitch and break the fine mask made of fermented butcher broom berries and dried water mint grown in marshes where men have drowned. It's a paste worn out of respect and a protection from those you serve. You scrutinize her eyes for tears, her hair and eyebrows waxed slick for any sign of dishevelment.

The purity of the body matters most. A single tear can sour the offering. A single hair can spoil the soul being presented to the gods…what a refined palate they have. But your daughter wears a stone face. Her eyes are opaque; her body is poised as if this is the easiest thing in the world to do. The ceramic knife you've shaped and baked yourself sits like a natural extension of her arm.

You remember what it took you to bake your own mother into a cake. No matter how many times you performed the ritual under her guidance, nothing prepared you for the moment when you saw her body on the table. Perhaps you can teach your daughter to love your art. Perhaps she belongs by your side as a Cake Maker, even though you pride yourself on not needing any help. Perhaps she hasn't agreed to this apprenticeship only out of grief. Perhaps, perhaps…

Your heart prickles at seeing her this accomplished, after a single lunar cycle. A part of you, a part you take no pride in, wants her to struggle through her examination, struggle to the point where her eyes beg you to help her. You would like to forgive her for her incapability, the way you did back when she was a child. You want her to need you—the way she needed your husband for so many years.

No. Treat him like any other. *Let your skill guide you.* You take your knife and shave the hair on your husband's left arm with the softest touch.

You remove every single hair on his body to use for kindling for the fire you will build to dry his bones, separating a small handful of the longest hairs for the decoration, then incise the tip of his little finger to separate skin from muscle.

Your daughter mirrors your movements. She, too, is fluent in the language of knives.

The palms and feet are the hardest to skin, as if the body fights to stay intact and keep its grip on this realm. You struggle at first but then work the knife without effort. As you lift the softly stretching tissue, you see the countless scars that punctuated his life— the numerous cuts that crisscross his hands and shoulders, from when he challenged the sword dancers in Aeno; the coin-shaped scars where arrowheads pierced his chest during their voyage through the Sear of Spires in the misty North; the burn marks across his left hip from the leg hairs of the fire titan, Hragurie. You have collected your own scars on your journeys through the forgotten places of this world, and those scars ache now, the pain kindled by your loss.

After you place your husband's skin in a special aventurine bowl, you take to the muscle—that glorious muscle you've seen shift and contract in great swings of his dancing axe while you sing your curses and charms alongside him in battle. Even the exposed redness of him is rich with memories, and you do everything in your power not to choke as you strip him of his strength. This was the same strength your daughter prized above all else and sought for herself many years ago, after your spells and teachings grew insufficient for her. This was the same strength she accused you of lacking when you chose your mother's calling, retired your staff from battle, and chose to live preparing the dead for their passing.

Weak. The word still tastes bitter with her accusation. *How can you leave him? How can you leave us? You're a selfish little man.*

You watch her as you work until there is nothing left but bones stripped clean, all the organs in their respective jars and bowls. Does she regret the words now, as she works by your side? Has she seen your burden yet? Has she understood your choice? Will she be the one to handle your body once you pass away?

You try to guess the answer from her face, but you find no solace and no answer. Not when you extract the fat from your husband's skin, not when you mince his flesh and muscle, not when you puree his organs and cut his intestines into tiny strips you leave to dry. Your daughter excels in this preparatory work—her blade is swift, precise, and gentle.

How can she not? After all, she is a gift from the gods. A gift given to two lovers who thought they could never have a child on their own. A miracle. The completion you sought after in pain, a bone-penetrating bliss that filled you with warmth. But as with all good things, your bliss waxed and waned as you realized: all children have favorites.

You learned how miracles can hurt.

You align his bones on the metal tray that goes into the hungry oven. You hold his skull in your hands and rub the sides where his ears once were. You look deep into the sockets where once eyes of dark brown would stare back into you.

His clavicle passes your fingers. You remember the kisses you planted on his shoulder, when it used to be flesh. You position his ribcage, and you can still hear his heartbeat—a rumble in his chest the first time you lay together after barely surviving an onslaught of skinwalkers, a celebration of life. You remember that heart racing, as it did in your years as young men, when vitality kept you both up until dawn. You remember it beating quietly in his later years, when you were content and your bodies fit perfectly together—the alchemy of flesh you have now lost.

You deposit every shared memory in his bones, and then load the tray in the oven and slam shut the metal door.

Behind you, your daughter stands like a shadow, perfect in her apprentice robes. Not a single crease disfigures the contours of her pants and jacket. Not a single stain mars her apron.

She stares at you. She judges you.

She is perfection.

You wish you could leave her and crawl in the oven with your husband.

Flesh, blood and gristle do not make a cake easily, yet the Cake Maker has to wield these basic ingredients. Any misstep leads to failure, so you watch closely during your daughter's examination, but she completes each task with effortless grace.

She crushes your husband's bones to flour with conviction.

Your daughter mixes the dough of blood, fat, and bone flour, and you assist her. You hear your knuckles and fingers pop as you knead the hard dough, but hers move without a sound—fast and agile as they shape the round cakes.

Your daughter works over the flesh and organs until all you can see is a pale scarlet cream with the faint scent of iron, while you crush the honey crystals that will allow for the spirit to be digested by the gods. You wonder if she is doing this to prove how superior she is to you— to demonstrate how easy it is to lock yourself into a bakery with the dead. You wonder how to explain that you never burnt as brightly as your husband, that you don't need to chase legends and charge into battle.

You wonder how to tell her that she is your greatest adventure, that you gave her most of the magic you had left.

Layer by layer, your husband is transformed into a cake. Not a single bit of him is lost. You pull away the skin on top and connect the pieces with threads from his hair. The sun turns the rich shade of lavender and calendula.

You cover the translucent skin with the dried blood drops you extracted before you placed the body in the purification vat and glazed it with the plasma. Now all that remains is to tell your husband's story, in the language every Cake Maker knows—the language you've now taught your daughter.

You wonder whether she will blame you for the death of your husband in writing, the way she did when you told her of his death.

*Your stillness killed him. You had to force him to stay, to give up his axe. Now he's dead in his sleep. Is this what you wanted? Have him all to yourself? You couldn't let him die out on the road.*

Oh, how she screamed that day—her voice as unforgiving as thunder. Her screaming still reverberates through you. You're afraid of what she's going to tell the gods.

You both write. You cut and bend the dried strips of intestines into runes and you gently push them so they sink into the glazed skin and hold.

You write his early story. His childhood, his early feats, the mythology of your love. How you got your daughter. She tells the other half of your husband's myth—how he trained her in every single weapon known to man, how they journeyed the world over to honor the gods.

Her work doesn't mention you at all.

You rest your fingers, throbbing with pain from your manipulations. You have completed the last of your husband's tale. You have written in the language of meat and bones and satisfied the gods' hunger. You hope they will nod with approval as their tongues roll around the cooked flesh and swallow your sentences and your tether to life.

Your daughter swims into focus as she takes her position across the table, your husband between you, and joins you for the spell. He remains the barrier you can't overcome even in death. As you begin to speak, you're startled to hear her voice rise with yours. You mutter the incantation and her lips are your reflection, but while you caress the words, coaxing their magic into being, she cuts them into existence, so the veil you will around the cake spills like silk on your end and crusts on hers. The two halves shimmer in blue feylight, entwine into each other, and the deed is done.

You have said your farewell, better than you did when you first saw him dead. Some dam inside you breaks. Exhaustion wipes away your strength and you feel your age, first in the trembling in your hands, then in the creaking in your knees as you turn your back and measure your steps so you don't disturb the air—a retreat as slow as young winter frost.

Outside the Bakery, your breath catches. Your scream is a living thing that squirms inside your throat and digs into the hidden recesses of your lungs. Your tears wash the dry mask from your cheeks.

Your daughter takes your hand, gently, with the unspoken understanding only shared loss births and you search for her gaze. You search for the flat, dull realization that weighs down the soul. You search for yourself in her eyes, but all you see is your husband—his flame now a wildfire that has swallowed every part of you. She looks at you as a person who has lost the only life she had ever known, pained and furious, and you pat her hand and kiss her forehead, her skin stinging against your lips. When confusion pulls her face together, her features lined with fissures in her protective mask, you shake your head.

"The gods praise your skill and technique. They praise your steady hand and precision, but they have no use of your hands in the Bakery." The words roll out with difficulty—a thorn vine you lacerate your whole being with as you force yourself to reject your daughter. Yes, she can follow your path, but what good would that do?

"You honor me greatly." Anger tinges her response, but fights in these holy places father only misfortune, so her voice is low and even. You are relieved to hear sincerity in her fury, desire in her voice to dedicate herself to your calling.

You want to keep her here, where she won't leave. Your tongue itches with every lie you can bind her with, spells you've learned from gods that are not your own, hollow her out and hold onto her, even if such acts could end your life. You reconsider and instead hold on to her earnest reaction. You have grown to an age where even intent will suffice.

"It's not an honor to answer your child's yearning." You maintain respectability, keep with the tradition, but still you lean in with all the weight of death tied to you like stones and you whisper. "I have told the story of your father in blood and gristle as I have with many others. As I will continue to tell every story as best as I can, until I myself end in the hands of a Cake Maker. But you can continue writing your father's story outside the temple where your knife strokes have a meaning.

"Run. Run toward the mountains and rivers, sword in your hand and bow on your back. Run toward life. That is where you will find your father."

Now it is she who is crying. You embrace her, the memory of doing so in her childhood alive inside your bones and she hugs you back as a babe, full of needing and vulnerable. But she is no longer a child—the muscles underneath her robes roll with the might of a river—so you usher her out to a life you have long since traded away.

Her steps still echo in the room outside the Baking Chamber as you reapply the coating to your face from the tiny, crystal jars. You see yourself: a grey, tired man who touched death more times than he ever touched his husband.

Your last task is to bring the cake to where the Mouth awaits, its vines and branches shaking, aglow with iridescence. There, the gods will entwine their appendages around your offering, suck it in, close and digest. Relief overcomes you and you sigh.

Yes, it's been a long day since you and your daughter cut your husband's body open. You reenter the Baking Chamber and push the cake onto the cart.

*Women outnumbered men on the main floor.
I focused on them, their happiness, their
sweat, their bare shoulders. Anything to not
see the men, writhing and radiant in too-tight
T-shirts. Ten percent of the men in any room
at any given moment were secret police, if you
believed the propaganda. And the Observers
filed past us all, shielded from sin by fear and
a velvet rope. A little girl with a long blonde
braid, too young to wear a wimple but not by
much, held her father's hand tightly.*

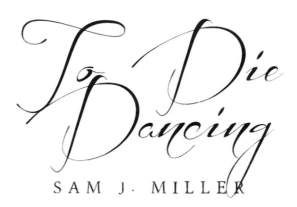

# To Die Dancing

SAM J. MILLER

HALF A BLOCK AWAY I could feel it already, the old giddiness, the limb-tingling bliss at being about to dance, to sweat, to shake my body beside other bodies, and that's when I knew I was in true mortal peril. I walked slower, then stopped, and took ten deep breaths, until the urge subsided. I waited until I felt nothing.

*Don't be fooled,* I told myself, arriving at the end of the long velvet-roped line. An old hotel, transformed for one night into a living museum. *This is all a sham. Come morning it will disappear again. And no matter how many times they promise tonight will have no consequences, you know they'll be watching. Once they know what you are, they'll follow you until they find something. Mess up once and it's the camps for you.*

Already a bassline was thumping from inside. Donna Summer? No. Too early in the evening for Donna. Donna you saved until the place was packed. Memory kindled long-dead smells, forbidden artifacts: pleather and hair products, sweat and smoke and scotch, poppers and nail polish and spilled beer.

Above the archway, a banner: DEGRADATION EVE. Projectors covered the place's entire majestic façade in swiftly-churning images. Disco divas and Playboy bunnies, arched backs and permed hair, fashion spreads and money shots. Alternating with bloody fetuses and ravaged wombs and brutal vid-clips of assault. To remind us all how vulgar and vile and degrading things had been, before.

*You were a fool to have come,* I told myself. *She won't be here. You've kept your head down and your ass safe for ten years, and tonight you're endangering yourself for nothing.*

But I had to know. And if Ummi didn't show up, here, tonight, I could finally be certain she was really gone.

Cops strutted across the street. The western fringe of midtown Manhattan still throbbed with an ebbing Saturday buzz. Curfew would come soon. Already the officers had stopped a group of construction workers for on-the-spot dupe scans. One by one the men pressed their cell phones against a nightstick for half a second. The State's backdoor Bluetooth channel would be copying every byte of data and running it against state-of-the-art sin-scan algorithms for offending content. Vintage or imported images of women with bare arms, for example, or knees, or hands. Texts with suspicious phrasing. App log-times during worship hours.

The line behind the velvet rope was for Observers; a dressed-up anxious crowd, frightened and excited by the proximity of the forbidden. Women in their wimples; men in the drab charcoal-and-olive palettes of Party power players. Laughter, nervous and swiftly stifled. They had come for the spectacle of it, to smell the stink of sin, to watch an elaborate reenactment of the Bad Old Days. Lots of them had brought their children. And then, as one, their spines straightened and their faces became deadly serious: instructions, no doubt, coming in through their earbugs.

My *Participant* badge let me breeze past them. I scanned faces, tried to imagine what was happening behind each one. People my age knew what to expect, could remember the time when this happened every night. I wondered what the younger ones thought. Some were still toddlers at the time of the Revival, and had spent their formative years hearing stories of the barbaric degeneracy of places like these.

One man cruised me, his eyes bold and firm, and I felt an inner tremor of terror for him.

*Do you have a death wish, man? How have you survived the last ten years? You don't know who the hell I am—I could be secret police, or some random zealot citizen. Even the possibility of 'deviant mental activity' could get you hauled downtown and hooked up to the Fruit Machine for testing.*

A gaggle of Participants bunched up at the entrance, signing waivers and waiting for body scans.

"You look scared," a man said, tough, straight, with Jersey vowels. No doubt it was the nostalgia, not the money, that induced him to volunteer as part of the spectacle. Club Night with the Fellas, 'banging chicks,' whatever it was that boys like him did then.

I asked "Aren't *you?*"

"Petrified, bro. Had an aunt, back then, was a Born Again. When I was ten she took me to one of them, whaddaya call it, hell houses? Like haunted houses, but, you know, all religious and stuff. Adulterers burning in hell, drug addicts peeling their own skin off? That kind of stuff. Scarred me for life. And tonight that's going to be me. Traumatize some little kid who never saw nobody dance before."

Scanned and waivered, we were each provided with a one-night Amnesty for any forbidden acts in which we engaged while inside the designated space for dancing. In digital and hard copy.

"Got a cigarette?" asked a forty-something woman in a bright pink wig and a short skirt still creased from the drawer (or, more likely, secret under-the-floorboard stash) where it had spent the last decade. Bizarre to see her knees, when on any other night baring the ankles was enough to earn you five lashes. I laughed, out loud, at the incongruity of it, like seeing a ghost, these six or seven re-educable offenses she was committing at once.

"Be careful," I said, handing her one.

She tucked the cigarette behind her ear and winked at me.

Whitney Houston called out from inside: one long *whooooo-oooo*—

As one, the crowd gasped. Participants and Observers. None of us had heard a recording of a woman's voice in years, outside of scratchy cassette tapes and secret computer files we could be re-educated for owning. The kids on the line looked nervous, the way you do when you do something technically illegal. Jersey Boy and Pink Wig cheered, as did a couple other Participants, chests already puffing out with long-forgotten freedom. I wouldn't let myself. I would keep my focus. I wasn't there to have fun or feel free; I was there for Umout. I went inside.

Graffiti covered the walls of the low-ceilinged hallway: slurs for women, *for a good time call*—, promises of sexual savagery. The stink of actual piss was in the air. Recorded voices barked threats and catcalls. I breezed past the slow trickle of Observers moving through checkpoints meant to make them spend as much time as possible in this grotesque hall. Whitney Houston sounded flat and muted through the wall, a ghost voice, singing about losing control, about men, about power, and powerlessness. A door opened and the beat got sharper, and I passed through.

"Clive," someone said, and I was shocked at the hot rush of hate that shot through me.

"Clive!" he said, again, and I turned, terrified, because I hadn't counted on this variable. My self-control only extended so far.

"Jeremy," I said, gritting my teeth, trying to smile, failing.

"I saw your name on the list," he said, drunk, pathetic, with a politician's fake cheer, in the mopey-dog voice I had first heard at planning meetings for protests of the very people he now worked for. "But I didn't think it'd be you. Some other Clive Loff, I told myself."

"It's me." I looked at Jeremy, possibly the most powerful closet case in the Republic, and his proud smile, and a horrible thought hummingbirded into my brain. "Did you help put this together?"

"I did," he said, and my suspicion that Degradation Eve was intended in part to flush out deviants and get good blackmail shots hardened into certainty. Jeremy had always been good at getting ahead, especially if other people got hurt in the process. It was why he was where he was.

"Good to see you, Clive," he said, and extended his hand. I held on, willing him to make eye contact, but when he did I couldn't ask the questions I wanted to ask. *Why are you doing this? How do you live with yourself? And what the hell did you do to Ummi?*

Chubby Jeremy was gone. This Jeremy had lost so much weight I could see his cheekbones. Working inside a system that wants you dead will do that to you. He'd have been hot, if he didn't look so sallow and beaten. And if I didn't hate him as much as he hated me.

He paused, waiting for something more from me. Finally he added, "I can't believe I'm actually going to be able to dance, without worrying about getting arrested for it."

"Don't they work for you, Jeremy? The ones who do the arresting?"

"It's not—" he said, then frowned, fiddled with his hands. I recognized the face he was making, the strenuous mechanics of rationalization. Back then he had worked for the most powerful woman in city politics, who rose to power by saying what men wanted to hear, a family-values schoolmarm vixen crowing Creationism and demanding the removal of songs sung by women from the radio. Whenever I needed to feel better about things I'd imagine what her face looked like, in the moment when she realized she was getting exactly the world that she wanted, and that there would be no place for her in it.

I pushed past him. "I'll see you around," he called after me. "And try to have fun, okay, Clive?"

Stepping out onto the dance floor, I scanned the crowd. I watched bodies bob and shake. Faces tilted and twisted. Men shrieked; women bellowed. Ummi wasn't there, but that didn't mean she wouldn't come. She had to come. If she was alive, if she was free, if she was still here, she'd come.

My earpiece crackled and cleared itself of static. Spot-specific, triggered by wifi through the legally-mandated backdoor that allowed the Republic and its authorized agents to assert total control over every device. A man's voice, wide flat Midwestern syllables:

*Hard to imagine, that sights and sounds like these were once commonplace. Hard to believe that people tolerated such behavior, and that a godless government allowed it. Which is why, as we celebrate our first glorious decade, it's important to look back and remember. Why we fought, and how much we've won. How far we've come.*

I turned and watched the pink-wigged woman step out onto the dance floor. My heart broke, seeing her face. Her smile, like meeting a lover she thought she'd never see again. The promise of Saturday night, eleven p.m., a throbbing dance floor.

It had all been pretend, until this moment. I didn't believe in any of it. I didn't let myself hope that I might be able to get this close to the joy and bliss and freedom that had gone out of the world. But here it was. Here we were.

Early still; a small crowd. The DJ was good, probably the best they could find—so many had fled. Each song nudged the energy a tiny bit higher. I followed the woman to the bar, where she legally bought an alcoholic beverage for the first time in ten years. The men around her thought nothing of it; they did it all the time, but I saw the light in her eyes.

The main dance floor had been the enormous lobby of a posh and decadent hotel. Above it were twenty stories of open space, twenty mezzanines looking down on it, each of them now a crowded dance floor. The new government had kept the entire building empty. It still stunk with the mold and rot of ten useless years.

Women outnumbered men on the main floor. I focused on them, their happiness, their sweat, their bare shoulders. Anything to not see the men, writhing and radiant in too-tight T-shirts. Ten percent of the men in any room at any given moment were secret police, if you believed the propaganda. And the Observers filed past us all, shielded from sin by fear and a velvet rope. A little girl with a long blonde braid, too young to wear a wimple but not by much, held her father's hand tightly.

I headed up to the second floor and scanned the crowd. Still no sign of Ummi.

Ummi was my best friend, the fiercest person I had ever met. A dancer. A genius. Punk royalty, six feet tall, piercings and ink you could never quite pin down or remember right from day to day. I spent more time with her than anyone, and even I couldn't be sure that the intricate tribal patterns and cursive quotations on her arms didn't shift slightly each time I looked away.

I was a graphic designer, then. By night I made flyers for protests, went to the meetings she dragged me to. We all worked hard, in our own ways, to fight the fundamentalist drift. We could see the writing on the wall, but we didn't know what it said. We couldn't have known how bad things would get. Everything happened so slowly, a far-right politician elected here, a Supreme Court decision there, an unpunished upsurge in hate crimes, the Modesty Movement, the Promise Militias. Until all the pieces were in place for the Revival.

On the second floor the dancing got dirtier. Couples bumped, grinded, dry humped. One by one I watched Observers' faces redden. Some forgettable scrap of diva-pop throbbed. A Britney or a Debbi or a Tiffani. Its appeal had baffled me then and it baffled me now. Except now, knowing the terrible fate that befell all those women, the flimsy song had a certain fresh poignancy. I kept climbing.

By floor fifteen, I knew she wasn't there. But I couldn't stop moving. Scanning every face. Participant and Observer alike, because it wasn't completely unimaginable that one of Ummi's admirers had risen to a place of some prominence in the new Republic, and offered to save her life by marrying her, although the risk of wedding a well-known woman artist would have been considerable. I'd spent a decade standing still, never visiting any of our old haunts or otherwise hunting for her, convinced the risk was too great for both of us. Now I couldn't stop moving. The actors on the topmost floors were masked, acting out mock-rapes and murders. My flesh crept as I hurried past, scanning body types, scouring exposed flesh for matching tattoos and finding none. On the twentieth floor I walked to the railing and stared down at the yawning gulf of screams and laughter and music and fevered, doomed joy.

"Attendance is triple our projections!" Jeremy said, appearing beside me suddenly. I sniffed for sulfur but didn't smell any.

"And the night is young," I said.

Was he sweating? From fear, probably. Maybe he had created a monster. Across town there was a rival event, the First Annual Celebration of Christian Art & Values, where men and women wore modest clothes and listened to the safe, male voices of legal music. If Degradation Eve was a big enough success, and the Celebration of Christian Art & Values bombed, it would become an embarrassment. The Revived Republic might have dissident threats under control, but the halls of government were themselves a terrifying and unstable place. Power struggles, interfaction posturing. Bloodbaths still happened, from time to time, and an ambitious little backstabber could climb the ladder fast by making a big enough stink about an evening of government-sanctioned gender treachery. Heads might roll. Jeremy's might. Mine might.

"Are you having fun?" he asked. He was closer to me than he needed to be, and smiling unwholesomely. His victory, he thought, was nigh. Any minute now I would finally fumble, and he could destroy me.

"Tonight isn't about fun," I said.

"You should try to have fun, Clive. We may never have the chance again."

I didn't know what to say to that. Sometimes I had felt sorry for Jeremy, back when he would come to meetings ill at ease inside the suit he was forced to wear at work, assuring us even as we called him out on his boss's latest sell-out move that he could do work within the system that would complement what we did outside it. There had to be some internal flicker of genuine radicalism in there, at war with the cowardice that let him delude himself so extensively.

From behind him, he produced two drinks. "Here's to one last night," he said, handing me one.

I clinked my glass against his, but then I set it down on the railing. We were not in this together. I had something Jeremy didn't have. I had this fire, Ummi's fire, the flame of freedom, corny as it sounds. One day it would happen, an uprising, a collapse, and I would be ready for it, and men like Jeremy would end up against the wall.

To tune him out, I turned up my earbug.

*This is the so-called freedom that women had back then. Freedom to wear provocative clothing, and to be assaulted for it. Freedom to go out after dark, where nothing good waited for them. Freedom to end a pregnancy, because liberal politicians peddled the lie that employment had more to offer women than motherhood.*

Still standing beside me, Jeremy pulled out his phone and doodled around on it. For a powerful closet case whose whole life had to be about fear of exposure, he was startlingly cavalier about using his swipe code in front of people. Then he shrugged apologetically, as if apologizing for ending the marvelous conversation we were not having, and put the phone to his ear and walked off.

Watching him leave, I saw the blonde-braided little girl again. Sobbing now, watching snarling male actors hold a woman down. She tried to turn away, but her mother turned her back.

I realized: if anyone had access to the kind of personal data that would help me figure out what happened to Ummi, it was Jeremy.

For the next hour, I followed him. Staying far enough back that he'd never notice me. Watching him drink. Knowing he'd let his guard down sooner or later. Waiting for when I could snatch his phone.

Three unmistakable guitar chords. A cheer went through the crowd.

Donna Summer. "Hot Stuff."

"This song is doubly seminal," Ummi once joked, drunk, when this song came on. "Seminal in that it's hugely influential, and also in that it's about semen."

I wanted so badly to hit the floor. To dance, to let myself go. But I couldn't. I wouldn't let Jeremy see me like that. The absurd, paranoid thought popped into my head: what if this is all for me? A Jeremy plan to get me to make the mistake he'd spent so long waiting for? The one that would let him destroy me like he destroyed Ummi? Ridiculous, of course, but hate is always ridiculous, and his hate for me had been pretty profound.

It had happened so slowly. And then it had happened so fast. Telecomms down; rumors of coups and outbreaks; a nation terrified of the dark without the light of their cell phones.

*We may not know what's going on, but we know what to do about it*, someone said, in those early days of desperate, secret meetings. *We take to the streets.* I remember it being Ummi, but now I wonder if that's not me aggrandizing my friend.

We knew there were pitched battles happening in Washington D.C., and in some state capitals. We knew that their victory was by no means certain. We knew that the commissioner of the NYPD had already declared his allegiance to the new Republic, but that we still had a shot. So Ummi and I and a couple dozen of our most trusted activist friends started putting something together.

And all of them vanished. All except me.

I knew it was Jeremy. Somehow he'd sniffed it out, and traded the intel for one of the handful of Amnesties the fundamentalists dangled before known subversives and degenerates who helped them in those last, crucial months. Left me unscathed so suspicion within the movement would fall on me, which it did, which didn't matter, because we weren't a movement anymore, we were all scared rabbits hoping no one would come along to snap our necks. And then—boom. Ten years passed. Ten years of toiling in the Salt Mines, working from my Bronx basement apartment for the mandatory eleven hours a day. Scanning code for cracks in the Firewall of Jericho, which protected our people from foreign malware and accurate information.

Back on the main floor, I followed the barely-remembered logic of hotel layouts to where I knew the offices would be. A cop saw me coming down the service hallway, came forward to block my path.

"Evening, officer," I said, not even tempted, after all these years of disciplined practice, to let my eyes wander to where his uniform cupped his package so precisely. Every month there were show trials for disobedience, with sentences including losing one hand, or one testicle. Nothing like a secret police force to keep everyone on their toes, including the actual police. "Jeremy around?"

Was I really going to do this? Was I really going to steal Jeremy's phone and use it to track down a subversive? Because if I did, I'd be kissing my ass goodbye. All those careful, careful years wasted. I'd be of no use to the eventual insurrection, dead or in prison. Or maybe sent to a Resettlement Zone, an open-air prison where Unrepentables picked cotton or gleaned scraps of food and tech from the mountain of garbage dumped daily over the wall.

The cop shook his head. "Come back a little later."

"Will do, officer," I said. I had to make eye contact to do it, and his were dazzling. Deep brown, framed in endless lashes. His jaw, bearded like a black seal's pelt, sent blood to where there hadn't been blood in a long time.

Michael Jackson, when I got back to the main floor. "Billie Jean." Bassline like lust itself: feral, insatiable, looping endlessly back on itself. Black music hadn't been devastated as badly as music by women, but there had still been plenty of death sentences handed out by officials and vigilantes alike, along with the millions of Resettlement orders. And it went without saying that you'd never hear anything so hungry and complex on the radio now. The chorus came on and I bit my lip to keep from singing.

*What is the point?* I asked myself. *Why even bother to stay alive? This isn't living.*

I knew the night had been a bad idea. I should have trusted my gut and stayed away. The music was messing with me, stirring up things I needed to keep a tight lid on if I wanted to stay alive. The hope that Ummi might show up had been an absurd and desperate one.

Madonna, then. "Like A Virgin." My heart hurt with wanting to dance. I watched them, out on the floor, the men. But mostly, strangely, the women. The men I had fantasized about so much that seeing them now felt familiar. The women, on the other hand, were like a species I believed to be extinct. My mouth would not shut. Their bodies, their faces. Their joy. Their fearlessness, their life. The dance floor was a black hole, determined to suck me in, but once I succumbed I would never surface again.

And—was that Jeremy, out there, dancing? Red in the face and wet with sweat? *Smiling?*

I kept my gaze focused on the wall ahead of me. Reading statistics on rape and single motherhood, and the well-worn slogan: *A woman's right to raise a child on her own was the right to ruin two lives.* Anything to keep from looking back at the gleeful seething of the dance floor. Light specks peppered my field of vision. Mirror balls had descended from the ceiling by now, hundreds of them, staggered throughout all twenty stories of empty space, dragged up no doubt from one of the regime's subway-tunnel storehouses. What other wonders were down there, what artifacts of freedom and excess slowly dying of loneliness?

A woman danced on a pedestal, naked but for two ostrich-feather fans. Her dark skin made her stand out in that sea of white. A forbidden flash of pirate radio politics echoed in my head, from the early days, before private radios were seized—a stern woman declaring that *the executive fiat of the Resettlements has only slightly accelerated the implacable economic attrition of gentrification.* I mumbled the words out loud, but quietly, marveling that it had once been possible and even commonplace to express complex concepts openly.

I turned around and headed back to where the cop had blocked me.

An hour had passed; if Jeremy wasn't back, I could push a little harder. Demand he summon Jeremy, threaten him perhaps. I had let fear paralyze me for far too long. Perhaps this could be the beginning. The moment when the spark within me kindled into flame. The night when the resistance finally kindled into action.

And then I saw her. The same little girl, blonde-braided, sobbing still, dragged brusquely forward by her father. She saw me staring, and started crying even harder.

When I got to the office hallway, the cop was gone.

"Jeremy?" I called, into the darkness. No one answered.

I called his name again, then entered the empty offices. I used my cell phone's flashlight feature. Stacks of photos lined desks: forbidden images of women, basemented somewhere since the Revival. I thought about stealing a photograph, Gisele Bundchen modeling jewelry or Elizabeth II modeling old age, but it would only be a liability. One more thing to worry about, each time my number came up for a random home inspection.

A light was on, way back in the warren of desks and cubicles. I walked toward it.

Jeremy and the police officer, up against a wall. *Finally*, I thought, *that evil queen is getting arrested*. Except that's not what was happening.

They kissed passionately and fearlessly. There was something chaste about it, the gentle way the cop's hand pressed to Jeremy's cheek, and something that was more erotic and forbidden than fucking would have been.

Something shifted in me, seeing it. The Jeremy I knew would never have had the courage to do something so bold, so dangerous. How had he dared? What sorcery was this? I watched, slack-jawed, aching for it.

"Shit," the cop said, seeing me, pulling away.

"Shit," Jeremy said. "No, Will, listen—"

But the cop sprinted out of the room. Jeremy slumped back against the wall, then slid down it to sit on the floor.

"You look like you need this," I said, handing Jeremy a cigarette.

"Thanks," he said, and accepted the light I offered him. His smile was sad and beautiful. "Hell of a party, huh?"

His lack of shame didn't shock me. Half an hour before, it would have. But now I knew that everything I thought about Jeremy had been wrong.

"How did you talk them into this?" I asked, spreading my hands to indicate Degradation Eve in its entirety.

He shrugged. "I took advantage of their arrogance," he said. "They believe their own PR. They really think all this music and dancing is so degrading and barbaric that anyone who sees it will be disgusted. I got the idea reading about the Degenerate Art exhibit. The Nazis put on a big show of all the art they hated—Jewish, modernist, Bolshevik, primitivist—intending to make fun of it, but instead people attended in huge numbers."

"What happened to Ummi?" I asked in a quiet voice.

"She's in Canada," he said. "I got her out."

*Out.*

Something very happy and something very sad settled in my stomach.

"How?" I whispered.

"Someone snitched. Gave the cops all the info on the planned action. I heard about it through my job. Couldn't stop it, but I could save a couple people."

"Why should I believe you? How do I know it wasn't you who snitched? How do I know she's not dead by now?"

Jeremy shrugged.

"And me? You saved me, too?"

He nodded, avoiding eye contact.

"Why would you do all that? You hated her. You hated *me*."

He laughed. He looked at me. His expression went from startled to puzzled to resigned. "I *love* you, Clive. I've always loved you."

I waited for laughter, or a mocking punch in the arm. None came.

"It's all for you, Clive. This whole thing."

"That doesn't…"

I couldn't finish the sentence. I couldn't think. My mind tried to play back every Jeremy memory I had, but it sputtered and gasped uselessly like a car engine on a cold morning. I sank to my knees before him.

"You really never knew?"

My head shook itself: *No.*

"I guess *you* hated *me*," he said, tucking in his shirt where it had come untucked. "I guess you just assumed it was mutual."

"You went along with it," I said. "With everything. How could you do that?"

"So did you, Clive."

"Not like you. Not by working for them. Not by signing death warrants or whatever the hell you do—"

"I've been able to do a lot of good things for a lot of people, because of who and where I am. Ummi would be dead now if it weren't for me."

"No. No. You—"

"It's not like you wake up one day and everything's terrible, and you have to say 'Yes' or 'No' to it," he said. And he was right. Even after the takeover, things took a long time to get really bad. Even before. I heard stories on the news, about crazy politicians getting elected in faraway states, or insane unconstitutional laws being passed, and I thought, *Damn, that sucks for those people*, but I never thought it would ever actually affect us.

"What could we have done?"

"Exactly," he said. "That was your attitude."

Jeremy was right. I had dressed him up in my own worst qualities, endowed him with all that was small and cowardly and pitiful in myself. I looked down at my own silent, obedient hands.

"Ummi's still fighting," he said. "Up in Canada, there's a whole network of people. It's still dangerous. Canada is terrified of angering its powerful neighbor, word is they're thinking of deporting all the Republic refugees. But she's still trying. She hasn't given up. She isn't hiding in a hole somewhere."

His eyes were hard and accusing and I could not think of a single thing to say.

"This is silly," he said. "I didn't want this to be a fight. It's a goodbye, really."

I looked at him.

"Do you remember the night of the Supreme Court decision victory party? What you told me?"

I remembered the party. I didn't remember telling him anything. I opened my mouth but could not say so.

"We were on the dance floor. You had just hooked up with some random super-hot guy. I congratulated you on it, and you said *'This is the kind of moment where I could just die. From happiness. Dancing, you know?'*"

It sounded like me. It was dramatic enough, meaningless enough.

"I'm an idiot," he said, standing, disgusted—in himself, having finally glimpsed the real me. "I don't know why I thought you'd be strong enough to take advantage of this."

I had so many questions, but only one came out. "Why didn't you ever say anything? Ten years—you could have found me at any point."

"I knew you had made your choice."

And I had. He was kind, not to spell it out. I chose to give up completely. I chose to never be happy. I chose to go along, to get along.

Jeremy stood up. "The party's about to come to a stop."

"It's barely two," I mumbled. "Thing's supposed to go on all night."

He looked me up and down, showed me a smile full of pity and contempt, got up to go. "You missed your last chance to dance, Clive."

I walked the floor in a daze, after that. Drinking, watching faces transfixed, ecstatic, rhapsodic. Hours might have passed.

Finally: Donna Summers again, "Last Dance," and a groan of pain and pleasure went up from all the older men and women who knew what this song meant, that we had reached the end of the night, that our revels now were ended, that this insubstantial pageant would fade.

But something felt wrong. It was too early for "Last Dance." We still had two hours to go before the party's scheduled end. Had the local Commander finally put his foot down? Were the Gestapo lining up even now, outside?

Someone screamed, high above me. A whooping, drunk, encouraging scream that spread through the crowd. I craned my neck and scanned each successive balcony in turn. All of them packed with people, everyone dancing, everyone blissfully in the moment except for me.

Eight stories up, I spotted him. Jeremy waved, standing on the railing at the edge of the balcony. He continued to dance at the edge of the abyss, and all around him people cheered.

I turned away. I watched the faces of the beautiful men and women around me. I thought of the little girl with the blond braid, and the little girl down the hall from me who was not allowed to learn to read. And the woman next door, and her nightly screams. And all the women I saw on the street and subway every day. And how I had been so focused on my own tragedy, my shitty job and empty pockets and soul-skinning loneliness, that I had never let myself see how good I had it. How much worse how many other people had it.

I had always believed, bizarrely, that I was somehow carrying a spark of revolution inside me. But fire isn't fire if it doesn't burn.

When Jeremy leapt, I wasn't watching.

When he hit the ground, and the screams started, I was still trapped inside the dawning epiphany of what I was.

And hours later, when the ambulances and cops had gone and the paperwork was filled out and the witness depositions deposited, and the press had left the scene for the official announcement from the Commander, I went up to the roof. A woman sat there, shoulders heaving with sobs. I didn't recognize her until I saw the pink wig wadded up and clenched tight in both hands.

"Hey," she said. "Is it time to go? I'm sorry, I've been up here for a long time."

"No," I said. "It's not time. Not yet."

She didn't know what had happened inside. She was crying about everything else. I looked: no blood I could see on the soles of my feet. Or my hands, for that matter. She pulled the cigarette from behind her ear. I patted my pockets in search of matches, but she already had it lit.

She needed a hug. I wanted to hug her. I almost did. I took a tiny step in her direction, before I remembered that the secret police could have been watching from any one of the dozen taller buildings around us. So we stood there. I hoped she could see, or guess, what was going through my mind: how sorry I was, for all of this, and how badly I wished that things were different.

*Except it doesn't matter what's in people's minds. What matters is what they do. And don't do.*

Sunlight showed us more and more of our city, unchanged by the evening's revels. More and more of myself. My fire would not blaze up and burn anything down. I would go on like this, like so many others, praying for an asteroid or divine intervention to fix the things I was too afraid to fix myself.

She handed me her cigarette, half-smoked. Her smile was full of pity, for a creature not strong enough even to weep.

*Wyatt is laughing and seems fully normal,
even though I wikied all this shit about
post-Edit malaise, how people feel like they
lost their tab, but in their head, and they're
patting every part of their brain trying to find
it. And his mom, when she chatted me, she
said that he might be sad. Might be distant.
But everything seems alright. We talk shit.
We laugh. We pick skinspray off ourselves
and flick it at each other.*

# RICH LARSON

FOR SOME REASON I THOUGHT Wyatt would look different after getting Edited, but when he steps out onto the porch of his parents' reefhouse summer rental, swilling a Corona and swiping my we're here skype off his tab, he's the same as ever. Still tall and bony with gray eyes and pale blonde hair that looks like it'll stick to your hand but doesn't.

He stuffs his tab into the pocket of his chinos and gives us a wave. "Boys."

Dray springs past me and up the porch in three lanky strides, wrapping Wyatt up like it's been a year instead of a month, then snapping off a slick twisty custom dap, because Dray has a custom dap with everyone and the motherfucking mailman.

"Wyatt, bru, look at this place," he says, rubbing his hand along the organic coral railing, mottled purple like the rest of the reefhouse, everything grown from some big name designer geneprint because Wyatt's parents only ever snag the chicest. Dray wraps his hand around the back of Wyatt's neck and sticks foreheads with him. "We are going to bang some bitches here, bru."

Wyatt mirrorgrins, catching my eye in a way that makes me not think about bitches, but more about the last time me and him sparked up on his mom's ponic and fooled around in his room.

"Yo," Dray says, going serious. "You got scars?"

Wyatt wriggles away then, muttering like no, no it was all nano, of course there's no scarring.

By this time I'm up the rippled steps and acting fully glacial even though it's good to see Wyatt again, like really good. "What's doing, Y," I say, cookie cutter dap, precise half a hug, stepback. "You still remember me?"

Wyatt grins again. "It's vague and shit. But yeah."

Dray's already loped past us into the reefhouse, crowing about throwing some ball on the wall screens, about cracking the 18+ thumblock on the minibar.

Me and Wyatt follow him in, backs of our hands not quite touching.

WE DECIDE TO SWIM WHILE there's still sun, so the three of us grab trunks and dart off through the backdoor of the house, which shutters shut behind us, and out to the pale gray beach.

THERE'S A RUSTY BOOTH FOR skinspray, because the water's not so user friendly anymore, even though it's not as bad as that webdoc where they pull that pilot whale out the Pacific and its hide is all bubbling and falling off in chunks.

Wyatt strips down as pasty as ever and me and Dray bust him on it like always, like whoa, polar, and it feels like a standard scene except Wyatt doesn't go red and squirm like usual, instead just smiles this new kind of smile I can't quite lock.

Dray molds a handful of the gritty orange skinspray to his crotch while the gel is setting, so he comes out of the booth with this wobbly skinspray cock hanging off him. We splash around in the waves, dunking each other and pretending to drown to fuck with the little paddlebot lifeguard, until Dray's fake dick dissolves and the water gets chilly enough to slice under the sunshine and turn my toes all thick and cold.

Then we slosh out back to the sand and camp down, talking shit about the NBA draft and that seven-footer from Senegal who doesn't want to get a nerve mesh for like, religious reasons. Then about the two girls a little ways off who are cam-chatting someone in a foreign language. They're both wearing black bikinis and one has an animated tattoo of a flowering vine slithering up and down her leg, which makes Dray pantomime humping his towel.

Wyatt is laughing and seems fully normal, even though I wikied all this shit about post-Edit malaise, how people feel like they lost their tab, but in their head, and they're patting every part of their brain trying to find it. And his mom, when she chatted me, she said that he might be sad. Might be distant.

But everything seems alright. We talk shit. We laugh. We pick skinspray off ourselves and flick it at each other.

EVENTUALLY DRAY CAN TAKE THE tattoo no more, and he pressgangs Wyatt and me to go mack on the girls with him. They turn out to be Finnish, holidaying for the summer, and also sisters. Both of them speak airtight English, but that doesn't stop Dray from pulling up Finnish-English babel apps so he can goof on them with some butchered phrases like "are you into four-ways" and "your smile gives me butterflies."

Normally Wyatt would just be basing him, but this time he dives right in, touching the tattoo girl's arm, winking, getting both of them to laugh. Like he's just realizing for the first time that he's tall (first on the team to slam, even though he only does it in practice) and rich (see: parents getting him Edited for his sixteenth and then setting us up in their reefhouse for the first weekend back) and handsome.

Eventually I get bored and slide off back to the water. From a distance I can tell the Finnish girls are still digging Wyatt, but the one who was giving me looks before points over to me and I hear "Your friend? What of your friend?"

Dray looks back and throws me a salute, then says, "Not his thing, yo. Pink is not his favorite color." Then explains further with some charades.

Him and Wyatt come join me a minute later with Finns in tab.

"Her sister's only fourteen, but whatever, right?" Dray says, shrugging. "Still sexy."

Somehow, nonverbally, it is cement that Wyatt gets the girl with the tat, whose name is Viivi, and Dray gets the little sister, whose name is Heli.

"Viivi's got a tight little ass on her," Wyatt says, looking at me when he says it with an edge I am not used to hearing. "Cannot wait to plow that." He thumps my shoulder, like I'm in on it, and lies back in the sand. He stays eyes shut and smiling until his parents skype to check in on him, then he knocks us fists and heads down the beach with his tab.

For a while me and Dray talk about a Bulls-Satellites final, how brag it would be for Thon Maker to get one last ring. Before we knew Wyatt, me and Dray were best friends. Same shitty burb, same shitty elementary, playing pick up on the big cement block behind the school with its one rusty hoop.

"His shoulders are different," Dray breaks out. "Used to slouch them when he asked a question, like, trying to suck it back in."

Dray's canny. A lot of people don't know that.

"Smiles different, sometimes," I say. "You ask what all they did?"

"No, bru. You should ask." He pauses. "If you could get Edited, what would you change? Like, if you could Edit anything you wanted."

I watch Wyatt dragging his feet in the wet surf, shoulders thrust back. I think about my cramped shitty house that he still treats like a museum, like, afraid to touch shit, peering out of the corner of his eye at the mold bloom on my ceiling and the bare wiring on the walls. I would want to make it so I didn't notice that. Or notice how his parents look at me sideways sometimes, or how he talks so different with his rich boys.

"I'd be funny," Dray says. "Like, really funny. Really sharp. Always say the smart thing. That'd be brag."

"You are funny, shithead."

"But, like, really funny," Dray insists. "What would you get?"

"Nothing, bru," I say, tucking my hands under my head. "Don't be fucking with perfection."

WE GO BACK TO THE reefhouse once Wyatt's done his skype. Then we dig the other Coronas out of the fridge, which is one of those sexy gel fridges where the stuff hangs suspended in little air bubbles, and fire up the hot tub.

The scaldy hot water and the glacial beer do their tingly headrush thing, and the steam cloud makes it feel easier to ask questions. When Dray slops over the side to go piss off the porch, I twist to Wyatt and tap my temple.

"What all did they change when they went in there, Y?" I say.

Wyatt's head lolls back on the edge. "Just a basic Edit, mostly," he says. "Chemo plug for anti-anxiety. Some body language modulation. Bigger memory retention, better spatial reasoning." He goes quiet for a second. "And I don't feel things as hard. Like, the shitty things. Bad memories. I remember feeling bad, but I don't feel bad remembering. Yeah?"

Our legs brush together under the water, hairs all swirling up on each other.

"And the good ones?" I say.

"Success, boys," Dray announces, back with a shit-eating grin and a frosty bottle of Jager. "Thought I was going to have to go chop someone's thumb off." Wyatt shifts over to make room, and Dray ends up between us.

Dray throws his chats with the Finnish girls up on the wallscreen, so we all get to witness the slow erosion of their plan to sneak out and meet us. By this time we are all tranqed enough to not care, not that I ever did.

"Still a brag first night," Wyatt says. "Like old times, yeah?"

"Brag," Dray says. "I'm going to have a place like this when I'm rich, yo. And I'll fly them Finns over on sub-orbital."

Wyatt does that new smile again, and I lock down the word for it. Permissive. It rubs me so wrong I take two chugs in a row to get the flow back.

It works: soon we're all laughing, all blurred, and it feels almost like we're drinking for the first time again. I remember Wyatt slipped his parents some bullshit about a midnight pick-up game and instead we all got pulped at this party, and Wyatt finally admitted he never invited us over after ball because he was ashamed of his big swanky house, and I almost hit him, but by the end of the night we were all level.

That's when I started liking him, not just for setting screens tight but also for his slow-mo straight face jokes and the way he flopped his arm around me to slur secrets.

I slurred some back, and in a week it got so my hands had a particular zone on his hipbones and kissing him was easy. When my sister got fucked up on pills and had to go to emerg, for some reason I told Wyatt first. He came over still digging the crusts out of his eyes.

Dray flicks out, sliding down the side of the tub, mumbling about learning Finnish, not to impress nobody but because it's a brag-sounding language. We get him nested on the couch with a bunch of fluffy white towels and turn him on his side, because Dray has been known to up his guts when Jager is in play.

"Dart to the beach again?" Wyatt says.

I feel a little bad leaving Dray, but I'm drunk, so only a little. We pull on some clothes and stagger on out, still dripping. The beach looks good at night, with the tide coming in soft and foamy and smoothing big arcs on the sand. The moon is nearly full, circled up by these jagged-looking clouds.

We plow some seats in the sand, which still feels warm, and watch the buoys at the edge of the swimming area bloom on one by one, bright yellow. The lifeguard is still paddling back and forth, making ripples in the water.

"I missed you," I finally say, because the week in hospital and the three in neural recovery almost did feel like a year.

"I missed you too," Wyatt says, and then we're kissing, his dry lips on my lips and my hand on his hip. It doesn't feel right. When my tongue touches his lips he shivers, not a sexy shiver, but a shiver like he just touched something dead.

He pulls away.

"Sorry, bru," he says. "Thought maybe I could. Can't." He puts a finger to his skull, where there is no scarring because they did it all with nano, and I get it now why Dray's body was always between ours.

"They did that too?" I ask dumbly.

"My parents thought it would be better," he says. "Simpler. Sorry."

"They knew about you and me?" I say.

He shakes his head, and that makes it worse, because it means he didn't tell them. "Nothing like that," he says. "It's just simpler, this way. You know, for later in life. Always liked girls more anyway, yeah?"

There's this new thing swelling big and inky in the space between us, black and bitter so I can almost taste it.

"Oh, yeah," I say. "Good call. Way simpler. Simpler the better. Your rich boy life is way complicated."

"I didn't know if it would take, or whatever," Wyatt says. "I thought maybe—"

"That's why me and Dray are your boys, right?" I say. "We keep it so simple. Couple

clowns from the lowburb to make you happy. Help you remember how good you got it."
I'm almost spitting the words. "That's what this weekend is, right? Therapy. To get you
out of whatever post-surgery funk your mom fucking chatted me about."

"She what?" For the first time, Wyatt flushes like he used to, goes blotchy red. "I had
to beg them to let me do the weekend with you. Fucking beg. They wanted me in SAT-
prep." Then the flush is gone again, quicker than should be possible, and he gives his new
smile. "We're still friends, bru. Right?"

I can't make him mad anymore, or hard, or anything else. But I wonder now if I ever
did. If this is Wyatt with something broken, or if this is Wyatt pure, like, Wyatt with the
paint stripped. If Wyatt was sad after surgery because they Edited me out, or if it was
just chemicals getting level in his head.

"Sorry," Wyatt says again. "Didn't think you'd care so much." He grabs my hand
and weaves the fingers tight. I look at his bony white knuckles on my brown ones and
wonder how different you have to be before you're a different person.

"I don't have some swanky surgeon to just turn that shit off when it's not simple," I
say. "I don't get to turn none of it off."

We sit there in the sand, and I can almost hear the countdown ticking through
his head. Like, this many minutes to still be a good person, this many to still be a good
friend.

I don't wait for zero. I take my hand back and get up, brush off. I go back up the
beach, watching the clouds eat the moon, Edit it right out the sky like it never was there,
not really.

*I looked down and noticed a pair of feet poking out from the bushes my father had planted by the side of the house. Sliding aside the screen, I leaned farther out, forgetting my fear of being seen, and that was when I first saw your white chest, your body alight in an almost lunar glow. You must have heard me, because you swept away the leaves of the bush with one arm and I saw your face staring up at me. It was like I was seeing my own reflection upon the surface of the lake in front of the house.*

# Envious Moons

### RICHARD SCOTT LARSON

EVERY NIGHT THAT SUMMER I looked across the yard from my bedroom window into Callie's, which glowed like something you could see from space. She was the prettiest girl in town, and there she was right next door, dancing around her bed, all pink sheets and teddy bears, swaying to music I couldn't hear. She was almost always wearing a white bathrobe, and I imagined I could smell the freshness of her pale skin underneath, the polished armor of it.

I was the kind of boy who didn't inspire a second glance, but everybody knew Callie. You must have known her too—why else would you have come? Her picture was always in the local paper, something about a beauty pageant she had won in the next county over, or a cheerleading competition where she had performed a particularly daring trick. She had even played Juliet in the school play, which everyone in town went to see. The production didn't include Shakespeare's original ending because a student had recently committed suicide in the high school gymnasium, so when Juliet woke up in the family crypt, Romeo was still alive, waiting for her there in the darkness.

I had caught my first glimpse of Callie at the supermarket early the previous year, when we were still new to town. We had moved because my father got reassigned to a new factory location out west of the city, past the river, too far to drive each day from our old apartment. A new development was going up around a small lake, and he said he had gotten a good price. We drove out and stood there in the empty lot where our house would eventually stand. "Just imagine," said my father, gripping my shoulder. We looked out at the lake, the more untamed edges of which were already being smoothed down by bulldozers into the perfect circle it would eventually become. Later I would imagine that it had always been that way.

Callie moved to our neighborhood shortly after our house was finished. She lived with her grandparents, old people who were always early to bed, never seeming to keep track of where Callie went off to after dark. And she was always going somewhere, always with boys from around town. In the supermarket with my mother, my eyes burned as I watched her flirting with the boys shelving boxes of cereal, boys chopping meat behind the deli counter, boys bagging the groceries at the checkout lines. They fell over each other for her attention, trying to make her laugh, to make her see something special in them. I recognized the hunger in their eyes. And then one night the light in the bedroom next door caught my eye from where I lay unsleeping in my twin bed against the wall, and I saw her there at the window staring dreamily out into the tiny space between us.

I knew she couldn't see me—saw that she was instead looking across at her own reflection in my window, occasionally putting a hand to her face or absently smoothing her hair—and I waited there, watching, until she turned off her light and went to sleep. Then I finally unclenched my fists and returned to my own bed.

THE NIGHT YOU CAME, I was watching Callie through the window as usual. And I knew from the way she danced in front of the mirror that the boys were on their way to pick her up. The boys always came for her, arriving in their fathers' cars, loud and bright in the Saturday night darkness. Sometimes it was only one boy, nervously clutching a flower or a wrapped gift. But sometimes they came paired or in groups, calling up to her from where they half-parked in the driveway. I knew there were parties in the rich neighborhoods a few exits down the highway, parties I heard about afterwards at school—gossip in the hallways about who had hooked up with whom, which party guest had gotten the drunkest, which girls had gone topless in the pool. And I knew that sometimes kids drove out to the state park, drinking and smoking all night beneath the stars, never thinking about those they hadn't invited.

Tonight it was a group of boys, their movie star faces calling her name and urging her down to them. I heard them before I saw them, the engine noise of the car roaring into the quiet circle of the neighborhood. Then the light of their headlights brightened the bend toward the north side of the lake, and finally the car itself pulled into Callie's driveway—a black SUV, polished and shining, reflecting the moonlight.

Callie came to her window to watch them arrive, still in her white bathrobe, craning her neck to look toward the front of the house. I shrank away into the shadows behind my own window, crouching beside my plastic laundry hamper. But she would never have looked in my direction anyway.

"Callie!" came the cry from the driveway, the boys leaning out the windows of the car and slapping the side of the passenger door. I recognized a few guys from school, Nathan and Jared, or was it Derek—all of them athletes who were unashamed in the showers after gym class, their perfect bodies begging to be seen. Nathan had played Romeo opposite Callie in the school play, and I remembered the way the girls in the audience leaned forward in their seats when he delivered his most heartfelt lines, as if he were speaking directly to them. "Arise, fair sun," he said, "and kill the envious moon"—the words, from his mouth, sounding almost like a song.

Callie laughed from the open window. "Just a minute!"

Earlier she had pulled dresses from the closet and spread them out on the bed, and now she held them up to her chest one by one, striking poses as she examined herself in the mirror. The boys whistled for her from the car below, their faces turned up to the house and their eyes catching the light from the street lamps, glowing like excited fireflies. Watching the boys, I didn't see Callie finish putting on her outfit, but finally I noticed her bedroom light wink out and a few seconds later she was dashing down the steps from her front porch. She had chosen an airy floral dress, backless except for the thin straps of her bra clinging to the tops of her shoulders, bright red like a dare.

"You'll wake up the whole neighborhood with that screaming," she said, squealing as the boys opened the door and all those hands reached out from the darkness to pull her inside. I held my breath as the car sped back out toward the highway, voices trailing away into the night until I was left alone with the muted neighborhood, the empty house below me, Callie's dark bedroom next door. I felt a tug somewhere inside, the urge to take off running, part of me already racing after them into the night.

LIKE ALWAYS, I WAITED AT the window for them to come back. I passed the time by imagining what they were doing in town together, maybe sinking into seats in a crowded movie theater, everything dark, hands descending into secret places. Sometimes while waiting for Callie I would be reading an old paperback at the window, or sometimes I would doze off with my head against the wall, knowing I would wake up when the car returned. But that night I couldn't concentrate on anything except the world outside. I looked down the street at all the other houses, the lights in the windows winking on and off like machines sending coded messages up into space. Then I was peering again into Callie's empty window, my face almost pressed to the screen, when something caught my eye from below.

I looked down and noticed a pair of feet poking out from the bushes my father had planted by the side of the house. Sliding aside the screen, I leaned farther out, forgetting my fear of being seen, and that was when I first saw your white chest, your body alight in an almost lunar glow. You must have heard me, because you swept away the leaves of the bush with one arm and I saw your face staring up at me. It was like I was seeing my own reflection upon the surface of the lake in front of the house.

You held my gaze unblinkingly for a long moment before scampering back into the bushes, then dashing toward where the backyard met the woods.

None of the lights in the house were on. I had been upstairs since dusk, after my parents had left for bowling night with my father's work buddies, and I also knew to keep the lights off in empty rooms to save money on electricity. I made my way through the hallway and down the stairs by memory, counting the steps on the staircase, then finally turning and walking into the living room. Through the windowed sliding door to the back patio I could see the yard faintly lit in the moonlight. Cheap lawn furniture we had bought at the department store in town was scattered across the concrete patio and in the freshly mowed grass. The line of trees behind the house stood tall and black.

I side-stepped along the wall of the living room past the small fireplace and the entertainment system. I stopped next to the patio door, keeping myself carefully obscured by the curtains. I heard nothing from the yard except the night sounds of unidentified insects calling out to each other, the occasional train whistle from the tracks running alongside the highway. I reached for the curtain hanging at the edge of the window and I pulled it aside slowly, incrementally, in a way I hoped was imperceptible from outside.

I sighed when I saw the empty yard, disappointed to see that you had gone.

I let the curtain fall back into place and I stepped toward the kitchen. I had skipped dinner again, but I knew there were microwaveable meals waiting for me in the freezer. Then I felt your gaze upon my back just before I flipped the lights on, and I turned sharply to see you standing at the glass door, looking in at me from the dark. You looked to be my age, and we carried ourselves with the same thin frame, slightly stooped at the shoulders. But you seemed breakable, like you needed someone to help keep you intact. The lightness of your face bore the weight of wet, overgrown hair. You were naked but seemingly unashamed, your arms hanging limply at your sides.

I went to the window and looked out at you, our faces mirrored in the glass. I opened my mouth to speak, but then I heard your muffled voice. "You don't need to cry out. I'm not going to hurt you."

Even now, I don't know what compelled me to open the door. I don't know if I would do it again—or is that something I tell myself, a way of not taking blame for what happened? But you kept casting glances back around to the side of the house, toward Callie's, tensing at what I imagined were the sounds of an approach. And I was afraid you would run away before I got to speak to you.

Your skin was so wet. The water ran down your face from your matted hair and gathered in little pools at the base of your neck. You needed help. I felt the coldness of you through the glass, my own almost primal urge to protect you guiding my hand as I slid open the door. Then you crossed into the house, your hand lightly grazing mine as you passed me.

UPSTAIRS IN MY ROOM, I pulled out a pair of pajamas from my dresser and turned to where you waited in the doorway, naked and pale, as if you needed to be invited inside.

"Here," I said, holding out the clothes. And in a moment you had concealed your damp body in my pajamas, the same striped pattern as the ones I was wearing. Together we moved soundlessly over the carpet to the window. You gripped the windowsill tightly, your hands curling into pincers.

"What's out there?" I asked. "What are you running from?"

My stomach was clenched like a cramped muscle. No one but my parents had ever been in my room, and here you were so close to me, wearing my clothes. I saw into your mind as if I lived there, and I saw that you also knew the danger of bringing buried thoughts out into the world. You caught your lower lip with the edge of your teeth. Then you shuddered and turned away.

"I'm so cold," you said.

I reached out to warm you and my mind went to Callie, her window across the yard dark and empty. She and the boys would have been finishing a movie by then, or maybe just getting to a party, doors being flung open for them, music and happy voices inviting them inside. There would be dancing in dark rooms, bodies pressed against one another, faces lit up briefly in flashes of neon before disappearing again into shadow.

We were still at the window when we heard the sound of the garage door opening downstairs. My parents were home already, which meant it was later than I thought. You looked questioningly into my eyes. My mind raced and my palms were wet as I thought quickly about what to do. I finally said, "Stay here, just stay here," and I crossed the room and stepped into the hallway. As I pulled the door slowly shut, you narrowed into a sliver of window and body, your eyes big and floating.

"Keep quiet," I said. "You can lie down on my bed if you're tired."

I thought for a moment of turning on the small television, something to make noise in case you stumbled against unfamiliar furniture, my video game controllers tangled on the carpet begging to trip you and send you hurtling to the floor, my books tossed chaotically across the floor like an obstacle course. I felt a desperate desire to hide you, having taken on the responsibility of keeping you unseen. But already I heard the door opening from the garage into the kitchen. I closed the bedroom door softly before descending the stairs, and when I looked from the landing I saw your wet footprints marking your path through the living room. I hoped they were invisible to someone who didn't know to look.

I watched from the staircase as they came into the kitchen from the garage, my father laughing as my mother explained away a poor bowling score. "I was trying to let you win," she said, "but you were just terrible! Barb and Mike were so embarrassed. The other team beat us by a mile."

"Did you see their faces when you threw that gutter ball?" he asked. "No, you couldn't have. Your jaw was on the floor."

"I thought you were going to cry," she said, pointing at him and laughing again. I flinched at the loudness of their voices.

My father opened a can of beer from the fridge and passed it to her before opening one for himself. "I'm a sensitive guy," he said. "That's why you married me."

"I thought I married you for your money."

He snorted and reached for her waist. "All those tips I was getting at the diner?" He pulled her close and I tensed at a muffled sound from my bedroom, a low moan. My mother glanced toward the staircase, but she didn't see me hiding there in the dark.

"Do you think he's okay?" she asked my father.

"It's just a phase," he said, trying to kiss her neck. "The whole shut-in thing. I went through it too."

"I hope so, but—" Then she giggled when he tickled her. "You'll make me spill my beer."

"He'll tell us when he's ready," said my father.

"If that's even what it is."

I was imagining you waiting for me in my bed, noiseless as a ghost. You were like a secret memory, something possibly from a dream. I suddenly needed to throw open my door to prove to myself that you were real. But then what? They would come upstairs, concerned about me as always, and they would see two of me standing there in the dark room—would see me doubled, broken apart.

Instead, I waited. I couldn't let them know about you. I wouldn't have even known how to tell them. Some things can't be said without giving something else up, closing a door forever. But when I saw them holding each other and smiling into each other's eyes, I wanted to break down the walls of the house to show them my secret self, the one hidden away.

"Enough about this for now," said my mother. She kissed my father lightly on the mouth and then hung her purse by the door. "I'm exhausted."

They moved together into the living room, still clutching their beer cans. I backed up the stairs as they approached, keeping always to the shadows. I made sure they didn't notice your footprints and then I retreated silently back to my room like someone deep underwater clawing to the surface, pushing away the depths.

You seemed smaller when I returned, sitting on the edge of my bed with your head in your hands. But when I entered the room, you stood and walked with me back to the window.

"Did you come from the lake?" I asked quietly.

You squinted at me, our faces so close. In the dim light from outside, you seemed haunted. I thought maybe you were a ghost who had come to haunt our house. Maybe ghosts sought out new houses to haunt, sick of all those old cobwebbed attics and creaky staircases. Maybe they wanted something all their own.

"Are you a ghost?" I asked.

You laughed a hoarse croak and then fell to coughing. I winced at the sound of your retching, but I saw that you were trembling and I put my hand to your back to steady you. You felt skeletal beneath my hand, a cocooned creature having just emerged from the dark into new flesh, not yet knowing how to make yourself strong.

"You've been so kind to me," you said, and I pressed my finger to your lips. Something flashed in your face when I touched you  something I recognized.

"I need to return this kindness with one of my own," you said.

I remember your face at that moment, your jaw clenched resolutely. You wanted so badly to help me. "I don't need anything. Just stay here. I'll hide you," I continued eagerly. I felt the breath coming out of you like something fungal, amphibious, the dankness of something long buried. "I won't let anyone find you," I said.

My mother knocked on the door. "Are you okay in there? Who are you talking to?"

I scrambled to my feet just as she opened the door without an answer from me. She stood in the doorway in her nightgown, the expression on her face concealed in the dark. I smelled the beer on her breath even from across the room. She didn't step further inside, and I imagined a gulf of water between us, moonlight dappling a route across the still expanse.

"You know I'm here if you want to talk," she said.

Something must have awakened in her, some sense of my secret self burrowing into the dark house and taking root there. I imagined her eyes crawling out of their sockets and roving through the shadows of my room, trying to exhume something I had hidden. But she only looked at me with a curious sadness, like she wanted to say something else but couldn't find the words. And when I glanced quickly around the room, I saw that you had disguised yourself once more.

"I know," I said.

She sighed and her face shrank away. "I'll see you in the morning," she said. "I'll make pancakes."

Then she quietly pulled the door shut behind her and you crawled out from under the bed, looking gravely into my eyes. The stillness of our secret was an island we could live on forever, floating unseen in the midst of a violent sea crashing always at our shores.

We settled close to each other once more at the window, kneeling together on the beige carpet. I wonder if the world felt as charged for you then as it did for me, both of us electrifying the darkness with our secret.

"What were you doing at the window when you saw me?" you asked.

I looked again out into Callie's dark bedroom. I told you about her face, her hair, the way her body looked when she slipped out of the bathrobe and wrapped herself up in one of her thousands of dresses—the curves of her, the way she held womanhood up like a gown, something expensive in a store I wasn't allowed to enter. I felt like I could tell you anything. And I told you how much the boys wanted her. I told you how it felt to wait for them to come back with her, those boys who came and called her name, then ushered her out into the world with them always at her side. The boys beneath the spotlight of the streetlamp glowing like the main attraction.

Then you said to me, "I know what you want."

The car the boys had been driving earlier suddenly roared back into the neighborhood, and we both shrank away from the glare of the headlights. We breathed heavily from the sides of the window as we watched Callie emerge from the car, laughing as one of the boys held out his pursed lips for a kiss. She dashed toward the house, the boys clamoring from the driveway, whistling and calling out, "We can't live without you!" They pretended to weep, spurned lovers cast aside. Nathan did his best Romeo, his arms outstretched as if to pluck her from a balcony.

You said again at my side, "I know what you want. I know what I can do for you."

I felt a warmth seeping from your body like you were on fire, but I wouldn't have stamped you out. I would have let you burn and burn for as long as you wanted. But then you stood up abruptly, stepped back into the shadows, and disappeared out the door.

I didn't dare call out to you, but I was so scared, so scared that I had lost you. The boys were still there in the car, watching as Callie teased them from the porch—a porch I couldn't see from my vantage point, but still I imagined her there as I watched the boys, imagined her returning their kisses and posing, hands on her hips, daring them to follow her and knowing all the while that they couldn't. Then Callie was inside and the boys were gone, disappearing around the north end of the lake and back out toward the highway. But when I looked across at the house I saw that Callie's bedroom was lit up like a bonfire, like a place to warm up from the cold, and you were looking at me from her window, your face framed by the darkness of the night that pressed in hard at the edges of you like a vise.

Callie was on her way upstairs, maybe turning down her hallway right at that moment, her bedroom door just a few steps away now—

But then you smiled at me, the lights went out, and I saw only my reflection staring back at me across the yard.

I CLOSED MY EYES AND thought of the lake out there in the night, now tamed, a round window made to match the shape of the pale moon above. I waited for my heart to stop hammering away at the cage my body had made of it. I imagined you dashing through the dark of Callie's house and diving once more to the depths of the lake, leaving only me to know your secret. And my mind flew forward to next Saturday night, the boys racing back down the street in their car, hollering excitedly over the noise of the engine, their voices rising to a thunder as they came closer. They would pull halfway into the driveway next door and call out her name, banging the sides of their car with anxious, ready hands.

But this time no one would answer. The house would stay dark. The window would be empty.

Then the boys would turn and see me up there in the window next door, where I would have been waiting for them all along. They would call my name, whistling and cheering, and then they would wait for me down on the street as I made myself ready for them, their hands excitedly slapping the sides of the car and filling the night with the sound of their love for me, their perfect faces catching the light as they gazed up at my window.

"You'll wake up the whole neighborhood with that screaming," I would say after dashing down from the porch to meet them, squealing as they opened the door, all those hands reaching out from the darkness to pull me hungrily inside. The engine would have been idling, thudding like the heart of a racehorse ready for a sprint, and then we would drive off together into a world that the beautiful boys were so excited to show me.

We would never talk about the girl next door. Eventually we wouldn't even remember her name.

*The young man is dressed as if for a stage play:
a loose brown tunic, leather bands around his
wrists, black hair cut short. His eyes reflect
the light of the small terracotta oil lamp in
his hand. Peasant boy, I think, looking at his
bare muscled legs and arms. I'm not surprised:
the Domkerkhof attracts both low and high
alike, and in his loose clothes he looks like the
Ganymede of the ancient Greeks, just before
Zeus abducted him. Our unnatural desires are
nothing if not quintessentially human.*

# PAUL EVANBY

*Anno Domini 1729*
*Utrecht, The Republic of the United Netherlands*

SOMEONE FIRES A SHOT FROM the church tower. I look up, because that's what you do when they take aim at you, but nothing is visible in the darkness above the hanging lanterns. The open square offers no cover, so I press my back against the rough stone wall surrounding the cathedral ruins, still warm from the summer sun.

A hand grabs my arm and pulls me aside. I barely manage to avoid stepping into a patch of fresh horse dung. A drunken laugh sounds from across the street.

"The laws of the divine nature in action," Raphael whispers in my ear. His perfume almost masks the reek of the manure. "Hide."

"What is it?"

Raphael Peixoto's face is hidden in the shadows under the brim of his hat, but I don't need to see the wry smile around his mouth to know it's there. After he pulls me through the overgrown gate into the ruins, I wait for his Spinoza. The philosopher is always on his lips, and Raphael has a quote for every precarious situation, no matter the time.

But once inside, he pushes me against the wall and presses a finger against my mouth. "Beware the impersonal wrath of God in the trajectory of a leaden ball, Gysbert."

For years the ministers have been fulminating about the wrath of our Lord, brought down on the Republic by the moral failings of its people, but this pistol shot? "Only the *custos,* you pompous fool," I whisper. High above us, we hear the man cursing "sodomites and bougers" as he chases trespassers off his gallery. He is notorious for his short and violent temper. The days when the Dom Tower guard ran his own tavern in the second-floor chapel are long gone.

"Darkness doesn't make you invulnerable, dear boy," Raphael insists, peering upward.

"I didn't know you cared."

"Nothing whatsoever. Still, best to hide that pretty face." Again the sardonic smile, then he disappears behind a bush.

WE'VE BEEN WALKING THE CLOISTERS and the Domkerkhof churchyard, two Academy students in search of some dirty work after a day listening to professors droning. It doesn't usually take long before someone approaches me, attracted by my youth and my clear countenance, unmarred by the pox. But for some reason the night watch has been out in force all evening, and the guards' whistling and rattling have scared away most of the regulars. I walk around for a while, before deciding to call it a night.

Two watchmen enter the ruins, carrying lanterns. One remains standing before the gate, while I see the other accosting someone with a hat like Raphael's.

*Where is Raphael?* I whisper his name and realise I am alone in the dark. The watchman's lantern moves in my direction, bobbing slowly. Suddenly I am rigid with panic, unsure where to go, certain I cannot stay here. I have visions of being arrested and interrogated, having to face the incredulous looks of my friends, the disapproving gazes of my professors. From the corner of my eye I see an arm beckoning from behind the Holy Font, but I hardly notice.

"Gysbert! This way!" Raphael's voice tears me loose. Quickly I shuffle in his direction.

The Holy Font is not actually a baptismal font, but our name for a broken, slanting, and half-buried column popular with devotees of certain acts the custos would no doubt find horrifying. Quite certain the trail of fluid running down its side isn't rain water, I hesitate before crouching behind it. Only when I see the guard looking in my direction, I duck down.

Too late. Has he spotted me? We try not to breathe as we listen to the footsteps approaching through the grass.

But the lantern bobs past. I nudge Raphael and nod at the darkened gate. "Coast is clear."

His breath hisses between his teeth. "No. That's the trap. They're waiting outside." He points at a narrow opening next to another pillar stump. "We go past the Thomas chapel."

"And then? The Munster Gate is closed by now."

He grins. "But have you seen the ivy on the wall there? Come on."

I watch how he quickly moves over to the pillar stump. There he looks around, before beckoning me. I get up, but immediately a loud voice commands us to come out, by order of the bailiff. I drop to the ground again. When I peer through the shrub, a watchman is standing next to the pillar stump, and Raphael is gone.

I crawl backwards, my coattails brushing the dirt, until my shoes touch the crumbling remains of a wall. The rough ground scrapes my hands painfully, and suddenly I smell my own sweat.

A third lantern appears. On my knees I shuffle sideways, trying to hide under a huge wall ornament partially buried in the grass. By now I've completely lost my bearings: the ruins of the former cathedral are a place of pits, unexpected corridors, and black holes. And in the darkness, we like to joke here, all holes are the same.

I crawl underneath yet another shrub, losing my hat to the bramble and tearing my stocking. Then the ground gives way.

I grab at the branches, but immediately I slide down into a pit. Sand covers my face as I claw upwards. Spitting and coughing, I slither down a steep incline, until I finally land painfully on a floor of damp earth.

When I've wiped enough grit from my eyes to look around, I see what appears to be a subterranean passage. Next, a pair of sandal-shod feet. I look up. A swarthy face gazes down at me in astonishment.

THE YOUNG MAN IS DRESSED as if for a stage play: a loose brown tunic, leather bands around his wrists, black hair cut short. His eyes reflect the light of the small terracotta oil lamp in his hand. *Peasant boy*, I think, looking at his bare muscled legs and arms. I'm not surprised: the Domkerkhof attracts both low and high alike, and in his loose clothes he looks like the Ganymede of the ancient Greeks, just before Zeus abducted him. Our unnatural desires are nothing if not quintessentially human.

When he speaks I don't recognise his strange tongue, though it has a hint of Spanish.

"Who are you?" I ask. "Don't you speak the language?"

He is silent, his eyes blinking rapidly. His next words are Latin.

A learned peasant boy, then. For a moment I'm so surprised his words slip past me. It must be some Vulgar dialect, because I have difficulty following it. "Nil intellego," I say. "Tardus. Tardior." *Slower.*

Whistles and muffled voices sound from above. The night watch is still there.

Touching the cold stone wall, at first I guess I'm in a crypt underneath the ruined nave. Do they know of this place? Any moment now I expect them to call down, demanding that I come out.

I look at the stranger's face. At least he doesn't know who I am, and that somehow reassures me. "I need help," I say. "Hide me. Please."

As HE WALKS AHEAD OF ME, the dark unfolds into a narrow corridor with openings on both sides. Pulling aside a curtain, he ushers me into a smell of leather, wax and old sweat. Dim light reveals neatly made bunk beds and empty coat pegs along the walls. I recoil when my hand brushes against a mail shirt hanging from one of the pegs. But most unsettling is the corner fireplace, which seems to double as a kitchen: a piece of dark bread and a chunk of dried meat lie on a wooden plate. The room looks and smells as if it's been lived in for ages. This is not a crypt.

"What is this place?" I whisper. "Who are you?"

His answers come rapidly, and my sadly underused academic Latin is hardly up to the task. He tells me I shouldn't be here—something I wholeheartedly agree with—because my clothes are *barbarica*. His *cohors* is charged with guarding the *traiectus*. I am lucky that his *centuria* is out, otherwise I would have been removed from the *castellum* immediately. He is the only one left, because…. The rest of his words flow past me in a meaningless stream.

He must be insane, living underground, imagining himself to be…what? A Roman legionary? Nevertheless I decide to play along, because listening to his raving is preferable to spending the night in a cell underneath City Hall. So I tell him I'm being chased by enemies, but I don't say who. His grin is more uncertainty than mirth.

There is some parchment on a low table, next to a reed pen and an inkwell. I see some kind of map or diagram, but when I lean in to look closer, he pushes me away. "Praeteritum arcanum adhuc," he says. *The past is still secret?* What does that mean? For a moment there is something else in his eyes, something complex, old, ancient. Then it's gone.

I step back. There's a stack of parchment in a corner, and I see more under the beds. Unsure about how to continue, I ask his name. When he tells me, I'm not sure I hear him correctly. But I repeat after him: "Ilurtibas," and he nods and grins again. He can hardly be called handsome, yet each time he grins he raises his left eyebrow, which gives him a pleasantly rakish look.

"Gysbert Coolsaet," I say, laying my hand on my chest.

He tries, but his tongue is so used to his soldier's Latin and his own strange vernacular that it's hard to recognise my name on his lips.

"And where are your comrades?" I ask, as casually as possible. I don't want to run the risk of confronting a roommate who fancies himself the king of Spain.

A shadow passes over his face. "I don't know."

"Well…when will they be back?"

Confusion in his eyes. "I don't…. They left in the past, and the past is hidden. Yesterday…last week…" He shakes his head. "Centuries ago? Anyhow, I couldn't join them. So I started writing. To pass the time."

I gaze at the stacks of parchment. Time has certainly passed here.

And that's it. Even my tolerance for insanity has its limits. "I'm sorry. I'm tired and cold." My legs feel as if they are about to give way. "Are we safe here? Can I take some rest?"

He points at one of the low bunks, saying that it's probably all right to sleep there.

WHEN I WAKE UP, MY teeth are chattering, though I have my coat wrapped tightly about me. The fireplace is cold. In the faint lamplight I see him watching me from a bunk across the room. He has a thin blanket, which I eye longingly.

I'm not used to sharing a bed with a soldier, not even a scholarly one, but I'm relieved when he beckons me over.

WE END UP IN EACH other's arms, fumbling and uncomfortable, our bodies somehow unwilling to come together, despite the cold and the closeness of the cramped bunk. After a while we lie still, as if poised in equilibrium. And we talk.

At least, we try. But his Latin is not an academic language. Strange meanings emerge from everything he says. Every word we speak, every gesture we make takes on special urgency, because we have so little common ground.

He tells of battles, campaigns, friendships, loss. Time becomes fluid when he speaks of centuries that might have been days, and nights that stretch on forever. Repeatedly he refers to himself as a *praeteritorum custos*, and gradually I realise he does not just think of himself as a soldier, but as a watchman: a guardian of things past.

"But what is there to guard?" I ask.

"All of it," he says, making a sweeping arm gesture. And again that ancient wisdom in his face, as if the young soldier is only a disguise. But it's just shadows, I know, and my imagination.

"This is a place of gods. Mithras was here, Wodan, and Hercules Magusanus. But before we arrived, before the Batavi and the Frisii lived here, gods were worshipped whose names even Jupiter and Minerva don't know. The god of the flight of the ruff in autumn. The goddess of the wind in the young reed. The god of the path the shadows of moving clouds trace across the fields. Their holy places, long gone. Their remains sink deeper and deeper. They must be protected."

"Against what?"

"The past must not be disturbed."

I am too tired to keep questioning. Drifting in and out of sleep, at one point I start awake from a dream in which I see Raphael waving at me from the bushes, before his face changes into that of a watchman. At the same time I'm always aware of Ilurtibas's warm and muscular body—right next to me, but somehow ages removed.

A PUNGENT SMELL OF BURNING wood wakes me. Ilurtibas is poking up the fire, his silhouette black against its light. The darkness in this place still feels like something timeless and eternal. My shoulders are stiff from the cold. I sit up and straighten my clothes. "I have to leave," I say. "Probably morning by now. Is there another way out?"

He nods silently, keeping his back turned to me. A more obvious expression of unease is hardly possible, so I get up, ready to leave.

But when he slowly rises and turns around I step back in shock. Instead of Ilurtibas's youthful face, a grey-haired old man looks at me. He wears the same tunic, but it hangs loose on his gaunt frame.

"Who…?" I have to clear my throat.

"I am called Ilurtibas. I think you…know me."

I shake my head. "You are not…where is Ilurtibas? I need him to show me the way out."

"And you think I don't remember? A senile old man, is that what I am?" He clacks his tongue. "Have it your way. But you're right, it is time for you to leave now. Come." He steps into the corridor and snaps his fingers with barely concealed impatience.

I hesitate. Waiting here for Ilurtibas would be the sensible thing to do.

The old man keeps looking at me. "You have trusted me this far, Gysbert. Why doubt me now?" The corners of his mouth turn up as he raises his left eyebrow. And the smile that yesterday was rakish, is a sardonic grin on this face: the bitter joy of someone who has seen too much. But it's the same grin.

As HE WALKS AHEAD OF me in the corridor, we pass other rooms similar to his. "Empty *contubernia*. None have returned yet." In his aged voice it sounds like a ritual incantation repeated daily.

Around the corner, I grow more mystified with every room we pass. There is a storeroom filled with jars of grain, another one with dried meat, stockfish, cabbage. One room looks suspiciously like a heathen temple, and there is even a simple bathhouse. But no sign of other people, anywhere.

At the end of a long passage we come to a low arch. And beyond it, the labyrinth starts.

It exists as little more than glimpses caught in the lamplight, as it moves and shifts along tunnels and pathways. The whole place seems to be made of walls, pillars, and arches, whole or broken, a bricolage of stone and masonry. Walls are built on top of each other, through each other, or next to rows of bricks supported by layers of pebbles, scattered over blocks of tuff. We pass the immense foundations of the Dom Tower, burrowing down through it all. When we go deeper, the walls become wooden stakes.

I come to a dead stop, wrapping my arms around me, shivering. Is this still Utrecht? "Where are we?"

"History," says the old man. He draws up his shoulders. "It sinks ever deeper. Look." He points at a rift in the wall.

Lights. Lights glimmering in the deep. Like looking down on the stars of an underworld firmament. But I've seen enough now. "Get me out of here," I whisper.

He nods. "The past wants to remain hidden." When he looks at me, it's as if his eyes have seen that past, all of it. His gaze bores into me, and I turn back to the rift again, afraid he sees too much. Then he beckons, and we walk along a broad tunnel to a double gate of weathered wood. "This is the *via principalis*. I can't leave the castellum. You must find your own way out." He puts a hand on my shoulder.

I pull open the gate and step into a draughty corridor. When I glance back at him, the old man is gone. It's the young Ilurtibas standing there, an unreadable expression on his face. Before I can ask him where he was, he raises his hand and pushes the gate shut.

AFTER WE DELEGATE TERVAERT TO fill us another bottle of Rhine wine at the tavern, I throw in an offhand remark: "Well, what about that rumour of a secret subterranean labyrinth?"

The morning's lectures concluded, four of us are spending a sunny afternoon under the trees of the pall-mall court just outside the city walls, watching the youths swing their mallets, whistling at the girls. I haven't seen Raphael for days, but ever since I emerged from the strange underground warren, I've been thinking of Ilurtibas's words.

"Rumour?" Cuylman's speech is slurred. His soiled wig is hanging lopsided on one ear. Three sheets to the wind already, and the pockmarks on his face have taken on a purple hue. "There's all kinds. All kinds of. Stuff. Beneath the Domkerkhof. That's not rumour. That's fact."

"Such as?" Nieuwmeyer demands. I wait in silence. Cuylman is the man to ask, I know, given his other interests besides drinking and whoring.

"The Dom wasn't the first cathedral built there. Actually."

"First to collapse when the bishop sneezed, though," Nieuwmeyer snorts.

"Franks. Franks had some kind of castle." Cuylman pushes a finger in his ear and wiggles it vigorously. "And the Romans."

I try not to show my surprise. "What about the Romans?" I ask.

Inspecting the brownish glob on his finger, Cuylman says, "Latest thinking, they had some kind of garrison here. Camp or some such. Lots of coins around."

"Coins?" Nieuwmeyer rubs his nose. "Know your Pliny, old man. Roman soldiers were paid in salt."

Cuylman gives him a glassy stare.

Then Tervaert returns from the Maliehuis with two flasks of wine. "Call that a rumour?" he says, refilling our cups. "Let me tell you gentlemen a rumour. Have you heard about Peixoto?"

"What's he done now?" Cuylman asks.

"Appears to've gotten himself collared near the Vreeburgh privies, a few days ago."

I feel every hair on my arms standing up. Raphael. Rumour has transformed Domkerkhof into Vreeburgh, but I dare not correct it. I take a swig of wine to hide my apprehension.

"Privies? What's wrong with the canal?" Nieuwmeyer, always slower on the uptake.

"That's disgusting," says Cuylman. "No surprise from a cursed Israelite, but really…a filthy *bouger*? Never expected that." He leans heavily against the wooden fence surrounding the playing field. "Now, him!" he blurts, pointing over the fence. "Him I'd suspect."

An elderly man with an old-fashioned black wig and a walking stick strolls along the path, two servants at a respectful distance behind him. The embroideries on his elegant pale blue justaucorps and waistcoat glitter in the sunlight, and his buckled shoes are perfectly polished.

"Renswou, Baron Big Nose," says Tervaert. "Well, what do you expect? Plenipotentiary for Utrecht at the Peace of 1713, no? That close to that many foreign diplomats, anyone's bound to pick up some of their…habits."

"Prattle," I say. "That's sixteen years ago." But I'm not even fooling myself. I've seen the baron strolling the Dom cloisters, I've recognised the look in his eyes, the hunger, the dull resignation to the certainty that his wealth will buy him everything but true companionship, genuine brotherly love. I've even heard whisper why he is called "that gentleman with the big nose."

"So where's Peixoto?" Nieuwmeyer asks.

"Locked up at Catheryne Gate, I presume. Maybe City Hall." Tervaert smirks.

The world seems to recede. As I close my eyes and steady myself against a tree, a memory surfaces: Raphael Peixoto, two years my senior, opening a tavern door and motioning me into a new world which I had never known existed. The Wine Wreath near Saint Paul's Gate offered drink, merriment, and what Raphael called "the dirty work." At first I loathed the ostentatious effeminacy of many of the regulars—the powdered perruques, the rouged cheeks, the vulgar perfumes—but then I found that the company of stable hands and cab drivers could be just as fulfilling. My world expanded, and I, Gysbert Coolsaet, son of a respectable merchant family, learned things about myself which would otherwise have been kept hidden, locked away as unspeakable secrets, silently poisoning my being.

"What's this, Coolsaet?" pulls me back to the present. "Can't hold your drink? Gentlemen, the boy is in need of a glass of orgeat!" Tervaert starts bawling the latest drinking song.

Cuylman is sitting in the grass with his chin on his chest, which allows me to make a joke of it, but the joy of the afternoon has evaporated. I excuse myself, pleading academic duties.

As I cross the Malie Bridge and look at the arbours and pleasaunces on the Lepelenburgh bulwark where the well-to-do are enjoying themselves in the sun, oblivious to anything beyond their garden fences, I feel as if I'm invisible. I want to scream, I want to tell somebody about Raphael, I want to ask what's going to happen to him. I'm not even sure if it's Raphael I care about, or the sudden revelation that whatever happens to him, might at some point also happen to me.

If my faith were stronger, I would pray. If I were a papist, I would go to confession. But prayer has not helped me in the past, and I'm not sure that God even listens to someone like me. I hope Raphael's God listens to him. His father is one of the Jews of the Portuguese nation, allowed back into Utrecht during the great speculation craze of 1720. They needed his money then. They don't need him now. They certainly don't need his son.

IN MY ROOM ABOVE THE wine merchant's shop, I try to concentrate on my reading. Raphael has lent me his copy of Spinoza's *Opera posthuma*. The infamous freethinker's *Ethica* distracts me for a while, but my thoughts keep wandering, so later that evening I go out and roam around the city for a while. The urge to talk to someone has become unbearable, but I don't dare trust anyone not to hand me over promptly to the bailiff— the only difference between a Jew and a sodomite being, as far as my social circle is concerned, that a sodomite might actually be willing to part with a guilder or two in exchange for his pleasure.

Of course I end up on the Domkerkhof again. The shrub behind the Holy Font is undisturbed, the tunnel entrance surprisingly easy to find. As I slide down the hole, I don't even wonder why no one else has discovered this tunnel. In a place like this, apparently other laws hold.

Before I can lose my way in the dark he appears in front of me. It is Ilurtibas, but he is neither the young man nor the old codger. This is Ilurtibas in the prime of his life, a soldier and legionnaire. "Quis es?" he demands in a deep and resonant voice, and it's almost as if the echoes call the corridor behind him into being, as if nothing existed there before his footsteps solidified it.

"A friend of mine has disappeared," I blurt, ignoring his question. Lord, but the relief of getting that off my chest, even in halting Latin!

In his contubernium I ramble on about Raphael, about how we met during a lecture on Saint Augustine, how he showed me what lay beyond the limits of my world, how he taught me to navigate the currents of our dark desires. I tell him how I feel about Raphael—something I have never told Raphael himself. I tell him that I sometimes imagine us to be Achilles and Patroclos, or Alexander and Hephaistion, and I try to explain why that feeling makes me stronger, as if it helps me to become a better man. Other people would be shocked at what they'd perceive as a tale of innocent Christian youth corrupted by the perverted Jew, but Ilurtibas just listens.

I'm not sure he truly *hears*, though. His face is still a hard mask. Finally he asks, again, "Who are you?"

Have I misunderstood after all? "Gysbert Coolsaet," I say, unsure. "Remember?"

"That is what you have told me. But you shouldn't be here. I know who let you in, and that shouldn't have happened. It's my duty to throw you out."

"Ilurtibas…" I shake my head in exasperation. Now that my story is done, the questions return. "Who are you? Every time you look different. I've heard tales of witchcraft, but this…and your writing…" I glance at the parchment on the table. When I look up, I involuntarily take a step back, and hit my head on the edge of a bunk bed. The soldier is gone, and now the old man is standing in front of me again.

He looks past me. "Not my duty to tell you. Not anymore. The duty used to be everything, long ago. The watch, the camp life." His gaze glides across the parchment. "The *historia*. But now I only have to make sure there's a proper ending." He looks up at the low ceiling. "History moves in waves, you know, one flowing over the other. A new wave washes away the sediment of an older one. But never completely. There are places in this world where waves meet and strengthen each other, where they rise up in a peak in which time is bundled together, into a single point full of meaning and possibility." He gestures at the sheets on the table. "The history of this place turns into the future. It is a *Metamorphoseon* my spirit has moved me to write, in which all things are turned into new and strange forms. I see now that you have not been written yet. I thought you were just a local who had wandered in by chance. But no one else has done so in centuries. You belong to later times, the waves above, the higher layers, the temples of that new god, the cruciform foundations."

I'm surprised at how much I want to accept his words. He sounds like a doting old man, but I remember the labyrinth outside this room, this barracks, and there is seductive logic to it.

This time he does not stop me. The handwriting is dense, virtually unreadable, and what little I can make out is colloquial and full of neologisms—Ilurtibas is no Spinoza or Ovid. It appears to be a painstaking description of the tunnels, in dated entries. As I leaf through a few pages, I see Julian dates but no *ab urbe condita* or even a single consular year, no starting point to his calendar. There are maps that seem to change from year to year, as if the maze is in constant transmutation.

Feeling slightly embarrassed, I ask, "Who was emperor when you...?"

"The august Antoninus Heliogabalus is princeps," he says without hesitation in a deep and powerful voice. I don't dare to look up, but I know the soldier is standing next to me again.

As I try to remember the position of Heliogabalus in the ranks of the heathen rulers, Ilurtibas grabs my shoulder so hard it hurts. I look up in surprise, and now it's the young man looking down anxiously. "Who is princeps...where you are from?"

It's difficult talking to three different people at once. How to explain that his empire fell apart a long time ago? "We..." I begin. "The Dutch people only recognise the absolute authority of our Lord Jesus Christ the Redeemer. Our leaders are just regents."

I expect him not to believe me, but he nods slowly. "New gods have taken over. Old ones are buried. Again." He sits down. Elbows on his legs, he stares at the ground. "I didn't know. Not really. But it's clear, isn't it?" He looks around the small room, the empty bunk beds, the dark doorway. "Buried," he whispers. "It's been so silent here. More silent every day, ever since you turned up."

I sit down next to him, self-consciously putting my hand on his shoulder. "Ilurtibas..."

But he turns away and says gruffly, "Get out."

As DAYS AND THEN WEEKS pass, eventually panic gives way to reason, a relentless academic detachment forcing me to think things over logically. I ask around, only to realise that I don't know any of Raphael's friends. Our fellow students just repeat the rumours Tervaert has been spreading with obvious relish. I visit Raphael's rooms, but his landlady only scowls at me. When I muster up the courage to inquire at the Magistrates'

Court, it leaves me none the wiser. At night I roam the Domkerkhof in vain.

And finally I decide on another way.

THE DOM TOWER CARILLON ANNOUNCES the half hour when I see Baron Renswou alighting from his carriage. He takes a pinch of snuff from a small jewelled box, then enters one of the coffee houses on the north side of the Domkerkhof. I take up position against the ruined wall, underneath a relief showing three women spinning a single thread. The pagan image depicting the inevitability of fate seems fitting all of a sudden.

I try to keep an eye on the entire street. This is not a reputable area, and already I see some drunks brawling on a nearby corner. High above me I hear the tower custos screaming again. He must have a clear view of the men using the place as a rendezvous spot. I pull my hat down over my forehead. The cheap wig and smelly clothes I'm wearing belong to the wine merchant's assistant. I must avoid another confrontation with the night watch.

When Renswou comes out, I follow him as he makes his way past the tower to Oudmunsterkerkhof square, and on through the cloister gate. He turns right, so I go left, staying in the shadows, hurrying along the walls surrounding the moonlit courtyard. On the other side I slow down and lean against the cloister wall, hands behind my back, one leg casually crossing the other—the way I've seen them do it, the baron's boys.

Other men walk past, arms akimbo, elbows stuck out with clear intent, trying to catch my eye, but I carefully ignore them. I've been here so often, but suddenly it feels like the first time again, the day after Raphael had explained what was going on, giving advice, warning about who to avoid.

From the corner of my eye I see Renswou approaching. Heart pounding in my throat, I force myself to relax. The wig itches fiercely.

He walks past me, and I remain motionless, waiting. A moment later he approaches again, closer this time. Then I feel his shoe stepping on my toes.

I push up the brim of my hat. He looks into my eyes. For a moment I'm afraid he will see *me* instead of the simple boy I'm pretending to be. But his hunger is unmistakable. Suddenly I feel pity, followed by misgivings over what I'm about to do.

He turns and walks off. I push myself away from the wall.

In his carriage, riding slowly through the countryside just outside the city, the old baron mutters what he wants me to do, and what his driver is going to pay me afterwards. He turns around and pulls aside his justaucorps. I make as if to oblige, but instead I lay my hand over his mouth, push him into the cushions and whisper, "I don't want money." He struggles, but not very hard. He is used to this game. Gently I pull off his wig, exposing a blotched pate. I can feel his surprise. "I want information."

Wɪᴛʜᴏᴜᴛ ʜɪs wɪɢ ʜᴇ ʟᴏᴏᴋs thin and frail in the little moonlight that enters the carriage. "You should make inquiry at the Magistrates' Court."

"I have. They won't tell me anything."

He shakes his head. "What do you think I can do, boy?"

"You have influence in government. You could find out…."

"I can tell you what they will probably do to your friend if he confesses to his unspeakable sin. At best he will spend the rest of his life rasping brazilwood, or he will be banished. More likely, being a Jew, he will be executed."

I am stunned. While Renswou fumbles for his snuff box, I try to regain my voice. "His unspeakable sin, but…it's your sin as well." *And mine.*

"How dare you?" he snaps. "What I do is of no concern to the likes of *you.* Anyway," he lifts a thumb tipped with sweet-smelling powder to his nose, "no doubt your friend is in solitary confinement under City Hall by now. He will be tried in secret and *extra ordinaris.*" He inhales and closes his eyes, the better to enjoy the tobacco. "If he is found guilty, you will not hear of him again."

I ᴅᴏ ɴᴏᴛ ᴋɴᴏᴡ ᴡʜɪᴄʜ Ilurtibas I will meet when I walk into his contubernium— the boy, the soldier, or the sage. He sits hunched over his parchment like an archetype, scribbling with his reed pen, observing, measuring, and fixing the history of his subterranean world.

"Those tunnels outside the gate," I ask him. "Where do they lead? How far?"

For a moment I'm afraid he won't answer me. But when he looks up, his face is that of the soldier. It isn't unfriendly, but it looks tired and resigned.

"I don't know," he says, and he puts down his pen with a controlled and patient movement, as if he is a busy father who knows he must make time for his children. "I am not allowed to leave the castellum. I must guard…."

"I need to get to into the City Hall cellars," I interrupt him. "Northwest of here. Maybe one hundred thirty *passus.*"

He frowns. "The gate road," he says. "Just outside the *porta sinistra.* It runs west to the *vicus.* There's a path north, along the wall. But it only leads down to the river."

"River? What river?"

He shows me a plan of the castellum and the vicinity, in brown ink on parchment. I try to reconcile his topography with my crowded Utrecht inner city. I feel faint, unsteady, as if I am torn between two realities. A river ran there, hundreds of years ago?

But I see Raphael's face before me, and imagining what they'll do to him is worse than actually knowing. "Show me that path," I say. "Please."

Again we follow the via principalis to its end. As he pulls open the gate, he looks back at me. "What if you get caught?"

"I won't," I say, desperately feeling for the certainty in those words.

"Is this friend really that important to you?"

"I…" What more can I tell him that I haven't already? What language does he understand? "He is my brother-in-arms."

He is silent. Then he turns away and points into the dark. "Go then, fool. There's your path." Before I know it he is gone, leaving me standing with a small oil lamp in my hand.

"Ilurtibas!" I call after him, but the corridor has already disappeared.

THE ONLY SOUNDS IN THE damp tunnel are my breath and the shuffling of my shoes on the sandy floor. I don't know how far I walk before it forks into a number of narrower passages with small holes in the walls. I press my eye to one of them and draw a sharp breath. Three women are sitting chained to the floor of a bare room.

Dungeons. I must be under City Hall already. Frantically I start looking through every one of the spy holes.

I HARDLY RECOGNISE HIS FACE under layers of grime. Raphael lies alone in a tiny cell. His lower legs are blackened and bloody.

I have to call his name four times before he reacts.

"Father?" he whispers. "Have you come?"

The dullness of his voice scares me. "It's me. Gysbert. Are you hurt?"

"Gysbert?" He rolls aside, curls up and turns away, as if he does not want me to see him. Then he reaches out one hand to me. "Gysbert, I've written letters, I've asked the warden, but…" A tremor in his voice. "Everyone here calls me filthy names. Father won't come. He won't see me. I've begged him to, I only ask for a visit. A clean shirt. A bit of money. But he won't…" His voice breaks and he falls silent.

"What have they done? Why are you here?" My teeth are chattering, but not from the cold. What happened to the cheerful, insouciant young man I knew? How have they managed to break his spirit so thoroughly?

"Thumb screws," he whispers. "Flogging. Shin screws. But after the strappado, I couldn't hold out any longer. Gave them names. May have given them yours, can't… can't remember." After a while he continues, "Why won't Father come see me? Just once? Maybe bring a clean shirt?"

"Raphael! Listen! What's going to happen? Is there a date set for the trial?"

The painful sound in his throat is laughter, I realise. "Trial? Trial was last week. Our sin isn't tried in public."

"But, then…what?"

"Tomorrow…" he whispers. He pushes himself up to look at me. I try not to recoil from the naked desperation in his eyes. "Go. Ask Father to come quickly. Please. Ask him to bring a clean shirt."

But Raphael's father is out of town. When I call at his house, Gideon Peixoto is in Antwerp and will not be back for some days. His wife tells me that no letters have arrived from City Hall. She immediately starts writing a request to the Magistrates' Court, dismissing me with an accusatory look that suggests my bad influence is entirely to blame for her son's predicament.

Back in my room, I sit motionless on a stool. The darkness swirls around me, conjuring up images of Raphael's torture, mingled with visions of Ilurtibas's "hidden history." I'm so exhausted I can't tell which is which.

Noise from downstairs startles me awake. Gruff, insistent male voices interspersed with the habitual sarcasm of the wine merchant's wife. Then they come stumbling up the stairs. And I remember Raphael's words, ominous in their simplicity. *I may have given them your name.* Before the consequences of that remark sink in, I'm at the side window, pushing up the sash. Someone raps on the door. "Mister Coolsaet?"

The narrow alley is pitch dark.

"Mister Coolsaet! By order of the bailiff of the city of Utrecht…" When I let myself drop, a cart breaks my fall, but I cry out as my foot doubles under me.

A hoarse shout above me. Then, someone at the window. "He's down there! Get him!"

Ignoring the pain in my ankle, I limp into the dark as fast as I can. Behind me I hear pounding on the locked alley door. I curse myself for my carelessness—but I'm also stunned. How can this be happening to me, a respectable citizen from a reputable family?

The other end of the alley opens on the Old Canal. Escape, for now. But nauseating fear gnaws its way up out of my stomach. There is nowhere to go. My friends, my family—the bailiff's men may be lying in wait anywhere.

"He betrayed you," says Ilurtibas the soldier.

"He was tortured."

"But he wasn't strong enough. He betrayed you and yet you wish to save him."

I know I should flee, leave the city, maybe even the country. If I have committed a crime, then the fact that I committed it with a Jew makes it twice as grave. Why am I still here? "But I can't leave him to his fate," I say. "I owe him this."

I expect disapproval in his eyes, but to my surprise I see understanding: friendship means loyalty. He nods resolutely. "Then it's your duty."

And somehow his words transform it into a commitment, weighing on my shoulders like chainmail. Fleeing the bailiff wouldn't be half as difficult as fleeing my responsibility now. I close my eyes. "But how?"

That sounds like a request for help, which I tell myself wasn't intentional. But the words are hanging between us now, and there I leave them.

Of course it's not that easy. When I open my eyes again, the young Ilurtibas stands before me with a brooding look on his face. "You've met the old one," he says.

"The...yes."

He bites his lip. "You see? He thinks I don't know. He thinks he is the end of everything. But I write the historia too, and I read his words. They're always *conclusions*. As if he is the end of everything, and after him there's nothing."

I remain silent.

He takes hold of my shoulders. "Do you understand what that means for *me*?" he asks ferociously. "I'm only here to support his decisions. As if I only exist to give meaning to his life." There is a fierce longing in his eyes now. "I had a life, myself. I was a legionary. We are from Hispania, *pia fidelis*, faithful and loyal. We're only auxiliaries, without rights in Rome. They promised us citizenship after our service is done. But how can I earn that honour when I'm buried here?" He grabs my head with both hands and pulls it even closer. "Your friend betrayed you. And now you want to help your betrayer. I have never witnessed such an act of...friendship, of humanity." He steps back and turns away. "You must save him."

"I know."

"For me," he whispers.

The only sound in the room is the crackle from the fireplace. I feel I should go. Find Raphael and get him out, somehow. No plan, no courage, but I take a deep breath and step towards the door.

The old man Ilurtibas blocks my way. He looks past my shoulder. "It's more difficult for some, you know," he says pensively. "Especially the boy... He isn't used to seeing people. You've given him things to think about. Is that good? We will see. He is still dreaming. Just like you. As he gets older he will learn the meaning of duty, and it will chafe him like a pair of ill-fitting *caligae*, but it will also give him purpose. He will find tranquility in the daily watch, in the compiling of the historia."

There is a note in his voice that makes me wish it was that simple for me. But my task is of a different order. "And you?" I ask.

He produces a sheet of parchment covered in diagrams and symbols. I recognise the layout of the castellum, but with a map of the city superimposed. The route to City Hall is outlined in red ink. A web of narrow tunnels is drawn between and underneath the prison cells. One of the cells is marked with a strange sigil.

The ink is still wet. I look up.

"Me?" He smiles. "My task is nearly done. I only have to make sure there's a proper ending. As always."

THE MAP GUIDES ME ALONG the threads woven between the cells. Unlike the first time I was here, I see where to go now. In some places the corridors are no broader than shoulder-width. Steep and narrow stairs sometimes make me stumble, almost spilling oil on the parchment. The architecture here seems to shift as I move through. I'm quite sure there are some passages I walk more than once. But when I round the last corner after one particularly twisted series of gangways, there he lies.

Somehow I have entered Raphael's cell. I look around, feeling the edge of the opening through which I came in, to make sure I can find it again. Ilurtibas's command of geometry is powerful but unstable.

Raphael lies curled up on his side, facing the wall. I kneel down and gingerly touch his shoulder. "Raphael, it's me."

Again it takes me several tries to coax a reaction out of him. When he turns his head and sees me, he closes his eyes. "They've got you too," he whispers. "Gysbert, I'm sorry, I'm so sorry...."

"No! I'm here to rescue you. We're going to leave. Can you get up?"

"There's no leaving this place." I can hardly hear his words, whispered into the filthy straw underneath his head. "Lasciate ogni speranza, voi ch'entrate."

"That's the spirit. Quotes," I say, joking to ward off his despair, and mine. I start hauling him upright. "Quotes all the way to Paradiso."

"It's too late. Listen!" He grabs my wrist. "Can't you hear them?" He stares at me, his eyes wide open. I hear footsteps approaching in the corridor, muted voices, keys clinking.

No time to lose. "Come on. Now!" I pull his arm over my shoulder and slowly get to my feet, trying to support him at the same time.

A key in the lock. Before we reach the back wall the door swings open. An astonished silence. Then: "What in the name of... You! Stand still!"

Another voice: "What's going on?"

We've almost reached the opening. I stretch out one arm to steady us against the wall. But there are swift footsteps behind me. Hands grab my shoulders and pull me back. Raphael slides to the ground. I thrust my free elbow backwards into the guard's chest, and I hear a satisfying grunt. But before I can reach down to Raphael, something connects with the side of my head. There is a moment of blinding light.

I WAKE UP TO THE sound of someone breathing heavily. A hard floor presses into my back. The small flame of an oil lamp throws flickering shadows against a rough, tuff-stone wall. I groan.

The heavy breathing ceases. "Awake?" Raphael's voice.

I turn my head. He is sitting against the wall, his ruined legs in front of him.

"What happened?" I manage. "Where are we?"

Raphael looks at me. "He went back, Gysbert. After carrying us here. He went back. He didn't need to, but he did."

"Who?" I ask, though there can be only one answer.

"He appeared out of nowhere, some rift in the wall I'd never seen before. So strange." He shakes his head. "Knocked them both down, then brought us here."

Pain throbs in my head when I try to get up. I have to pause and squeeze my eyes shut when I'm sitting on one knee. "How do you feel?" I ask.

"Gysbert…" He looks up at me. "He wants me to take his place. Says history must be guarded. Says he shouldn't have left his…his castellum, whatever that means." His grin is painful. "Like a fairytale, eh? A life for a life. Balance must be maintained, all that… As if there can be anything within Creation that is not in balance. *Ethica* says…" His voice fades to a mumble.

"Shh." I push myself up the rest of the way. "Rest. I'll be back for you."

"But it's useless. They'll find us here."

I see the oil lamp and the map lying next to it, neatly folded. "No, they won't," I say grimly. "You'll be safe here. Sleep." I grab the lamp and the map, and I start walking.

THE EARLY-MORNING CANAL SERVICE TO Amsterdam is packed. Inside the horse-drawn boat no one pays attention to two hungover students, and we try our best to look the part, in our shabby clothes and rumpled hats. The sweet pipe smoke filling the cabin helps me relax and accept the uncertain new reality in which I suddenly find myself.

I don't want to think beyond the next few hours. Handing Raphael the bottle of wine, I say, "We'll be there around two. Might as well take our leisure."

Raphael is still pale. He winces as he tries to arrange his legs more comfortably in his borrowed clothes, without causing the weals on his back to start bleeding again.

"What did Renswou say?" he asks.

The baron was none too pleased when I turned up on the doorstep of his townhouse that morning, demanding money and clothes in exchange for my silence about his scandalous behaviour. I feel sullied and ashamed by that bit of blackmail, but I also know Renswou will be the last one to get hurt.

"He told me the Dom Tower custos has been apprehended for disturbing the peace. The man is acting as an informer to save his own hide. There'll be public prosecutions. But we'll be safe in Amsterdam, for now."

"No." Raphael shakes his head. "No public prosecutions. Not in this God-fearing Protestant country. The *peccatum mutum* is the sin of Catholics and sybarites. Of the French, the Italians. They'll never admit its existence in the Republic."

The boat lurches. Raphael stifles a groan as his back shifts against the wooden boards.

"You could have stayed," I say softly. "Regain your strength. Guard the labyrinth, like Ilurtibas asked."

"I refuse that role," he mutters vehemently. "Let it lie unguarded. I pray for the day when an enterprising antiquary puts his shovel in the ground to open up history as it should. Otherwise nobody will ever know which Utrechtenaar they killed last night. Or how many more they will kill." He shivers. "They'll make sure nobody remembers us, you know. They'll burn our faces and bury us beneath the gallows. They told me that's how they do it." He pauses. "I pray for the day when anyone who even hears the word 'Utrechtenaar' will remember who they killed here. Finally he glances at me. "Will Amsterdam really be safe?"

What is "safe"? Did Ilurtibas believe himself safe in his barracks? I think back to the tunnels, the damp darkness, the close corridors magnifying the sounds of my feet and my panting. I run and I run, my lamp unsteady in my hand, the shadows dancing wildly just ahead. When I reach the cell, it's empty and the door is open. Am I too late? I search the rest of the dungeons, feeling like a ghost moving between the walls.

In the end I hear the execution chamber before I see it, and at first I don't dare to look through the hole in the wall. Finally I swallow and force myself to peer into the low, vaulted room.

I have seen executions before, large theatrical performances full of pomp and ceremony in front of City Hall: the bewigged magistrates appearing in their black blood-robes with red sashes, the presentation of the rod of justice, bells tolling, and the announcement of the sentence. The minister leading a communal prayer, the family members wailing.

But this is a sober and secret affair. A rabbi is saying the last prayer of the Israelites. A comforter-of-the-sick stands shuffling his feet behind him, and several guards are positioned against pillars. One of the few seated spectators must be the bailiff. A bored executioner leans against the back wall. I have to crane my neck to see the garrote standing next to him, and the person sitting on its narrow plateau.

He is not wearing his regular tunic, but a simple shirt. His hands are bound, lying in his lap, his feet strapped to the post of his seat. He sits upright, the thick rope already coiled around his neck.

How can they not notice this is not their prisoner? I want to call out to them, to set Ilurtibas free…only to have them go searching for Raphael again? I bite my lip and hit the wall with both fists.

The rabbi ends his prayer. The comforter, a layman clearly uneasy about the Jewish rites, steps to the front and asks loudly, "My son, for the sake of your immortal soul, do you repent of your hideous crime against God and nature?"

Ilurtibas stays silent. Then he looks straight at me. I press my forehead against the wall to look into his eyes, and I know he sees me. As the preparations draw to a close, I realise how presumptuous I am to think I could make his choice for him.

The executioner steps forward. Just before a black cloth is thrown over his head, Ilurtibas whispers two words at me. "*Mi contubernalis.*"

"My brother-in-arms," I say, as I pat Raphael on his shoulder. Whatever I tell him now, he knows it will only be to reassure him. I gaze out of the cabin's rear window across the water. The bubbles in the glass distort the silhouette of the Dom Tower receding in the distance, until I'm not sure if I'm seeing the tower, or just a gnarled dead tree trunk sticking up.

*Outside, the air is heat-dried and dirtier. Grace slits one eye—his old one, his real one. He faces a wide, paved street flanked by banks of windowless buildings, worn things built of metal and stone. They're so big, Grace can't see the rooftops. He can't see the sky through the atmosphere dome above the city, or the stars beyond. The noise is the worst of it, though, the hum of great engines, machines grinding. The air vibrates against his teeth as a vehicle big as one of the faithful's houses back home rumbles past. Grace stumbles backwards. A gust of hot air from a passing carriage stings his face.*

# A · MERC RUSTAD

WHEN GRACE OPENS HIS NEWLY crafted eye, the first thing he sees is wire. Thick cords of braided wire snaking like old veins up the walls. It's dim inside the surgical unit, but for all the black metal and mesh shelves, it *feels* clean, even in the heat. The air still has the unfamiliar taste of crude oil. Sweat sticks the borrowed clothes to his skin. He blinks, a flicker of pain in his head as the left eyelid slides down over cool metal buried in the socket.

He's awake and he's alive.

The anesthetic hasn't worn off. It's sluggish in his blood, an unpleasant burn at the back of his throat. It blurs the edges of his thoughts like too much bad wine. But it doesn't dull the deep-etched fear still unspooling through his gut. He survived the demon, survived his own execution. It's a hard thing to accept, even days later. He wants to touch the new eye, this machine part of his body, the forever-reminder what happened. Doesn't dare, yet.

"Back with us, eh?" says a raspy voice muffled by a respirator.

Grace turns his head, slow and careful. He dimly recalls the wire-tech mumbling about whiplash in his neck and the horrific bruising along his ribs and back where the welts are still healing. "Guess so."

The tech is a small man dressed in heavy surgical leathers that are studded with metal sheeting. Old blood speckles the apron and gloves; the metal and rivets are spotless. Only the skin on his forehead is visible under thick embedded glasses and a breather covering nose and mouth. "Nearly died on us, you did. Venom went right into the blood."

The demon's venom. Grace doesn't reach to touch his face where the sunspawn's claws took out his eye and split flesh to bone. He doesn't look down, either. A new shirt and worn jeans cover whatever scars the demon left on his belly and thighs. He shivers in the heat. He doesn't know if he can ever look at himself again; what will Humility think–?

Humility.

Grace trembles harder. Humility will never see him again.

*Don't think.* Harder a self-command than it should be. *Don't go back there.*

"He's tough."

The second voice jerks Grace's attention back to where he is. He turns his head again, wincing. He craves more anesthetic, and hates that he wants it. Numbness is just another way to hide.

Bishop stands near the narrow doorway, leaning against corded wire that bunches like supports along the wall. He's tall, broad-shouldered, dressed in travel-worn leathers with a breather mask over the lower part of his face. His mechanical eyes gleam dull green in the surgical bay's weak fluorescent glow.

Bishop–the man who saved his life. Bishop brought him here to this city, to the medical bay tucked somewhere in one of the vast districts that have no name Grace can recall. Grace's throat tightens. He ought to say something in greeting, or acknowledgement. All words feel hollow.

Bishop looks at Grace, unblinking, though he speaks to the tech. "Appreciate your help, Dee," Bishop says. "Your skill's always sharp."

"I do my best." The tech bobs his head. "Better if some of us live."

Grace flinches. He braces his hands on the metal gurney, gripping the edge until he can't feel the tips of his fingers. He should be dead–worse, even. Should be, and isn't.

Bishop straightens. "Grace, we need to go."

Grace shuts his eyes–the new optic sensor makes details too sharp, too real. He shoves himself to his feet. The world tilts.

Bishop's shoulder is under his arm before he falls. He can't recall if he walked into the Wire City or if he was carried. Not that he'll ask. *Forgive us our sins, oh Lord, forgive us–keep us safe from the Sun, from the Dark, and from our own–our own…*

He can't remember the rest of the litany, so he leans on Bishop and swallows down the shame of needing such help even to stand. His wrists carry the memory-weight of the heavy manacles that held him bound to the cross.

"Sorry about your boy," Bishop says to Dee in an undertone as he pivots towards the door. "Heard Jackob mention that."

Dee's throat clicks. "We can't save them all."

Grace tries not to flinch again. *God doesn't save the ones He should.* "How'd he die?" Grace asks, hoping that Dee's boy wasn't crossed and left as tribute to the demons that walk out from the sun.

"He didn't," Bishop says.

Outside, the air is heat-dried and dirtier. Grace slits one eye—his old one, his real one. He faces a wide, paved street flanked by banks of windowless buildings, worn things built of metal and stone. They're so big, Grace can't see the rooftops. He can't see the sky through the atmosphere dome above the city, or the stars beyond. The noise is the worst of it, though, the hum of great engines, machines grinding. The air vibrates against his teeth as a vehicle big as one of the faithful's houses back home rumbles past. Grace stumbles backwards. A gust of hot air from a passing carriage stings his face.

He can *feel* the space around him, despite the compact grid-like structure of the buildings. His home, Blessed Servitude, was a large town. But he was never lost inside the walls. Here, Grace has no reference points. It's a cavernous space that his senses are adrift in. Panic edges into him, sideways like it always does.

He needs to get away from here, but when last he tried to run, he was caught.

Bishop nudges him. Grace stumbles along, down a narrow alley.

Grace braces his legs and breathes deep. The city is too big to focus on, its massive presence overwhelming his senses. He needs something smaller, something saner. "What happened to the boy?" he asks, jaw gritted so his voice doesn't break.

Bishop shrugs. "The cityheart took him."

Grace grinds his teeth. "He's alive?"

Bishop's arm is tense. "Yeah, more's the pity. The cityheart takes easy targets. Kids, mostly. They're somewhere down inside, but the fumes kill them eventually."

Grace presses his spine against the alley wall. The metal is warm like sunbaked earth. He stares at Bishop, not hiding his anger. It's ingrained like fear into his heart. "No one does anything?"

Bishop's tone is flat. "There's nothing we can do."

"Nothing?" Grace should drop it. He's always been like this—clinging to the questions he shouldn't ask. Wanting what he can't have.

Bishop rubs his temple above the cluster of thin black-cased wires that trail from the corner of his eye down under his mask. "The cityheart shorts out Wired tech. Anyone dependent on it who goes down dies sure as not."

Grace digs his fingertips against the wall, the heat winding up his arms. "You're telling me everyone's going to leave the boy to die."

"Don't be so surprised," Bishop says. "No one intervenes in the offerings, either."

"Except you."

Bishop was once an offering and he escaped alive. Then he returned to Blessed Servitude, years later, faced down a demon and killed it to save a stranger. Grace doesn't know where that kind of strength comes from.

"I can't go into the cityheart." Bishop sighs. "Neither can Dee."

"Then let me," Grace says, before he turns coward.

Bishop shakes his head. "You'd–"

"Die?" Grace sets his jaw. "We'd not lose much, would we?"

Bishop is silent.

Grace turns his face away. He didn't mean it as a jab. He's shaking and can't make his body stop.

He was tried in Blessed Servitude and condemned to death; he was shackled to a steel cross as an offering for the demon. He deserved to die, and he was so fucking afraid of it. But then Bishop appeared from the wastelands, freed him and challenged the demon for Grace's sake. Grace fought at Bishop's side, unwilling to see someone else die because of him.

*You deserve to live*, Bishop told him when the fight was over, when Grace lay wounded, poisoned. Bishop offered him a choice between survival and mercy-killing. Grace knew he should have taken the knife, not Bishop's outstretched hand.

He still isn't sure he can believe Bishop's words. It's because of him Humility is dead.

"You gave me a chance," Grace says. He can't exist like this: breathing and walking and possessing space, all the while knowing that someone who aided him has lost family and no one else will *help*. "Dee should have that."

"I already paid Dee with credit," Bishop says. "You owe him nothing."

Grace jerks his head side to side and points at his implanted eye. Fuck the pain. "You paid him for parts."

Bishop grunts. "He stitched you up. It's his job."

"He saved my life." Grace can't meet Bishop's gaze again, or look up. There will be only steel and the glow of the dome above. He stares past Bishop at the seemingly endless line of flat doors set in the alley wall. "So did you."

Bishop is quiet again.

Grace swallows hard. "I need to make that matter, Bishop."

"It already does."

Grace concentrates on his breath. *Stay steady.* "I know." He doesn't believe it, and he hopes Bishop can't see that. "But if I can help that boy, I have to try."

Like his little brothers he left behind, like his friends and neighbors, his weakness will punish them more than it will ever hurt him. And he cannot endure that again.

Bishop turns his back on Grace. "If that's what you want, I'll show you where the access hatch is." His voice is tired. "You know you'll be on your own."

"I know," Grace says, and this time it's true.

"His name's Das," Bishop says.

The two of them stand by an open grate in a shallow circular indent between a crisscross of alleys. A few city workers in rubberized contamination suits watch. Musty air gusts up from the tunnel opening. Grace wonders how many willing suicides go down there.

"He was taken earlier this day. He won't have more than a few hours left."

"Understood," Grace says.

Bishop clasps his arm. Grace meets Bishop's eyes with effort.

"Good luck," Bishop says, quiet.

Grace nods, then lowers himself into the access hatch, down the short ladder to the dark tunnel below.

The access tunnel winds in a slow spiral downward. The first hundred feet are a sharp incline looping deep into the earth. It gentles out into an easy slope for the rest of the way. Dim red emergency lights line the tunnel and all he can think of is the blood spreading along the dusty ground.

Grace keeps a hand on the wall for balance as he walks. He's never liked enclosed spaces, but in the tunnel, he can't feel the city anymore. The relief is short-lived.

He steps into the huge, cavernous room that holds the cityheart and stops. The tunnel ends on a narrow platform that juts out over an abyss.

The cityheart is as big as a building, a cylindrical structure covered in riveted metal plates, rising from the center darkness. A giant fan turns methodically halfway up the bulk, stirring the thick, heavy air. Wire-mesh catwalks circle it, bare of railings. Huge throngs of corded, braided wires twist and loop away from the tower to jut out into the walls. Red emergency lights dip down, down along the cylinder's side, until it's too far to see anything more than a faint glow, and then blackness.

The machine, the cityheart, thrums with a giant, slow pulse. Each beat fills the air and reverberates in Grace's teeth.

He's never seen anything so massive and so *alive*.

His new eye goes dark. Grace starts, retreating into the tunnel again. Where can he run except back to the surface in defeat? No. Not like that. He makes himself stop. He squints, forced to turn his head as he searches the huge chamber.

There, lying in a small heap on the catwalk near the cityheart, is a child. Das? Grace spots no other bodies, but he doesn't look too deep.

[[Welcome.]]

The voice is not so much words as a great, intense weight that buries itself into his awareness. Yet he understands it the way he comprehends spoken language.

Grace sucks in a breath, unnerved. Wires of copper, steel, and a dark material he doesn't recognize peel away from the sides of the tunnel and gesture in a sweeping motion towards the great cylinder.

[[We get few visitors any longer,]] the cityheart says. [[Have you come for a purpose?]]

Unsteady, Grace takes a step forward. Wires turn like slender, delicate snakes, unwinding from the walls of the cityheart and the catwalks. They caress his back and shoulders. Grace startles and jerks away. He stumbles on the catwalk, his steps a shallow echo in the chamber.

[[You may stay. It is warm here and you will forget the world above.]]

*Easy death*, is what Grace hears, and he dares not answer. Bishop risked too much to save him once. But when he frees Das, Grace doesn't know what awaits him above. Bishop is lucky. Bishop knows his purpose, knows himself, knows what he wants.

Grace is lost.

"I can't." Grace points at the boy. "I came here for Das."

[[What awaits you upon return?]] The cityheart's voice is a deep purr. The wires creep forward again. [[Who will stay to see you rise? Is there truly anyone who will mourn your passing?]]

Grace flinches away. "Doesn't matter. Give me Das."

[[No. A child's mind is open and full of wonder, and wonder is a taste we have always craved. It is sweet and fresh, fleeting and delicate.]]

Grace swallows down bile. The cityheart's intense, vast hunger for the new presses against him. It craves things it has never seen or felt or imagined. It is…bored.

"We can make a deal." Grace edges along the catwalk; it's as wide as he is tall, but feels too narrow, and a misstep will plummet him into the abyss. "I give you something and you give me the boy."

Das is curled in a ball twenty paces away. Grace can't see if the boy is alive. *Lord, be kind. He doesn't deserve to die alone down here.*

[[And what could you offer, jaded as you are?]]

Grace shakes his head. If it only wanted a body, well, he was given to a demon already. The sunspawn's whispers still trill in the edge of his thoughts; recreated voices of the dead urging him to lie down and struggle no more. Does Bishop fight these thoughts every day? How does he live?

*Don't think about it.* It will paralyze him faster than firemoth venom. He was stung once as a boy, and only the curse of witch-breath kept him from dying in agony as his insides liquefied. That was the first time he met Humility—the older boy found him convulsing in the fields and carried him back to the safety of the town. Grace adored him and their friendship grew over the years until he loved Humility so fiercely it hurt.

"What haven't you seen before?" Grace asks, his voice hoarse.

[[That is an impossible question. You might be clever, old as you are.]]

Old? Grace almost laughs in surprise. He's not even twenty.

"I'm not from this city," Grace continues. "I've seen things no child could imagine."

There—Das shivers. The white gleam of an eye, red-rimmed with tears, peeks from over the boy's elbow where his arm is curled around his face.

The cityheart sounds curious now. [[What do you propose?]]

Grace takes a slow breath. One more step and he can reach down and scoop the child up. "Let me take him back. I'll give you—"

Wires snap away from the cylinder's walls and loop around Grace's wrists quicker than a blink. They pull his arms wide and pin him against the dully rumbling heart shell. Like he is being bound to the cross again. Grace chokes on a scream and throws his weight against the bonds in panic. Wire slices into skin. Blood wets his sleeve cuffs and drips to the steel floor.

[[Why should you give when we can take all?]] the cityheart murmurs, an honest question.

A gleaming needle-pointed wire hovers before his good eye.

Grace freezes. He can't abide the dark. When the demon wound its neural tendrils into his mouth and one ear, it easily found his fears pushed to the forefront of his mind. The dark, loss of sight, being left alone.

[[You are wise not to struggle. You will never remember what it is you lost.]]

The witch-breath in his blood—the heresy he was born with—strengthens his muscles and bones, makes him tougher, harder to kill. The Deacons found it easier to shoot Humility than him.

He strains and lifts one hand until his blood-slicked palm is between the wire and his face. Wire cuts deeper along the back of his wrist. The pain is not unbearable yet, and he welcomes it as distraction from the ache in his gut. "You're wrong," Grace says. "There is one thing you can never take."

[[Is there?]]

"I've seen the stars," Grace says. "But only with this eye. If you take that, you'll never know what they are."

The wire dips languidly and presses under his jawbone. With any pressure, it will pierce his throat, his tongue, and drive into his brain.

[[There are other ways.]]

"If you kill me," Grace says, "you'll never see."

[[And why is that?]]

"I told you. I'm not from your city. I'm not like the others. Can't you sense what's in my blood?" Bishop's scanners detected it easily enough. Surely a city can feel it too. "The witchery?"

The humming tone shifts a note. [[Others have given memories of stars. Lights in the night. Dim, warm, dull. There is nothing left of interest in them.]]

Grace's breath comes short, startled. "Those aren't stars." The ones he knows are cold and bright, spread vast across the dark sky. "You've only taken children from this city, haven't you?" The needle punctures skin, and blood trickles soft down his throat. "How many have been outside the walls or the dome? Any of them?"

A longer pause.

Grace fights for breath. "Let me leave with Das safe, and I will give you memories of the stars."

[[What leverage do you believe you have?]]

"Do you think you'll ever find another like me who comes down willingly?" Grace says. "You won't ever know what I've seen."

[[Perhaps.]]

Grace's muscles ache and the inexorable pull of the wires drag his arm back until he is pinned against hot, rusted metal. The needle flicks away from his chin and lightly touches the edge of his tear duct.

The same terror he couldn't fight when he saw the demon, its golden eyes alight in the sunset, burgeons in his chest once more. His knees give out. Wire holds him up, thicker cords sliding beneath his elbows and arms so the thinner wires don't slice through his wrists.

He shouldn't be afraid. The cityheart isn't a demon. It can't devour his soul. He can see Humility again—except if the cityheart gobbles his memory before it kills him, how will he remember who he loves, who he's looking for in Heaven?

Grace holds tight to the image of Humility's face: dark eyes and crooked smile, his jawline and the errant wisp of beard that always grew too fast to be kept shaved smooth. The wheat-shaped burn scar on his cheek and the way the left eyebrow was higher than the right. The confidence with which he walked; the calm he nurtured in his spirit so he would never be angry; the way his face lit up when he looked back at Grace.

"You can't have him," Grace snarls. "I already survived a demon digging though my head. You'll get nothing through force." It's a bluff. The sunspawn saw everything; the cityheart can do the same. "You kill me and you get nothing but a boy who's never seen the stars like I have."

The needle withdraws from the corner of his eye, and he feels it prick the base of his neck instead.

Grace grunts in surprise.

[[Very well.]]

Grace's voice catches. "How do I know you'll keep your word?"

[[Perhaps you will come back, when you understand how easy it is to forget.]] The cityheart almost seems amused. [[Remember the stars for us, and you and the child may go.]]

Sharp, violent pain slices into the back of his neck. The vast hunger of the machine hovers at the edge of his thoughts, waiting.

Das's life depends on him.

Trembling, Grace shuts his eye and remembers.

GRACE SAT ON THE ROOF of the old abandoned silo. It was flat, patched once or twice before it was left to the chokevine and creeping spider grass. The silo was the only tall structure in the Grove, and from this height, away from the light pollution inside Blessed Servitude, the huge expanse of the sky spread above them.

The stars were cold and bright, knife tips gleaming against black satin. No moon tonight to outshine them. Grace gazed up, unblinking, calmed by the open space he knew so well. Stars, he'd heard once, were distant suns in other worlds too far away to imagine. And the light that reached the sky came from the dying suns, corpse candles left by the ancient dead. It was just another story. Demons came from the sun, dull and hot as it faded. But demons didn't live in the stars. The stars were alive and bright, cold and beautiful.

Humility leaned his head on Grace's shoulder. "What do you think about when you look at the sky?" he asked.

Everyone was forbidden to be out past dark. Too many dangers lurked in the sand and along the roads. But Grace felt safe here, even with chokevine and ghost whippoorwill nests less than two meters below his feet on the side of the silo.

"I wonder what it'd be like to visit the stars," Grace said. "Just you and me."

Humility laughed. "How'd we get there?"

"We could walk," Grace said, smiling. "We could walk away from here, step onto the edge of the sky where it touches the horizon, and keep going 'til we touch the first star."

He didn't say, *We'd be safe and no one could take you away.*

He didn't say, *We'd never have to hide.*

He didn't say, *We'd never have to be afraid again.*

For a moment, Humility was quiet. Then he squeezed Grace's hand tight. "Maybe one day we will."

FASTER NOW, GRACE RECALLED THE moments he saw the stars clearest:

The nights he snuck away with Humility, hiding their time together with help from Humility's sister, who operated the delivery gates on the north wall.

The time he climbed up the Deacon's Clocktower and caught a glimpse of the sky during the Night of Reflection, when all lights were shut off.

That final night, when he and Humility gathered what belongings they could carry and snuck from Blessed Servitude, intent on stealing aboard a train to Pure Temperance where they would be unknown and free. They never saw the Deacons follow them. Grace kissed Humility in excitement as they neared the train depot. They were so close. Above them, the stars were bright, beacons of hope.

The Deacons came. Grace pushed Humility ahead of him as they ran. Gunfire chattered and something struck him in the back, flinging him to the ground. He didn't feel the pain at first. Not until he saw Humility fall, and saw the blood dark under the starlight.

The Deacons fished the bullet out of Grace's side, kept him alive, and brought him back to Blessed Servitude to pay for the crime of wanting to live with the one he loved. He was found guilty of forsaking his duty to Blessed Servitude and of unsanctioned intimate behavior. His sentence: he was to be an offering, staked to the cross at the edge of the road, and left for the demon that dwelled there. His death, his damnation, would be tribute to the demon and would ensure Blessed Servitude remained untroubled for another season.

And the final memory, the night Bishop killed the demon to save him and half-dragged, half-carried Grace to the Wire City. That one, brief glimpse was all Grace remembered before sunspawn venom and pain felled him unconscious: a splash of brightening sky and three stars sharp and knife-bright above the horizon. He could touch them, if he reached–

And then nothing.

THE WIRES RELEASE HIS ARMS. Grace pitches forward onto hands and knees and vomits. The air is hot, so close it presses like cloth against his nose and mouth. Grace fumbles at the back of his neck in search of the needle. It's gone.

The cityheart sighs, a deep, reverberating wave of pressure more than sound.

Grace wants to fold his arms over his head and scream. He knows the cityheart took something, but all he is left with is a word.

Stars.

He talked with Humility about it, and yet, all he remembers is lying on the flat silo roof and staring at the black, empty sky. The sky has always been dark at night. Hasn't it?

[[The child is yours. Go, before you tempt us with what else you have seen.]]

Grace chokes down a sob. He doesn't know for what he grieves—there are spots of emptiness where something was taken. He crawls along the catwalk, his one eye half-closed, scarcely able to see in the dim red light.

"Das." Grace curls his fingers around the boy's thin arm. "We're going back up."

IT'S A LONG CLIMB.

Grace is soaked in sweat, muscles trembling by the time he sees the change in light from the open access hatch. Das has crawled slowly ahead of him; Grace carried him when he could find the strength, but it isn't enough to last all the way.

"Grace?" Bishop's voice echoes in the tunnel.

"We're here," Grace manages. "Help him out."

Grace heaves Das up. The boy's foot kicks his face, jarring the dead metal eye. He grunts and turns his head. He's staring down the long, curving passage a step behind him. The incline would let him slide if he let go the iron rungs.

Just slide, down and down until he falls into infinite dark. There might be others down there, like Das; perhaps he might buy them free. If he let the cityheart take everything, perhaps it wouldn't hurt any longer.

"Grace."

Bishop's voice.

Slowly, Grace turns his face up.

Bishop leans down, hand extended. Again. *I'll help you, if I can,* Bishop told him. *If you want.*

Grace wants to know how Bishop can go on. How he can find any will to live when everything has been lost to him.

With a faint buzz and click, the wire eye flicks on again. Grace starts, almost losing his grip. His sight blurs a moment; his left eye is sharper, clearer with the metal and glass optic processing the thick air and smog. He can see farther.

He can see.

Humility's voice is clearer than the demon-song, and for a moment, it doesn't hurt so much to remember his voice. Grace focuses on that.

*I wonder what it'd be like to visit the stars. Just you and me.*

*How'd we get there?*

*We could walk.*

*Maybe one day we will.*

Grace takes Bishop's hand and lets Bishop help him up. The hatch clangs shut behind him.

Dee gathers Das up, incoherent words spilling between father and son.

A flicker of relief pushes back the hot, suffocating weight in Grace's chest. He almost smiles. It tugs at the scar along the corner of his mouth.

Bishop nods to him. "Glad you made it back."

Grace bows his head. Bishop has faith. In what, Grace doesn't know. But perhaps that's what lets him go on. Bishop believes Grace deserves a chance to live and find a purpose.

For just a moment, as he watches Dee lead Das back home, Grace can almost believe it. And one day, perhaps, he can find that first step and climb the black sky.

There is one thing he wants first, sharp and fierce.

"Bishop," Grace asks, all but a whisper. "Can you show me the stars?"

"They're hard to see in the city light," Bishop says quietly.

Grace's body sags. He leans on his thighs and fights down the yawning grief like a pit in his chest, opening wider.

Bishop lays a hand on his shoulder to steady him. "But I know a place that might work."

GRACE SCARCELY RECOGNIZES THE JOURNEY through the city. Fever claws at his blood. He refuses rest; he needs this first. He needs to know what the stars are like.

There is another climb, and he is aware of Bishop supporting him as they ascend the final steps and emerge from a tower onto a roof, flat and open, lined with gravel. The dome is a thin membrane here, nearly translucent, tinted red-orange from the city lights.

"Look up," Bishop says.

Grace tilts his head back. With his good eye, he can see nothing but the faint glow of light pollution. But with his new eye, wired like Bishop's, he sees the dark sky beyond. He focuses, slowly, accustoming his senses to the new perception.

There, in the distance, is a flicker of white light, tiny and almost lost in the blackness.

The heat lessens in his skin. He can breathe easier. He wants to keep breathing, to keep watching the sky.

The star gleams like a knife, bright and cold.

Grace smiles. "It's beautiful."

"It is," Bishop says. "It is."

*On my feet and playing host, I could reasonably meet them all eye to eye, count them off like call-over at school. Hereth and Maskelyne, who were not friends but nevertheless arrived together and sat together, left together every time. Thomson who rarely spoke, who measured us all through his disguising spectacles and might have been a copper's nark, might have been here to betray us all except that every one of us had reason to know that he was not. Gribbin the engineer and van Heuren the boatman, Poole from the newspaper and the vacuous Parringer of course, and Mr. Holland our guest for the occasion, and—And our unannounced visitor, the uninvited, the unknown.*

# The Astrakhan, the Homburg, and the Red, Red Coal

## CHAZ BRENCHLEY

"Paris? Paris is ruined for me, alas. It has become a haven for Americans—or should I say a heaven? When good Americans die, perhaps they really do go to Paris. That would explain the Hood."

"What about the others, Mr. Holland? The ones who aren't good?"

"Ah. Have you not heard? I thought that was common knowledge. When bad Americans die, they go to America. Which, again, would explain its huddled masses. But we were speaking of Paris. It was a good place to pause, to catch my breath. I never could have stayed there. If I had stayed in Paris, I should have died myself. The wallpaper alone would have seen to that."

"And what then, Mr. Holland? Where do good Irishmen go when they die?"

"Hah." He made to fold his hands across a generous belly, as in the days of pomp — and found it not so generous after all, and lost for a moment the practised grace of his self-content. A man can forget the new truths of his own body, after a period of alteration. Truly Paris had a lot to answer for. Paris, and what had come before. What had made it necessary.

"This particular Irishman," he said, "is in hopes of seeing Cassini the crater-city on its lake, and finding his eternal rest in your own San Michele, within the sound of Thunder Fall. If I've only been good enough."

"And if not? Where do bad Irishmen go?"

It was the one question that should never have been asked. It came from the shadows behind our little circle; I disdained to turn around, to see what man had voiced it.

"Well," Mr. Holland said, gazing about him with vivid horror painted expertly across his mobile face, "I seem to have found myself in Marsport. What did I ever do to deserve this?"

There was a common shout of laughter, but it was true all the same. Marsport at its best is not a place to wish upon anyone, virtuous or otherwise; and the Blue Dolphin is not the best of what we have. Far from it. Lying somewhat awkwardly between the honest hotels and the slummish boarding-houses, it was perhaps the place that met his purse halfway. Notoriety is notoriously mean in its rewards. He couldn't conceivably slum, but neither—I was guessing—could he live high on the hog. Even now it wasn't clear quite who had paid his fare to Mars. The one-way voyage is subsidised by Authority, while those who want to go home again must pay through the nose for the privilege—but even so. He would not have travelled steerage, and the cost of a cabin on an aethership is… significant. Prohibitive, I should have said, for a man in exile from his own history, whose once success could only drag behind him now like Marley's chains, nothing but a burden. He might have assumed his children's name for public purposes, but he could not have joined the ship without offering his right one.

No matter. He was here now, with money enough for a room at the Dolphin and hopes of a journey on. We would sit at his feet meanwhile and be the audience he was accustomed to, attentive, admiring, if it would make him happy.

It was possible that nothing now could make him exactly happy. Still: who could treasure him more than we who made our home in a gateway city, an entrepôt, and found our company in the lobby of a cheap hotel?

"Marsport's not so dreadful," the same voice said. "It's the hub of the wheel, not the pit of hell. From here you can go anywhere you choose: by canal, by airship, by camel if you're hardy. Steam-camel, if you're foolhardy. On the face of it, I grant you, there's not much reason to stay—and yet, people do. Our kind."

"Our kind?"

There was a moment's pause, after Mr. Holland had placed the question: so carefully, like a card laid down in invitation, or a token to seal the bet.

"Adventurers," the man said. "Those unafraid to stand where the light spills into darkness: who know that a threshold serves to hold two worlds apart, as much as it allows congress between them."

"Ah. I am afraid my adventuring days are behind me."

"Oh, nonsense, sir! Why, the journey to Mars is an adventure in itself!"

Now there was a voice I did recognise: Parringer, as fatuous a fool as the schools of home were ever likely to produce. He was marginal even here, one of us only by courtesy.

And thrusting himself forward, protesting jovially, trying to prove himself at the heart of the affair and showing only how very remote he was.

"Well, perhaps. Perhaps." Mr. Holland could afford to be generous; he didn't have to live with the man. "If so, it has been my last. I am weary, gentlemen. And wounded and heart-sore and unwell, but weary above all. All I ask now is a place to settle. A fireside, a view, a little company: no more than that. No more adventuring."

"Time on Mars may yet restore your health and energy. It is what we are famous for." This was our unknown again, pressing again. "But you are not of an age to want or seek retirement, Mr....Holland. Great heavens, man, you can't be fifty yet! Besides, the adventure I propose will hardly tax your reserves. There's no need even to leave the hotel, if you will only shift with me into the conservatory. You may want your overcoats, gentlemen, and another round of drinks. No more than that. I've had a boy in there already to light the stove."

That was presumptuous. Manners inhibited me from twisting around and staring, but no one objects to a little honest subterfuge. I rose, took two paces towards the fire and pressed the bell by the mantelshelf.

"My shout, I think. Mr. Holland, yours I know is gin and French. Gentlemen...?"

No one resists an open invitation; Marsporter gin is excellent, but imported drinks come dear. The boy needed his notebook to take down a swift flurry of orders.

"Thanks, Barley." I tucked half a sovereign into his rear pocket—unthinkable largesse, but we all had reasons to treat kindly with Barley—and turned to face my cohort.

On my feet and playing host, I could reasonably meet them all eye to eye, count them off like call-over at school. Hereth and Maskelyne, who were not friends but nevertheless arrived together and sat together, left together every time. Thomson who rarely spoke, who measured us all through his disguising spectacles and might have been a copper's nark, might have been here to betray us all except that every one of us had reason to know that he was not. Gribbin the engineer and van Heuren the boatman, Poole from the newspaper and the vacuous Parringer of course, and Mr. Holland our guest for the occasion, and—

And our unannounced visitor, the uninvited, the unknown. He was tall even for Mars, where the shortest of us would overtop the average Earthman. Mr. Holland must have been a giant in his own generation, six foot three or thereabouts; here he was no more than commonplace. In his strength, in his pride I thought he would have resented that. Perhaps he still did. Years of detention and disgrace had diminished body and spirit both, but something must survive yet, unbroken, undismayed. He could never have made this journey else. Nor sat with us. Every felled tree holds a memory of the forest.

The stranger was in his middle years, an established man, confident in himself and his position. That he held authority in some kind was not, could not be in question. It was written in the way he stood, the way he waited; the way he had taken charge so effortlessly, making my own display seem feeble, sullen, nugatory.

Mr. Holland apparently saw the same. He said, "I don't believe we were introduced, sir. If I were to venture a guess, I should say you had a look of the Guards about you." Or perhaps he said *the guards*, and meant something entirely different.

"I don't believe any of us have been introduced," I said, as rudely as I knew how. "You are…?"

Even his smile carried that same settled certainty. "Gregory Durand, late of the King's Own," with a little nod to Mr. Holland: the one true regiment to any man of Mars, Guards in all but name, "and currently of the Colonial Service."

He didn't offer a title, nor even a department. Ordinarily, a civil servant is more punctilious. I tried to pin him down: "Meaning the police, I suppose?" It was a common career move, after the army.

"On occasion," he said. "Not tonight."

If that was meant to be reassuring, it fell short. By some distance. If we were casting about for our coats, half-inclined not to wait for those drinks, it was not because we were urgent to follow him into the conservatory. Rather, our eyes were on the door and the street beyond.

"Gentlemen," he said, "be easy." He was almost laughing at us. "Tonight I dress as you do," anonymous overcoat and hat, as good as a *nom de guerre* on such a man, an absolute announcement that this was not his real self, "and share everything and nothing, one great secret and nothing personal or private, nothing prejudicial. I will not say 'nothing perilous,' but the peril is mutual and assured. We stand or fall together, if at all. Will you come? For the Queen Empress, if not for the Empire?"

The Empire had given us little enough reason to love it, which he knew. An appeal to the Widow, though, will always carry weight. There is something irresistible in that blend of decrepit sentimentality and strength beyond measure, endurance beyond imagination. Like all her subjects else, we had cried for her, we would die for her. We were on our feet almost before we knew it. I took that so much for granted, indeed, it needed a moment more for me to realise that Mr. Holland was still struggling to rise. Unless he was simply slower to commit himself, he whose reasons—whose scars—were freshest on his body and raw yet on his soul.

Still. I reached down my hand to help him, and he took it resolutely. And then stepped out staunchly at my side, committed after all. We found ourselves already in chase of the pack; the others filed one by one through a door beside the hearth, that was almost always locked this time of year. Beyond lay the unshielded conservatory, an open invitation to the night.

An invitation that Mr. Holland balked at, and rightly. He said, "You gentlemen are dressed for this, but I have a room here, and had not expected to need my coat tonight."

"You'll freeze without it. Perhaps you should stay in the warm." Perhaps we all should, but it was too late for that. Our company was following Durand like sheep, trusting where they should have been most wary. Tempted where they should have been resistant, yielding where they should have been most strong.

And yet, and yet. Dubious and resentful as I was, I too would give myself over to this man—for the mystery or for the adventure, something. For something to do that was different, original, unforeseen. I was weary of the same faces, the same drinks, the same conversations. We all were. Which was why Mr. Holland had been so welcome, one reason why.

This, though—I thought he of all men should keep out of this. I thought I should keep him out, if I could.

Here came Durand to prevent me: stepping through the door again, reaching for his elbow, light and persuasive and yielding nothing.

"Here's the boy come handily now, just when we need him. I'll take that, lad," lifting Durey's tray of refreshments as though he had been here all along. "You run up to Mr. Holland's room and fetch down his overcoat. And his hat too, we'll need to keep that great head warm. Meanwhile, Mr. Holland, we've a chair for you hard by the stove…"

THE CHAIRS WERE SET OUT ready in a circle: stern and upright, uncushioned, claimed perhaps from the hotel servants' table. Our companions were milling, choosing, settling, in clouds of their own breath. The conservatory was all glass and lead, roof and walls together; in the dark of a Martian winter, the air was bitter indeed, despite the stove's best efforts. The chill pressed in from every side, as the night pressed against the lamplight. There was no comfort here to be found; there would be no warmth tonight.

On a table to one side stood a machine, a construction of wires and plates in a succession of steel frames with rubber insulation. One cable led out of it, to something that most resembled an inverted umbrella, or the skeleton of such a thing, bones of wind-stripped wire.

"What is that thing?"

"Let me come to that. If you gentlemen would take your seats…"

Whoever laid the chairs out knew our number. There was none for Durand; he stood apart, beside the machine. Once we were settled, drinks in hand—and most of us wishing we had sent for something warmer—he began.

"*Nation shall speak peace unto nation*—and for some of us, it is our task to see it happen. Notoriously, traditionally we go after this by sending in the army first and then the diplomats. Probably we have that backwards, but it's the system that builds empires. It's the system of the world.

"Worlds, I should say. Here on Mars, of course, it's the merlins that we need to hold in conversation. Mr. Holland—"

"I am not a child, sir. Indeed, I have children of my own." Indeed, he travelled now under their name, the name they took at their mother's insistence; he could still acknowledge them, even if they were obliged to disown him. "I have exactly a child's understanding of your merlins: which is to say, what we were taught in my own schooldays. I know that you converse with them as you can, in each of their different stages: by sign language with the youngster, the nymph, and then by bubbling through pipes at the naiad in its depths, and watching the bubbles it spouts back. With the imago, when the creature takes to the air, I do not believe that you can speak at all."

"Just so, sir—and that is precisely the point of our gathering tonight."

In fact the point of our gathering had been ostensibly to celebrate and welcome Mr. Holland, actually to fester in our own rank company while we displayed like bantam cocks before our guest. Durand had co-opted it, and us, entirely. Possibly that was no bad thing. He had our interest, at least, if not our best interests at heart.

"It has long been believed," he said, "that the imagos—"

"—imagines—"

—to our shame, that came as a chorus, essential pedantry—

"—that imagos," he went on firmly, having no truck with ridiculous Greek plurals, "have no language, no way to speak, perhaps no wit to speak with. As though the merlins slump into senescence in their third stage, or infantilism might say it better: as though they lose any rational ability, overwhelmed by the sexual imperative. They live decades, perhaps centuries in their slower stages here below, nymph and naiad; and then they pupate, and then they hatch a second time and the fire of youth overtakes them once more: they fly; they fight; they mate; they die. What need thought, or tongue?

"So our wise men said, at least. Now perhaps we are grown wiser. We believe they do indeed communicate, with each other and perhaps their water-based cousins too. It may be that nymphs or naiads or both have the capacity to hear them. We don't, because they do not use sound as we understand it. Rather, they have an organ in their heads that sends out electromagnetic pulses, closer to Hertzian waves than anything we have previously observed in nature. Hence this apparatus," with a mild gesture towards the table and its machinery. "With this, it is believed that we can not only hear the imagos, but speak back to them."

A moment's considerate pause, before Gribbin asked the obvious question. "And us? Why do you want to involve us?"

"Not want, so much as need. The device has existed for some time; it has been tried, and tried again. It does work, there is no question of that. Something is received, something transmitted."

"—But?"

"But the first man who tried it, its inventor occupies a private room—a locked room—in an asylum now, and may never be fit for release."

"And the second?"

"Was a military captain, the inventor's overseer. He has the room next door." There was no equivocation in this man, nothing but the blunt direct truth.

"And yet you come to us? You surely don't suppose that we are saner, healthier, more to be depended on . . . ?"

"Nor more willing," Durand said, before one of us could get to it. "I do not. And yet I am here, and I have brought the machine. Will you listen?"

None of us trusted him, I think. Mr. Holland had better reason than any to be wary, yet it was he whose hand sketched a gesture, *I am listening*. The rest of us—well, silence has ever been taken for consent.

"Thank you, gentlemen. What transpired from the tragedy—after a careful reading of the notes and as much interrogation of the victims as proved possible—was that the mind of an imago is simply too strange, too alien, for the mind of a man to encompass. A human brain under that kind of pressure can break, in distressing and irrecoverable ways."

"And yet," I said, "we speak to nymphs, to naiads." I had done it myself, indeed. I had spoken to nymphs on the great canals when I was younger, nimble-fingered, foolish, and immortal. For all the good it had done me, I might as well have kept my hands in my pockets and my thoughts to myself, but nevertheless. I spoke, they replied; none of us ran mad.

"We do—and a poor shoddy helpless kind of speech it is. Finger-talk or bubble-talk, all we ever really manage to do is misunderstand each other almost entirely. That 'almost' has made the game just about worth the candle, for a hundred years and more—it brought us here and keeps us here in more or less safety; it ferries us back and forth—but this is different. When the imagos speak to each other, they speak mind-to-mind. It's not literally telepathy, but it is the closest thing we know. And when we contact them through this device, we encounter the very shape of their minds, almost from the inside; and our minds—our *individual minds*—cannot encompass that. No one man's intellect can stand up to the strain."

"And yet," again, "here we are. And here you are, and your maddening machine. I say again, why are we here?"

"Because you chose to be"—and it was not at all clear whether his answer meant *in this room* or *in this hotel* or *in this situation*. "I am the only one here under orders. The rest of you are free to leave at any time, though you did at least agree to listen. And I did say 'one man's intellect.' Where one man alone cannot survive it without a kind of mental dislocation—in the wicked sense, a disjointment, his every mental limb pulled each from each—a group of men working together is a different case. It may be that the secret lies in strength, in mutual support; it may lie in flexibility. A group of officers made the endeavour, and none of them was harmed beyond exhaustion and a passing bewilderment, a lingering discomfort with each other. But neither did they make much headway. Enlisted men did better."

He paused, because the moment demanded it: because drama has its natural rhythms and he did after all have Mr. Holland in his audience, the great dramatist of our age. We sat still, uncommitted, listening yet.

"The enlisted men did better, we believe, because their lives are more earthy, less refined. They live cheek by jowl; they sleep all together and bathe together; they share the same women in the same bawdy-houses. That seems to help."

"And so you come to us? To *us*?" Ah, Parringer. "Because you find us indistinguishable from common bloody Tommies?"

"No, because you are most precisely distinguishable. The Tommies were no great success either, but they pointed us a way to go. The more comfortable the men are with each other, physically and mentally, the better hope we have. Officers inhabit a bonded hierarchy, isolated from one another as they are from their men, like pockets of water in an Archimedes' screw. Cadets might have done better, but we went straight to the barracks. With, as I say, some success—but enlisted men are unsophisticated. Hence we turn to you, gentlemen. It is a bow drawn at a venture, no more: but you are familiar with, intimate with the bodies of other men, and we do believe that will help enormously; and yet you are educated beyond the aspiration of any Tommy Atkins—some of you beyond the aspiration of any mere soldier, up to and including the generals of my acquaintance—and that too can only prove to the good. With the one thing and the other, these two strengths in parallel, in harmony, we stand in high hopes of a successful outcome. At least, gentlemen, I can promise you that you won't be bored. Come, now: will you play?"

"Is that as much as you can promise?" Thomson raised his voice, querulous and demanding. "You ask a lot of us, to venture in the margins of madness; it seems to me you might offer more in return."

"I can offer you benign neglect," Durand said cheerfully. "Official inattention: no one watching you, no one pursuing. I can see that enshrined in policy, to carry over *ad infinitum*. If you're discreet, you can live untroubled hereafter; you, and the generations that follow you. This is a once-and-for-all offer, for services rendered."

There must be more wrapped up in this even than Durand suggested or we guessed. A way to speak to the imagines might prove only the gateway to further secrets and discoveries. If we could speak directly to the chrysalid pilots of the aetherships, perhaps we might even learn to fly ourselves between one planet and another, and lose all our dependence on the merlins…

That surely would be worth a blind eye turned in perpetuity to our shady meeting-places, our shadier activities.

Mr. Holland thought so, at least. "Say more, of how this process works. Not what you hope might come of it; we all have dreams. Some of us have followed them, somewhat. I am here, after all, among the stars," with a wave of his hand through glass to the bitter clarity of the Martian night sky. "How is it that you want us to work together? And how do we work with the machine, and why above all do we have to do it here, in this wicked cold?"

"To treat with the last first: Mr. Heaviside has happily demonstrated here as well as on Earth, that aetheric waves carry further after dark. We don't know how far we need to reach, to find a receptive imago; we stand a better chance at night. Besides, you gentlemen tend to forgather in the evenings. I wasn't certain of finding you by daylight."

Someone chuckled, someone snorted. I said, "I have never seen an imago fly by night, though. I don't believe they can."

"Not fly, no: never that. But neither do they sleep, so far as we can tell. All we want to do—all we want you to do—is touch the creature's mind, fit yourselves to the shape of it and find whether you can understand each other."

"I still don't understand how you mean us to achieve that?"

"No. It's almost easier to have you do it, than to explain how it might be done. We're stepping into an area where words lose their value against lived experience. It's one reason I was so particularly hoping to enlist your company, sir," with a nod to Mr. Holland, "because who better to stand before the nondescript and find means to describe it? If anyone can pin this down with words, it will be you. If anyone can speak for us to an alien power—"

"Now that," he said, "I have been doing all my life."

The run of laughter he provoked seemed more obligatory than spontaneous, but came as a relief none the less. Durand joined in, briefly. As it tailed away, he said, "Very well—but there is of course more to it than one man's dexterity with language. Our wise men speak of the, ah, inversion of the generative principle, as a bonding-agent stronger than blood or shared danger or duty or sworn word — but again, there is more than that. You gentlemen may be a brotherhood, drawn from within and pressed close from without; we can make you something greater, a single purpose formed from all your parts. The wise men would have me flourish foreign words at you, *gestalt* or *phasis* or the like; but wise men are not always the most helpful.

"Let me rather say this, that you all have some experience of the demi-monde. By choice or by instinct or necessity, your lives have led you into the shadows. This very hotel is a gateway to more disreputable ventures. There is an opium den behind the Turkish bath, a brothel two doors down. I do not say that any of you is a libertine at core: only that the life you lead draws you into contact and exchange with those who avoid the light for other reasons.

"I will be plain. Mr. Holland, you have a known taste for absinthe and for opium cigarettes. Mr. Parringer, laudanum is your poison; Mr. Hereth, you stick to gin, but that jug of water at your elbow that you mix in so judiciously is actually more gin, and you will drink the entire jugful before the night is out. Mr. Gribbin—but I don't need to go on, do I? You each have your weaknesses, your ways of setting yourselves a little adrift from the world.

"We need to take you out of yourselves more thoroughly in order to bind you into a single motive force, in order to create the mind-space wherein you might meet an imago and make some sense of it. I have brought an alchemical concoction, a kind of hatchis, more potent than any pill or pipe or potion that you have met before."

He laid it on a tray, on a table that he set centre-circle between us all: a silver pot containing something green and unctuous, an array of coffee-spoons beside.

"Something more from your wise men, Mr. Durand?"

"Exactly so."

"I'm not sure how keen I am, actually, to swallow some hellbrew dreamed up in a government laboratory." Gribbin leaned forward and stirred it dubiously. There were gleams of oily gold amidst the green. "Does nobody remember *The Strange Case of Dr Jekyll and Mr. Hyde?*"

"'Can anyone forget it?' should rather be your question," Mr. Holland observed. "Stevenson was as much a master of delicate, fanciful prose as he was of a strong driving story. But he—or his character, rather, his creation: do we dare impute the motives of the dream unto the dreamer?—he certainly saw the merits of a man testing his own invention on himself, before bringing it to the public." Even huddled as he was against the ironwork of the stove, he could still exude a spark of knowing mischief.

Durand smiled. "I would be only too happy to swallow my own spoonful, to show you gentlemen the way—but alas, my duty is to the device, not to the *entente*. You will need me sober and attentive. Besides which, I am not of your persuasion. I should only hold you back. Let me stress, though, that senior officers and common troops both have trod this path before you, and not been harmed. Not by the drug. Think of the hatchis as grease to the engine, no more; it will ease your way there and back again. Now come: I promised you adventure, and this is the beginning. Who's first to chance the hazard?"

There is a self-destructive tendency in some men that falls only a little short of self-murder. We have it worse than most; something not quite terror, not quite exhilaration drives us higher, faster, farther than good sense ever could dictate. Some consider it a weakness, evidence of a disordered nature. I hope that it's a badge of courage acquired against the odds, that we will fling ourselves from the precipice with no certain knowledge of a rope to hold us, no faith in any net below.

Of course it was Mr. Holland who reached first, to draw up a noble spoonful and slide it into his mouth. No tentative sips, no tasting: he was all or nothing, or rather simply all.

The surprise was Parringer, thrusting himself forward to do the same, gulping it down wholesale while Mr. Holland still lingered, the spoon's stem jutting from between his full contented lips like a cherry-stem, like a child's lollipop.

Where Parringer plunged, who among us would choose to hold back? A little resentfully, and with a great many questions still unasked, we fell mob-handed on the spoons, the jar, the glistening oleaginous jelly.

IT WAS BITTER ON MY tongue and something harsh, as though it breathed out fumes, catching at the back of my throat before it slithered down to soothe that same discomfort with a distraction of tastes behind a cool and melting kiss. Bitter and then sour and then sweet, layer beneath layer, and I couldn't decide whether its flavours were woven one into another or whether its very nature changed as it opened, as it bloomed within the warm wet of my mouth.

He was right, of course, Durand. Not one of us there was a stranger to the more louche pleasures of the twilit world. Myself, I was a smoker in those days: hashish or opium, anything to lift me out of the quotidian world for an hour or a night. In company or alone, sweating or shivering or serene, I would always, always look to rise. Skin becomes permeable, bodies lose their margins; dreams are welcome but not needful, where what I seek is always that sense of being uncontained, of reaching further than my strict self allows.

From what he said, I took Durand's potion to be one more path to that effect: slower for sure, because smoke is the very breath of fire and lifts as easily as it rises, while anything swallowed is dank and low-lying by its nature. I never had been an opium-eater, and hatchis was less than that, surely: a thinner draught, ale to spirits, tea to coffee. Sunshine to lightning. Something.

If I had the glare of lightning in my mind, it was only in the expectation of disappointment: rain, no storm. I never thought to ride it. Nor to find myself insidiously companion'd—in my own mind, yet—where before I had always gone alone.

Even in bed, even with a slick and willing accomplice in the throes of mutual excess, my melting boundaries had never pretended to melt me into another man's thoughts. Now, though: now suddenly I was aware of minds in parallel, rising entangled with mine, like smoke from separate cigarettes caught in the same eddy. Or burning coals in the same grate, fusing awkwardly together. Here was a mind cool and in command of itself, trying to sheer off at such exposure: that was Gribbin, finding nowhere to go, pressed in from every side at once. Here was one bold and fanciful and weary all at once, and that was surely Mr. Holland, though it was hard to hold on to that ostensible name in this intimate revelation. Here was one tentative and blustering together, Parringer of course . . .

One by one, each one of us declared an identity, if not quite a location. We were this many and this various, neither a medley nor a synthesis, untuned: glimpsing one man's overweening physical arrogance and another's craven unsatisfied ambition, sharing the urge to seize both and achieve a high vaulting reach with them, beyond the imagination of either. Even without seeing a way to do that, even as we swarmed inconsequentially like elvers in a bucket, the notion was there already with flashes of the vision. Perhaps Durand was right to come to us.

Durand, now: Durand was no part of this. Walled off, separated, necessary: to us he was prosthetic, inert, a tool to be wielded. He stood by his machine, fiddling with knobs and wires, almost as mechanical himself.

Here was the boy Barley coming in, no part of anything, bringing the hat and overcoat he'd been sent for. At Durand's gesture he dressed Mr. Holland like a doll, as though he were invalid or decrepit. Perhaps we all seemed so to him, huddled in our circle, unspeaking, seeming unaware. The truth was opposite; we were aware of everything, within the limits of our bodies' senses. We watched him crouch to feed the stove; we heard the slide and crunch of the redcoal tipping in, the softer sounds of ash falling through the grate beneath; we felt the sear of heat released, how it stirred the frigid air about us, how it rose towards the bitter glass.

"Enough now, lad. Leave us be until I call again."

"Yes, sir."

He picked up the tray from the table and bore it off towards the door, with a rattle of discarded spoons. Durand had already turned back to his machine. We watched avidly, aware of nothing more intently than the little silver pot and its gleaming residue. We knew it, when the boy hesitated just inside the door; we knew it when he glanced warily back at us, when he decided he was safe, when he scooped up a fingerful from the pot's rim and sucked it clean.

We knew; Durand did not.

Durand fired up his machine.

WE HAD THE BOY. Not one of us, not part of us, not yet: we were as unprepared for this as he was, and the more susceptible to his fear and bewilderment because we were each of us intimately familiar with his body, in ways not necessarily true of one another's.

Still: we had him among us, with us, this side of the wall. We had his nervous energy to draw on, like a flame to our black powder; we had his yearning, his curiosity. And more, we had that shared knowledge of him, common ground. Where we couldn't fit one to another, we could all of us fit around him: the core of the matrix, the unifying frame, the necessary element Durand had not foreseen.

DURAND FIRED UP HIS MACHINE while we were still adjusting, before we had nudged one another into any kind of order.

He really should have warned us, though I don't suppose he could. He hadn't been this way himself; all he had was secondhand reports from men more or less broken by the process. We could none of us truly have understood that, until now.

We weren't pioneers; he only hoped that we might be survivors. Still, we deserved some better warning than we had.

WE FORGET SOMETIMES THAT NAMES are not descriptions; that Mars is not Earth; that the merlins are no more native than ourselves. We call them Martians sometimes because our parents did, because their parents did before them, and so back all the way to Farmer George. More commonly we call them merlins because we think it's clever, because they seem to end their lives so backward, from long years of maturity in the depths to one brief adolescent lustful idiocy in the sky. When we call them imagos—or imagines—because they remind us of dragonflies back home, if dragonflies were built to the scale of biplanes.

Which they are not. The map is not the territory; the name is not the creature. Even redcoal is not coal, not carbon of any kind, for all that it is mined and burned alike. We forget that. We name artefacts after the places of their manufacture, or their first manufacture, or the myth of it; did the homburg hat in fact see first light in Bad Homburg, or is that only a story that we tell? Does anybody know? We let a man name himself after his children, after a country not relevant to any of them, not true to any story of their lives. We assert that names are changeable, assignable at whim, and then we attach unalterable value to them.

Durand had given no name to his machine. That was just as well, but not enough. He had given us a task to do, in words we thought we understood; he had laid the groundwork, given us an argument about the uses of debauchery and then a drug to prove it; then he flung us forth, all undefended.

He flung us, and we dragged poor Barley along, unwitting, unprepared.

It started with a hum, as he connected electrical wires to a seething acid battery. Lamps glowed into dim flickering life. Sparks crackled ominously, intermittently, before settling to a steady mechanical pulse. A steel disc spun frantically inside a cage.

Nothing actually moved, except fixedly in place; and even so, everything about it was all rush and urgency, a sensation of swift decisive movement: *that way*, through the run of frames and wires to the umbrella-structure at the far end of the table. There was nothing to draw the eye except a certainty, logic married to something more, an intangible impulsion. That way: through and up and out into the night.

And none of us moved from our places, and yet, and yet. The machine hurled us forth, and forth we went.

If we had understood anything, we had understood that the machine would bring an imago's voice to us, and we would somehow speak back to it, if we could think of anything to say. That would have been Mr. Holland's lot, surely; he was never short of things to say.

We had misunderstood, or else been misdirected. Unless the drug seduced us all into a mutual hallucination, and in plain truth our intelligences never left that room any more than our abandoned bodies did. But it seemed to us — to *all* of us, united — that we were shot out like a stone from a catapult; that we streaked over all the lights of Marsport and into the bleak dark of the desert beyond; that we hurtled thus directly into the static mind of an imago at rest.

No creature's thoughts should be…architectural. Or vast. At first we thought we were fallen into halls of stone, or caverns water-worn. But we had found our shape by then, in the flight from there to here; we might fit poorly all together, but we all fitted well around Barley. And something in that resettling, that nudging into a new conformation, caused a shift in our perspective. A thought is just an echo of the mind-state it betrays, as an astrakhan overcoat is a memory of the lambs that died to make it.

Where we fancied that we stood, these grand and pillared spaces—this was an imago's notion of its night-time world, beyond all heat and passion, poised, expectant. A memory of the chrysalis, perhaps.

Expectant, but not expecting us. Not expecting anything until the sun, the bright and burning day, the vivid endeavour. We came like thieves into a mountain, to disturb the dragon's rest; we were alien, intrusive, self-aware. It knew us in the moment of our coming.

I have seen set-changes in the theatre where one scene glides inexplicably into another, defying expectation, almost defying the eye that saw it happen. I had never stood in a place and had that happen all about me; but we were there, we were recognised, and its awareness of us changed the shape of its thinking.

Even as we changed ourselves, that happened: as we slid and shifted, as we found our point of balance with Barley serving at the heart of all, as we arrayed ourselves about him. Even Mr. Holland, who would need to speak for us, if anything could ever come to words here; even Parringer, whose motives were as insidious as his manner. There was an unbridgeable gulf between the imago as we had always understood it, flighty and maniacal, and this lofty habitation. A naiad in the depths might have such a ponderous mind, such chilly detachment, but not the frenzied imago, no. Surely not.

Save that the imago had been a naiad before; perhaps it retained that mind-set, in ways we had not experienced. Imagined. Perhaps it could be contemplative at night, while the sun burned off its intellect and lent it only heat?

It closed in upon us almost geometrically, like tiled walls, if tiles and walls could occupy more dimensions than a man can see, in shapes we have no words for. We should have felt threatened, perhaps, but Barley's curiosity was matched now by his tumbling delight, and what burns at the core reaches out all the way to the skin. We sheltered him and drew from him and leaned on him, all in equal measure; he linked us and leaned on us and drew from us, in ways for which there never could be words.

WITH SO MANY NAMES FOR our kind—leering, contemptuous, descriptive, dismissive— we know both the fallibility and the savage power of words. The map seeks to define the territory, to claim it, sometimes to contain it. Without a map, without a shared vocabulary, without a mode of thought in common—well, no wonder men alone went mad here. No wonder men together had achieved so little, beyond a mere survival. Mr. Holland might have flung wit all night with no more effect than a monkey flinging dung against a cliff-face, if we had only been a group forgathered by circumstance, struggling to work together. With the drug to bond us, with each man contributing the heart's-blood of himself in this strange transfusion, there was no struggle and we found what we needed as the need came to us.

Whether we said what was needed, whether it needed to be said: that is some other kind of question. Did anyone suppose that the confluence of us all would be a diplomat?

The imago pressed us close, but that was an enquiry. There was pattern in the pressure: we could see it, we could read it almost, those of us with finger-talk or bubble-talk or both. *What lives, what choices? Swim or fly, drown or burn? Swallow or be swallowed?*

We knew, we thought, how to press back, how to pattern a reply. Mr. Holland gave us what we lacked: content, poetry, response. Meaning more than words. Sometimes the map declares the territory.

*For he who lives more lives than one*
*More deaths than one must die.*

He would have turned the bitterness all against himself, but our collective consciousness couldn't sustain that. We all wanted our share, we all deserved it: all but Barley, who had no hidden other self, who'd had no time to grow one.

Suddenly he couldn't hold us together any longer. Fraying, we fled back to Durand, back to our waiting bodies — and the imago pursued, flying by sheer will in the dreadful night, wreaking havoc in its own frozen body. It followed us to the Dolphin and hurtled against the conservatory where we were anything but sheltered, battering at the windows like a moth at the chimney of a lamp, until the only abiding question was whether the glass would shatter first or the machine, or the creature, or ourselves.

# ABOUT THE AUTHORS

**Richard Bowes** has published six novels, four story collections and eighty short stories. He has won World Fantasy, Lambda, Million Writer and IHG Awards. A new edition of his 2005 Nebula nominated novel *From The Files Of The Time Rangers* will be out in 2016 from Lethe Press. His 9/11 story "There's A Hole In The City" recently got a fine review in the *New Yorker*. It's online now at *Nightmare Magazine*. Bowes is currently writing a novel about a gay kid in 1950's Boston. Recent/upcoming appearances include *Queers Destroy Fantasy*, *The Doll Collection* and *Black Feathers*.

**Chaz Brenchley** has been making a living as a writer since the age of eighteen. He is the author of nine thrillers, two fantasy series, two ghost stories, and two collections, most recently the Lambda Award-winning *Bitter Waters*. As Daniel Fox, he has published a Chinese-based fantasy series; as Ben Macallan, an urban fantasy series. A British Fantasy Award winner, he has also published books for children, two novellas and more than 500 short stories. He has recently married and moved from Newcastle to California, with two squabbling cats and a famous teddy bear.

**Jared W. Cooper** is a New Jersey-based editor and reviewer who might also be an actual bear. He drinks too much tea, loves the woods in winter, and can be found on Twitter @ jaredwcooper when he should be working

**Paul Evanby** is a Dutch writer with several novels (e.g. *De Scrypturist*) out from Meulenhoff Boekerij, as well as two short story collections. His Dutch short fiction has won the Paul Harland Prijs twice. His English-language stories have appeared in *Interzone*, *HGMLQ*, *Elastic Book of Numbers*, *Nemonymous*, and others. He is @evanby on Twitter.

**Jonathan Harper** is the author of the short story collection *Daydreamers*. He received his MFA from American University in 2010. His writing has been featured in such places as *The Rumpus*, *The Nervous Breakdown*, *Chelsea Station* and *Big Lucks* as well as in several anthologies. Visit him online at jonathan-harper.com.

**Rich Larson** was born in West Africa, has studied in Rhode Island and worked in Spain, and at twenty-three now writes from Edmonton, Alberta. His short work has been nominated for the Theodore Sturgeon Award, featured on io9, and appears in numerous Year's Best anthologies as well as in magazines such as *Asimov's*, *Analog*, *Clarkesworld*, *F&SF*, *Interzone*, *Strange Horizons*, *Lightspeed* and *Apex*. Find him at richwlarson.tumblr.com.

**Richard Scott Larson** holds an MFA from New York University. His fiction has appeared in *failbetter*, *Joyland*, *Strange Horizons*, *Hobart*, *Subterranean*, *Shimmer*, *Booth*, *Icarus*, and other venues, including a previous volume of *Wilde Stories: The Year's Best Gay Speculative Fiction*. He also contributes criticism to a variety of publications, including *Publisher's Weekly*, *Strange Horizons*, and *Slant Magazine*, and he was an Assistant Editor of a special "Queers Destroy Fantasy!" issue of *Lightspeed Magazine*. Born and raised in St. Louis, he now lives in Brooklyn and works for the Expository Writing Program at NYU.

**Paul Magrs** lives and writes in Manchester. In a twenty year writing career he has published a number of novels in a variety of genres, including books about transtemporal adventuress Iris Wildthyme and also the *Brenda and Effie Mysteries*, which are about the Bride of Frankenstein running a B&B in the seaside town of Whitby. He has also written fiction for young adults, including *Strange Boy*, *Exchange* and most recently, *Lost on Mars* (Firefly Press.) Over the years he has contributed many times to the Doctor Who books and audio series. He is the author of a beloved cat memoir: *The Story of Fester Cat* (Berkley.) He has taught Creative Writing at both the University of East Anglia and Manchester Metropolitan University, and now writes full time. His blog is at: lifeonmagrs.blogspot.co.uk/ and he can be found on Twitter and Facebook.

**Haralambi Markov** is a Bulgarian critic, editor, and writer of things weird and fantastic. A Clarion 2014 graduate, Markov enjoys fairy tales, obscure folkloric monsters, and inventing death rituals (for his stories, not his neighbors…usually). He blogs at The Alternative Typewriter and tweets at @HaralambiMarkov. His stories have appeared in *The Weird Fiction Review*, *Electric Velocipede*, *TOR.com*, *Stories for Chip*, *The Apex Book* *of World SF* and are slated to appear in *Genius Loci*, *Uncanny* and *Upside Down: Inverted Tropes in Storytelling*. He's currently working on a novel.

**A. Merc Rustad** is a queer transmasculine non-binary writer and filmmaker who lives in the Midwest United States. Favorite things include: robots, dinosaurs, monsters, and tea--most of which are present in their work to some degree. Their stories have appeared in *Lightspeed*, *Fireside Fiction*, *Daily Science Fiction*, *Escape Pod*, *Mothership Zeta*, and *InterGalactic Medicine Show*, as well as the anthology *The Best American Science Fiction and Fantasy 2015*. Merc has considered making their tagline "The Robot Who Makes People Cry With Their Stories." In addition to breaking readers' hearts, Merc likes to play video games, watch movies, read comics, and wear awesome hats. You can find Merc on Twitter @Merc_Rustad or their website: amercrustad.com.

**Sam J. Miller** is a writer and a community organizer. His fiction is in *Lightspeed*, *Asimov's*, *Clarkesworld*, and *The Minnesota Review*, among others. He is a nominee for the Nebula and Theodore Sturgeon Awards, a winner of the Shirley Jackson Award, and a graduate of the Clarion Writer's Workshop. His debut novel *The Art of Starving* will be published by HarperCollins in 2017. He lives in New York City, and at samjmiller.com.

**David Nickle** is an author and journalist who lives and works in Toronto, Canada. His stories have appeared on Tor.com, in numerous Year's Best anthologies and in two collections, *Monstrous Affections* and *Knife Fight and Other Struggles*. His novel *Eutopia: A Novel of Terrible Optimism* led Canada's National Post to call him "a worthy heir to the mantle of Stephen King." He is also author of *Rasputin's Bastards*, *The 'Geisters* and (with Karl Schroeder) *The Claus Effect*. With his wife, science fiction author Madeline Ashby, he co-edited the only-in-Canada anthology of James Bond stories, *Licence Expired: The Unauthorized James Bond*. He is a past winner of the Aurora, Bram Stoker and Black Quill Awards.

**Benjamin Parzybok** is the author of the novels *Couch* and *Sherwood Nation*. Among his other projects, he founded *Gumball Poetry*, a literary journal published in gumball capsule machines, co-ran Project Hamad, an effort to free a Guantanamo inmate (Adel Hamad is now free), and co-runs Black Magic Insurance Agency, a one-night city-wide alternative reality game.

**Bonnie Jo Stufflebeam**'s fiction and poetry has appeared in over forty magazines and anthologies such as *The Toast*, *Clarkesworld*, *Lightspeed*, *SmokeLong Quarterly*, *Hobart*, and *Goblin Fruit*. She lives in Texas with her partner and two literarily-named cats—

Gimli and Don Quixote. She holds an MFA in Creative Writing from the University of Southern Maine's Stonecoast program.

**E. Catherine Tobler** had never written a story with footnotes, until this one! Among others, her fiction has appeared in *Clarkesworld*, *Lightspeed*, and on the Theodore Sturgeon Memorial Award ballot. You can find her online at ecatherine.com and @ ecthetwit.

# ABOUT THE EDITOR

**Steve Berman** believes he has seen a ghost. Or a dead friend. He has been editing the *Wilde Stories* series since 2008, which was much after he had seen either ghost or dead friend. He resides in southern New Jersey within driving distance of the birthplace of the Jersey Devil.

# ALSO AVAILABLE IN THE WILDE STORIES SERIES:

WWW.LETHEPRESSBOOKS.COM

# MORE BY *WILDE STORIES 2016* AUTHORS FROM LETHE:

CPSIA information can be obtained at www.ICGtesting.com
Printed in the USA
LVOW07s1706310816

502664LV00010B/1053/P